By MARY CALMES

NOVELS
Change of Heart • Honored Vow • Trusted Bond

A Matter of Time Vol. 1 & 2
Bulletproof
But For You

Acrobat
The Guardian
Mine
Three Fates (anthology)
Timing
Warders Vol. 1 & 2

NOVELLAS
After the Sunset
Again
Any Closer
Frog
Romanus
The Servant
Steamroller
What Can Be

THE WARDER SERIES
His Hearth • Tooth & Nail • Heart in Hand
Sinnerman • Nexus • Cherish Your Name

Published by DREAMSPINNER PRESS
http://www.dreamspinnerpress.com

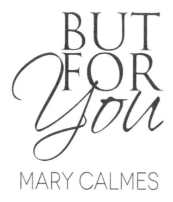

BUT FOR YOU

MARY CALMES

Dreamspinner Press

Published by
Dreamspinner Press
5032 Capital Circle SW
Ste 2, PMB# 279
Tallahassee, FL 32305-7886
USA
http://www.dreamspinnerpress.com/

Cover Art by Reese Dante
http://www.reesedante.com

ISBN: 978-1-62380-026-0

Printed in the United States of America
First Edition
October 2012

eBook edition available
eBook ISBN: 978-1-62380-027-7

Lee, Ellis, and Lisa, without you each doing your part, there would not have been a book. I can't thank you enough.

ONE

THE man was a pig, and it wasn't just me who thought so. Rosa Martinez, who lived on the other side of the Petersons, agreed with me. In fact, all the women who lived on our cul-de-sac were of the same mind. Oliver Peterson, whose wife had just caught him cheating on her—again —was filth. It wasn't the fact that they already had two children; it was the fact that she was currently pregnant with a third.

Sam, the love of my life, my partner, husband, and the guy who was parenting two small people with me, just shook his head the night before and kissed me breathless after telling me for the nine-hundredth time to please not get involved. Leave the neighbors alone; this was not *Housewives of Wherever*, we were not on reality TV. I had explained over the McDonald's that the man had brought home instead of having me cook—which, after the last time, we had both agreed would never happen again—that I was involved because I was her friend.

"No," he told me as we put the kids down. "You use that word so loosely. She's an acquaintance, Jory, she's not a friend."

"She's my neighbor, Sam, and her man's a dog, and if she needs my help with whatever, I'm gonna give it to her."

"I'm not saying not to be nice to her, but just don't stick your nose in their business."

I ignored him.

"Jory Harcourt!"

I gave him the most indignant look I could manage. "So I'm what, nosy now? I'm the busybody neighbor?"

He threw up his hands in defeat.

I gave him a superior grunt because I thought he was on his way out of the bedroom to check the house, make sure all the doors were locked, make sure the stove burners were all off, but then I realized he hadn't moved. "What?"

"You're very cute."

I squinted at him. "Thirty-five-year-old men are not cute."

"You'll always be the twenty-two-year-old club kid I saw for the first time lying in the street with a beagle on top of him."

"I thought George was a Jack Russell."

"Nope." He came toward me. "Beagle."

"Go away." I smiled at him, trying to shoo him out of the room. "Go make sure the zombie horde can't get us."

But instead of leaving, he grabbed me and slammed me up against the wall in our room. With his hot mouth nibbling up the side of my neck, his hands frantically disrobing me, and his hard groin pressed to my ass, my mind went completely blank. There was no way to concentrate when I had 220 pounds of hard-muscled man focused on getting me in bed.

But the next day, as I staggered around my kitchen—I never had been and never would be a morning person—and saw my neighbors on their front porch, Christie Peterson smiling tentatively, her husband scowling, I just wanted to go over and punch him out. I had an idea what I must have looked like: robe on, T-shirt and pajama bottoms under that, bunny slippers looking all bright-eyed and happy, I resembled the nosy neighbor in every sense.

A throat cleared behind me.

"Don't you have to go to work?" I asked pointedly. It was Wednesday, not Saturday.

The warm rumbling chuckle was next. "You think maybe now since you've got one kid in preschool and the other in first grade that you should start thinking about going back to working from your office?"

Obviously my sanity was in question, because I was still working from home. I hoped the look I gave him when I turned and squinted conveyed my displeasure.

He snorted out a laugh.

I all-out scowled at the supervisory Deputy US Marshal standing beside me at the kitchen sink. We had both been looking at the Petersons. "Why would you say that?"

"Say what?"

I growled.

He pressed his beautiful lips together in a hard line so he wouldn't smile.

"Sam?"

"No reason."

"Spit it out."

He cleared his throat. "I just think that perhaps you being home during the day is giving you cabin fever, and maybe you need to get back out in the real world and talk to the grown-ups."

I huffed out an exasperated breath. "Sam, just because I don't go to the office doesn't mean I'm starved for adult contact. I talk to Dylan every day, I talk to Fallon every day. They're my business partners, they need me, and they keep me involved with what's going on at the office."

"Okay."

"I send out more e-mails than both of them combined!"

"I'm sure you do," he said, sliding his hand around the back of my neck, then squeezing gently, massaging, and easing me closer. "I just think that maybe getting out of this house during the day would do you some good."

I batted his hand away, whirling on him. "I go to the store, to the park, drop kids off at school, pick them up... when do I not see people?"

He grunted, rolled his eyes, and put his coffee cup down in the sink before his dark smoky-blue eyes flicked to mine.

"No," I almost squeaked, turning to run.

So not fast enough.

You would think that a big man could not move like that, with so much speed, but Sam Kage's athleticism and strength were never to be underestimated. At forty-six, he was just as powerful as he'd been when I first met him, and I finally understood the whole getting better with age thing. The man looked the best he ever had, and he lived well in his skin, so content, so happy both personally and professionally.

I was so proud of him and told him so often. He was an amazing father, a wonderful husband, a great son, and the kind of friend anyone would be happy to claim. I was biased because I loved him, but still, I saw people look at him and knew the truth. Four years after beginning his new job as a marshal, he was now the supervisor of the Chicago field office, overseeing five other deputies and three clerks. I had thought once he moved up, he'd become a sheriff, but apparently all they did was add the "supervisory" in there. A sheriff was a totally different thing. It made no sense from a Western standpoint. In every movie I had ever seen, the deputy got moved up to sheriff. As usual, Sam had just shaken his head at me.

As I ducked around the island in the middle of the kitchen, I thought for half a second that I would get away from him, but as he grabbed, yanked, and pinned me against the refrigerator, I realized how wrong I had been.

"All I meant to imply," he began, tilting my head up with a hand on my chin, "was that since you have a six-year-old and a four-year-old now, you can do a half day at the office instead of working full-time from home. It might be nice after you drop them off to pick up a fancy cup of coffee and go to your office and actually see Dylan and Fallon and talk to them face to face."

I was really far too interested in his mouth to listen to him. He had the kind of lips made for kissing, plump and dark, and when he smiled, there was this curve in the corner that could break your heart. Not that the rest of his rugged features were without appeal. His dark smoky blue-gray eyes with the deep laugh lines at the corners, his long straight nose, the hard square jaw, and the thick copper-gold eyebrows were a treat too. And his voice, over the phone or in person, deep and husky, edged with a growl, could send rippling heat through my entire body. But the man's mouth, the shape of it, the feel of it... really, I was a fan.

"Are you listening to me?"

I lifted up from my height of five nine to his of six four, and he bent down at the same time. Our lips met and parted, and his tongue slid deep to taste me.

The sounds from the peanut gallery—choking and retching—and the tug on my robe instantly drained the heat from the encounter. Sam snorted out a laugh as he broke the kiss, both of us eyeing the short people standing close to us.

"That's disgusting," Kola assured me with a glare that a six-year-old shouldn't have had, full of judgment and revulsion.

"Why?" I asked snidely.

"Your mouth has germs," he informed me haughtily. "That's why you told Hannah not to lick Chilly."

"No, I told her not to lick Chilly because the cat doesn't like to be licked by her."

"He licks his body."

"He does," Hannah, our four-year-old, agreed with a nod. "Kola's right."

"But he doesn't want you to do it," I assured my daughter, directing my comment to her.

"How do you know?" Kola questioned.

"Yeah," Hannah Banana chimed in again, always her big brother's backup. "How do you know?"

I had to think.

Kola waited, squinting at me.

Hannah was waiting as well, one of her perfectly shaped dark brows arching. It was new. She had the same way of looking at me that her father did, like I was an idiot.

"Do not lick the cat! Nobody licks the cat!" Sam ordered when the silence stretched for too long.

I started laughing; only my husband would have to make such rules.

He looked down at his son, Mykola Thomas Kage, six years old going on forty, who was full of questions and opinions.

We had adopted him when he was three, from an agency in the Netherlands. When we had made the final trip to bring him home, he had seen us from the window of the orphanage director's office and run to the door to meet us. We had been there two weeks and he already called Sam Daddy, which Sam was madly in love with hearing. But though Kola had been taught the American word meaning father, it was not his, not the one he had grown up hearing and had been waiting to use for someone who belonged to him. So he had tried out the one he knew on me.

Pa.

So simple a word but it meant so much.

I had heard it in the streets when we visited, along with the more formal, *vader*, and seen kids run to their fathers using it. Not the papa I knew, not what Sam's father was called by his grandchildren, but instead just pa. When Kola called to me, I answered to it, and his face, the way it lit up, the absolute blinding joy, had been a gift.

Sam was Daddy, and Daddy represented Kola's new life and his new family in the United States, and I was the comfort of the old. I was Pa, and he had named me.

Of course it didn't matter to me what name he settled on. He could have called me Jory for all I cared; he was my kid, and that was all I gave a damn about. He was legally and completely mine and Sam's, and *that* was what mattered. And we were good, the three of us, until the first agency we had contacted back when we'd started the whole adoption process called to tell us that there was a little girl from Montevideo ready for adoption. I had forgotten about them because they had never come through, but that turned out not to be the case. You heard from them when it was time, and it finally was.

I was surprised, Sam unsure, until the professional but not personable and definitely not warm gentleman slid the picture across the desk for us. He needed to know if we wanted the little girl in the photograph.

Yes, we wanted the angel very much.

Our family went from three to four with the coming of the little sister that Kola wanted nothing to do with until we were all home under one roof. He resented all of us going to the airport to pick her up, hated her crying in the car, and was really annoyed that Sam was carrying her instead of him. He was starting to fret, it was all over his face—until Sam knelt and picked him up too. Kids are so funny. As soon as Kola figured out that Hannah was planning on sharing us with him, that she wasn't there to take his spot, that nothing was changing in the love department, just some tweaking in the time area, he decided he liked her. And now, with him at six and her at four, their bond was noticeable.

They fought like cats and dogs... but only sometimes. She cried, he moped, they chased each other and roughhoused, but nine times out of ten, I found her in his room in the morning. When we were out, he held her hand, he fixed things when she couldn't, and he was supremely patient when she was trying to impart some tidbit of information. I was like, *Spit it out, kid*, but Kola just nodded and waited until some incident about a bug on a flower was all communicated in excruciating detail.

He brushed her off if she fell down, made her remember her mittens and hat, and could be counted on to translate her wishes to others if Sam and I were absent. Dylan Greer, my best friend, was really surprised because she was certain that, sometimes, Hannah Banana—or B, as we all called her—spoke in tongues. But Kola would just say that she wanted milk or a crayon or a flashlight. And he was never wrong. He was an excellent big brother, and she adored him.

Hannah Regina Kage—her middle name after Sam's mother— had the most adorable little button nose on the planet. I would lean in to kiss her sometimes and nibble on her nose instead. It made her squeal with delight. Putting her toes in my mouth was also cause for raucous laughter. Even at a year old, she had a good laugh. It was not timid or soft. She was small, but how she expressed herself was big. People heard the deep, throaty sound and were enchanted. I had been under her spell at first glance.

In our neighborhood in River Park, sometimes people still looked at us when we were out walking. And most questioned Kola when they got close, since with his deep-set cobalt-blue eyes, sharp European features, and dark-brown hair, he didn't look like either me or Sam. But Hannah, who was half-Uruguayan, was obviously adopted. What was funny, though, was that people sometimes questioned whether Gentry—born with my brother Dane's charcoal eyes instead of my sister-in-law Aja's honey-brown ones—actually belonged to his own mother. I always wondered why people cared. If your kid was blue and you were orange, who gave a crap as long as you loved and cherished the blue kid? People still surprised me.

"Pa."

Hannah was looking up at me like I was the village idiot.

"What?"

"If Kola can't lick Chilly, you can't lick Daddy."

I had a terrible image of giving Sam a blow job just then, and he probably knew it, which was why he grabbed me and covered my mouth with his hand. "Will you two go finish your breakfast, please?"

They left then, but not without casting looks back.

Sam moved his hand but bent and kissed me. I received it happily, and of course, there was more retching.

"Kola Kage!" I admonished him even as I laughed. "Will you knock that off?"

"Ewww," Hannah squeaked out.

When I looked over at them, Kola was mixing his oatmeal with butter and brown sugar, making it burp with his spoon.

"Just eat it," I told him.

"I'm making it edible."

Edible. Damn kid and his damn vocabulary.

"Leave the Petersons alone," Sam sighed, long-suffering as he was.

"I am." I bit my bottom lip.

"Jory…," he cautioned me.

I tried for innocent.

"Daddy," Kola said, back beside us, looking up at Sam.

"Don't lick the cat," Sam reiterated, bending down to one knee as his son stepped into his arms and put his hands on his face. "All right?"

"Okay." Kola nodded.

"Okay," Sam sighed, pulling Kola close, hugging him tight for a minute.

"What's homonic?"

"I dunno." Sam yawned, leaning back so father and son could look at each other. "Where'd you hear it?"

"Pa told Auntie Dyl that Jake's parents won't let him come play at my house 'cause they're homonic."

Sam nodded. "That's homophobic, and that means that Jake's parents don't want him to come over because you have two fathers."

Kola squinted at Sam. "Why?"

"Some people just don't like it."

"Why?"

"Well, I think that some people are afraid of what it means."

He shook his head. "What does it mean?"

"That if you can have two fathers, maybe things are changing."

His scowl made his little eyebrows furrow. It was adorable. "I don't understand."

"I think you will when you're older, buddy."

"It's dumb."

"Yes it is," Sam agreed, hugging him again. "But I'm sorry."

"That's okay." He hugged Sam back tight, both arms wrapped around his neck. "Stuart and his mom are coming with me and Pa and Hannah and Uncle Evan and Bryce and Seth and Auntie Dyl and Mica and Mabel and Tess and her dad to the movies next Saturday, so Jake's the one who's missing out."

"Who's coming again?" Sam teased him.

"Stuart and his mom are coming with—"

"Stop," I cut Kola off. "Your father heard you the first time."

Sam grunted and looked up at me. "How come I didn't get invited to the movies?"

"First"—I smiled at him—"the Chipmunks give you hives, and secondly, won't you be fishing with Pat and Chaz that Saturday?"

"What Saturday are we talking about?"

"We're leaving tomorrow for Phoenix, for the reunion, and we'll come home Sunday."

"Yes, I know this."

"Okay, so then I'm talking about not this coming Saturday, since we'll be out of town, but the one after that."

"Oh, so that's right, then." He smiled brightly. "I'll be fishing. Sorry I won't make the movie, babe."

"Liar," I said flatly.

He cackled.

But it was going to be fun. I was going with my two kids, my buddy Evan was bringing his sons Bryce and Seth, and Dylan was schlepping her two kids: her son, Mica, who was her oldest, and Mabel, her daughter, who was the same age as Kola. It was unfortunate that they had made another *Alvin and the Chipmunks* movie, but all the kids were dying to see it, so we were making a day of it. I was still waiting to hear from Aja to see if she was coming along as well. I knew that Robert and Gentry were just as interested in helium-fueled rodents as the rest of our kids, but Aja wasn't, and she could use a day off.

Aja, who had been in the public school realm when she first married my brother, as first a principal and then assistant superintendent of schools, had found herself unable to enact change at that level. Aja could not amend policy or allocate funds, but instead of growing bitter about what she saw happening around her—the apathy and deliberate ignorance—she decided to do something about it. In her present position as the associate dean of education at De Paul University, training and inspiring the next generation of teachers, she was preparing bright minds for the real world as well as toughening skins. She armed them and motivated them and made sure they knew she would always be a resource for them even after they graduated. All that plus parenting two children, being a wife, attending a myriad of social functions with her husband, and the result was a worn-out Aja Harcourt. I wanted to help lessen her load.

As I was driving back home after dropping off Kola and Hannah—they both went to the same Montessori school close to Oak Park—I called Aja from the car and offered to take her two short people off her hands instead of having her join us. I was immediately called a saint.

"Jory, I need some me and Dane time."

"How 'bout I pick Robbie and Gen up next Friday after school and keep them until Sunday morning? We'll all go to brunch and you can have them back. But that gives you Friday night and all day Saturday. Whaddya say?"

I thought she was going to cry, she was so thankful.

"So is that a yes?"

"Ohmygod, yes, that's a yes!"

"You're starting to sound like me."

"Thank you, baby."

"What is family for?"

"But you're the only one I trust."

"That's not true." I smiled into the phone as I turned from the side street I was on into traffic on Harlem Avenue, heading for home. I went maybe ten feet before I and everyone else on the street came to a grinding halt.

"Yes, but since Carmen got her dream job globetrotting around the world and my folks fled to Florida and Alex to Delaware, you and Sam are the only family I've got here."

"You have a lot of other girlfriends," I told her as I tried to see what the problem was around the SUV in front of me.

"I know, but I would check in with the others, I don't need to check with you and Sam. He'll kill anyone that comes near my kids, and you worry more than I do."

"I don't worry."

She snorted out a laugh over the phone.

"That was very undignified," I said as I leaned back in the driver's seat of the sleek black minivan I utterly adored. Everyone else I knew had SUVs that were, I was certain, helping to destroy the environment. My minivan was not part of Satan's master plan, and I loved my car that proclaimed me married with children as well as safety conscious. I was looking forward to Kola starting soccer in the spring so the picture of domestic bliss would be complete. I had a sweater all picked out.

"You bring it out of me," Aja cackled.

"Whatever, I'll call you when I get back from the reunion on Sunday."

She started snickering.

"What?"

"Family reunion." She was laughing now. "Oh the horror!"

"It'll be fine," I told her as I noticed a man striding by my window. It was weird that he was walking down the middle of the street and not on the sidewalk, but since we were in gridlock, he was in no danger of getting run over. "Hey, your kids like Mountain Dew and Oreos, right?"

"They're staying with you for two days. Feed them whatever you want."

I was laughing when I hung up, but when the SUV in front of me suddenly reversed, crashing into my front bumper, I yelled and laid on my horn. But the car didn't stop—it kept grinding metal, and I realized that he, or she, was trying to get enough of an angle to go up onto the curb to the right.

I took a picture of the license plate with my phone, thanked God that my kids weren't with me, and was about to call the police to report the accident when I saw the passenger door of the SUV open. What was confusing was that the small woman who scrambled out had keys in her hand. It was like she had been driving but had not wanted to get out of the driver's side door. When she flung open the back door, a little rocket seat was visible: she had a toddler.

I got out fast and went around the back of my van—even as the guy in the car behind me honked, leaned out, and told me to get back behind the fucking wheel—and darted to her side.

She whirled on me with a can of pepper spray in hand.

"Wait! I'm here to help."

Her eyes were huge as she looked at me, shoved the can into my chest, and told me to look out for the guy so she could get her son out of the car. She had been too frightened to even open her door.

"What guy?"

"I don't know, some psycho. I think he killed the man in the car in front of me," she cried. "I think he has a gun or—oh God!"

Turning, I saw a man advancing on us. "Move your fucking cars!"

"Get inside!" I ordered her. "Lock it!"

She climbed into the backseat around her kid, and I heard the locks behind me as the man advanced on me fast.

He had a lug wrench, not a gun, and since I could run if I needed to, I went from terrified to annoyed very quickly. "What the hell are you doing?" I barked at him. "You're scaring the crap out of this lady!"

"Move your cars! This whole street is just full of fucking cars!"

He wasn't even looking at me; I doubt he could have told me where he was or what he was doing. Maybe the road rage had made him snap; perhaps something else. I didn't know and I didn't care—he was carrying around an automotive tool like a weapon. That was really my only concern. The lady in the SUV was freaked because her kid was in the car and this guy was acting crazy. If my kids were with me, I would have had the same reaction.

"Stop," I ordered him. "Don't come any closer."

He kept coming, and he raised the wrench like maybe he was thinking of braining me with it. I aimed the nozzle of the pepper spray and made sure to get his face.

His scream was loud and wounded, but he didn't drop the tool.

"What the fuck are you doing?"

It was the guy who had yelled at me earlier, whose car was in gridlock behind mine.

"You just attacked this guy?" he roared right before he hit me.

I went down hard, hitting the van as I bounced off it, but from my angle, I could see the guy I had sprayed coming at him.

Kicking hard, I knocked the guy who had just hit me off balance, and he tumbled to the ground beside me.

"What the fuck are you—"

"Look out!" I yelled as the guy with the lug wrench came after us.

"Oh shit," he screamed, scrambling back away from me, moving to run.

"Drop the weapon!"

"Get on the ground!"

Normally, policemen—even though I'm married to an ex one—are not my favorite people. As a rule, they catch me doing crap I shouldn't be but somehow miss everyone else talking on their cell phones, running red lights, and speeding.

But right at that moment, as I saw the uniforms, noted the drawn guns, and heard the orders being roared out, I was comforted.

The guy dropped the lug wrench and went to his knees.

"All the way down, face on the pavement!"

"You saved my life," the guy who hit me said.

"I—"

But something slammed the back of my head, and everything went dark.

MY HUSBAND, my brother, family, and friends would say that yes, Jory Harcourt is a trouble magnet, but I think it's more coincidence than anything else when fate decides to screw with me. Especially this time: I was going home from dropping off my kids, a trip I made

Monday through Friday, normally without incident. How was I to know that I would end up in the crosshairs of accidental crazy?

"A what?" the policeman who was taking my statement at the hospital asked.

"Trouble magnet," I told him as I sighed deeply.

"How did you get knocked out?" he asked me.

"I guess the lady I told to stay in her SUV, she opened the door really fast and I was sitting right beside her car and… you know."

He nodded. "I see."

"That's why vans are better, the doors slide," I educated him.

His smile was patronizing.

"I—"

"Jory!" His yell bounced off the walls, and I winced.

The officer looked startled. "Who was—"

"Scooch back," I ordered, and took a breath to get the required amount of air into my lungs. "In here!"

The curtain was flung open moments later and there was Sam, jaw clenched, muscles cording in his neck, eyes dark and full of too many things to soothe at once.

"Detective Kage?"

Sam turned to the officer.

"Oh, no, marshal." He tried to smile at my glowering man.

Sam's attention returned to me, and I smiled as I lifted my arms for him.

Moving fast, Sam closed the short distance between us and hauled me forward and crushed me against him.

It was not gentle; the entire movement was jarring and hard.

I loved it.

"Scared me," he said as he clutched me tight.

I knew I had, which was the reason for the grab. I leaned into him, nuzzled my face into the crook of his neck, and slid my arms under the suit jacket and over the crisp dress shirt. He smelled good, a faint trace of cologne, fabric softener, and warm male. I whimpered softly in the back of my throat.

"Those calls take years off my life, you know?"

"What calls?"

"The *Jory's in the hospital* calls."

I nodded, and there was a rumble of a grunt before he leaned back and looked down into my face. His eyes clocked me, checking, making sure I was whole and safe.

"I'm fine," I said as he lifted his hand and knotted it into my hair, tilting my head back as he examined my right eye and my cheek.

"Yeah, you don't look fine," he said, and his voice was low and menacing. "Who did this?"

"There was a guy behind me, and he didn't understand why I sprayed the man with the lug wrench, and he—"

"Stop," he cut me off, dropping his hand from my hair as he turned his head to the policeman. "Talk."

I could tell from his change of tone that he wasn't waiting on me, but apparently the officer could not. "Hello?" Sam snapped icily.

"Oh-oh," the guy stammered and then recounted to Sam the events of the morning.

"So the lady in the SUV knocked him out when she opened the door?" He was trying to make sure he understood everything.

"Yes."

Sam grunted.

"She's really sorry about it. She told me that your partner there saved her life."

That didn't make it any better, at least for Sam.

"My van is—"

"We'll take care of the van and get you a rental until it's fixed. Just don't worry about it."

"No, I know," I snapped at him. Sometimes—a lot of the time— Sam treated me like an invalid. It was happening more and more lately, like I needed to be taken care of, same as the kids, because I couldn't think for myself or reason things out. "I just wanted to know where my vehicle was towed to… Officer."

I had turned to the man in uniform, pinned him with my gaze—my question was directed to him—and he was still looking at Sam to see if he should answer me.

"Officer?"

"I can find out where the—"

"No," I shut Sam down, eyes wide as I waited. "Where's my car?"

"We, um." He coughed as he passed me a business card from his clipboard. "Had it towed to a garage downtown and—"

"Just stop," Sam barked at me, snatching the card away. "Sit here while I go find your doctor and figure out if you have a concussion or—"

"Sam—"

"After I get you home, then we'll worry about the damn van."

"I can—"

"Stop," he ordered again, and because I didn't want to have a scene, I went still and quiet and stared at the clock on the wall.

The officer muttered something and left, and Sam told me that he had to go and find out about the other people in the accident and would see about my release at the same time.

I stayed quiet.

"You're gonna sulk now?"

I turned my head and was about to say something when he lifted his hand.

"I don't wanna fight with you. Just let me do this."

"I'm not a child, Sam. I can take care of my own car. I can do—"

"So I shouldn't be here? I shouldn't have even come?"

"No, I just… lately it seems to be the *Sam Show* and not the *Sam and Jory Show*. You do everything, and I don't get why that's happening."

His eyes searched mine.

"Sam? Do you think I'm helpless?"

The glare I was getting would have terrified most people. But this was the guy who loved me, and as always, when I stopped and actually used my brain, I understood what was really going on.

He was terrified.

I had scared the crap out of him that morning, and because he was waiting for the other shoe to drop anyway… it was almost like he was expecting bad news. And he was—he was expecting the worst.

"You think me and Kola and Hannah could get taken away."

"What? No," he said quietly, not a lot of force behind his words. "No."

He was such a liar.

"I'm sorry," I said quickly, putting my hands on his heavily muscled chest, unable to stop myself from curling my fingers into his shirt, holding on. Yes, he was being overprotective, but not for the reasons I thought. He didn't think I was stupid; he just didn't want to let me, or his kids, out of his sight for any reason. Not ever. And because he was trying not to be suffocating, he was managing the exact opposite. "I wasn't thinking."

He took a breath. "What're you talking about?"

"The more you work, the more you see, the more you realize that this, what we have, is not the norm. Most people don't get the kind of happiness that we have, the home we have, so you get over protective and smothering."

He furrowed his brows, and I smiled up at him as I hooked my legs around the back of his thighs. He leaned closer, hands on either side of me on the narrow hospital bed. "You think you know me?"

I nodded, my fingers unclenching from his shirt. "Yes. I know you well."

He bent toward me, and I twined an arm around his neck to draw him close. His breath fanned softly across my face before his mouth settled over mine.

I loved to kiss him. Whenever, however, for as long as he'd let me or as long as he wanted to. I was his for the taking.

He swept his tongue in, mating it with mine, tangled, rubbed, pushed, and shoved. Our lips never parted, not once, even for air. I felt his arms wrap around me, crush me to his chest, and hold tight. I had a hand knotted in his hair, and the moan I couldn't stifle was low and aching. When he suddenly shoved me back, breaking the scorching, devouring contact, my whine of protest was loud.

He was flushed and panting, his lips swollen, his pupils blown as he stared at me.

I was breathing hard, my lungs heaving for air as I smiled at him.

"Crap." He finally managed to get out a word.

My smile was wicked.

"You're not supposed to kiss me at work."

"You kissed me," I reminded him.

"Crap," he said again and swallowed hard as he straightened up, stepping away from me, obviously fighting to get his body back under control.

"You can nail me in your car."

His frown came fast, and so did my grin.

"What?" I smiled wide.

"A Deputy US Marshal does not nail his spouse in the car."

I arched an eyebrow for him. "Are you sure?"

He pointed at me. "I will take you home to our bed and nail you."

"Oh yes, please." I waggled my eyebrows for him.

"Just sit there," he growled at me. "And wait while I get you signed out of here so we can go get the kids."

"Not today, Marshal," I told him.

He looked surprised. "You didn't plan to pick up your children today?"

"No, your mom's picking them up and then we're going there for dinner."

He squinted at me.

"You know she's a planner," I said cheerfully.

"Lemme get this straight," he sighed. "We're gonna be with them on a plane tomorrow, with them at a resort from Thursday to Saturday, and then with them again on a plane on Sunday coming home, but we're still eating with them tonight because they won't see us?"

"Your mom likes to coordinate and you know this, so just let it go."

"Why?" He was annoyed.

"Why does she like to plan things or why are we indulging her?"

"The second one," he grumbled. "Why do we do that?"

"Because we love her," I said like it was obvious.

"No, screw that. I'm gonna call her and tell her we—"

"Why would you rock the boat? Why would you upset the delicate balance of all things Regina?"

I loved his mother, Regina Kage, with absolute abandon, and of everyone—her own children, their spouses, and all her grandchildren combined—she and I got along best. The reasons for that were twofold: first, because I'd never had a mother and craved one like a drug; second, and most of all, because I didn't ever try to change her. We never fought; I allowed her to rearrange anything in my house she wanted, make suggestions on parenting—because really, her kids came out good, so where was the argument?—and most of all, when she fussed, whenever she fussed, I was at her disposal to lend a hand. We were good.

"Jory—"

"Let it go, Sam."

He rolled his eyes, but we both knew he wouldn't say a word. No one said a word to Regina Kage. We all did exactly as she wanted. She was the matriarch, after all.

"Seriously, though, we should cancel, you're in no—"

"I'm fine, and besides, I think she had trip itineraries printed up, and I want to make sure to get mine."

He was disgusted, but I got the smile I was after with the shake of his head, the *you are too much* and *I give up* one that I loved.

"So," I said softly as my gaze skated over him. God, I loved looking at him. The broad shoulders that the suit jacket accentuated, the snug fit of the tailored dress shirt over his massive chest, and the stubble that covered his square, chiseled jaw even though he'd shaved that morning before work.

"What?" he asked, and his voice was husky as he stared at me.

"You're gonna take me home?"

"Yes."

"And stay with me?"

"Yeah. I want to make sure you're okay."

I stared into those eyes that I loved as much now as I had the first time he'd kissed me all those years ago. "You're taking care of me again."

He grunted and it was all male, all growly bear. "And?"

"And it's nice." I smiled at him, taking a loose hold of his tie.

He sighed and I got a trace of a smile. "Okay, I'll be right back."

"Wait," I said before he could leave.

"Why? What?"

"Come gimme kiss."

"No." He snorted out a laugh and then bent and kissed my forehead before he walked out of the room.

I was lost in thought, every brain cell I possessed absorbed with Sam Kage and what I was going to do to him with an afternoon alone, when my name was called.

"Mr. Harcourt?"

When I turned, there was a doctor there, and I registered almost instantly that it really wasn't fair. He got to look like that *and* be brilliant? Normally you were smart or pretty, not both. He even had bright blue-green eyes. I noticed that because they were the exact shade of turquoise that I wanted when I was growing up. I had hated my brown eyes with a passion. Now things were different. My daughter and I had almost the same shade of deep chocolate brown with hints of gold, and the man who woke up in bed with me every morning never failed to mention that as eyes went, mine were his favorite color.

"Mr. Harcourt?"

"Yeah, sorry." I flashed him a quick grin. "That's me."

"Hi." He smiled warmly as he closed in, offering me his hand. "I'm Dr. Dwyer, and—"

"Jory, you—"

"Sam?"

My doctor called my man by his first name.

Sam stood there looking utterly gobsmacked.

Both men, my partner and the doctor, froze as they stood staring at each other.

What the hell…?

Doctor Dwyer had been interrupted by Sam's return, and Sam had apparently been quite startled to see the doctor when he came charging back into the room.

I kept looking between them, feeling weirder by the second.

"Kevin," Sam finally said.

The man took a step forward, and the smile, the light that hit his eyes, the shiver that ran through his long, lean swimmer's frame, was not to be mistaken for anything other than absolute, quivering, pulse-pounding, blood-racing joy. Whoever he was, he was deliriously surprised and delighted to see Sam Kage.

I waited and realized that I had stopped breathing.

Who was this heavenly creature, this doctor who was looking at Sam like he was the most beautiful thing he had ever seen in his entire life?

"You…." Sam sucked in a breath. "What are you doing here?"

"Jesus," the doctor gasped and rushed forward, arms lifted, ready to reach out and grab hold, reclaim.

Sam moved faster, meeting him and cutting him off, so basically, with his forward momentum halted, the good doctor was brought up short, almost to a jarring, lose-your-balance stop. Sam leaned, gave him the guy clench, tight-tight, then pushed off and back so Dr. Dwyer was basically left abandoned and bewildered, arms empty, looking lost.

"Nice to see you," Sam said quickly, stepping close to the bed and taking my hand at the same time. "Jory, this is Dr. Kevin Dwyer. We met in Columbia when I was there working that drug bust after Dom went into witness protection. He was with Doctors Without Borders at that time. What are you doing here in Chicago?"

Years ago, Sam had left me recovering in the hospital to track down a drug cartel in Colombia on a tip from his corrupt partner. We had been apart for three years, and at some point he had met the good doctor.

Dr. Dwyer seriously looked like someone had punched him in the gut or run him over with a truck. It was hard to tell which better described him at that moment. "I," he started but stopped, and then his eyes flicked to mine. "Jory?"

I smiled at him. "Yes."

He nodded. "Sam told me all about you."

And yet Sam had never, ever mentioned Kevin Dwyer to me. "Did you date?" I asked the doctor, because I didn't mess around.

"Jor—"

"No," he cut Sam off. "We lived together for three months."

And my world imploded.

TWO

"SPEAK."

"I'm not a dog, Sam."

He muttered something under his breath.

"I'm sorry?" I asked and realized my voice was much too sharp.

"I said...." He sighed, and only when I glanced over at him did I realize that his knuckles were white on the wheel. He was holding on tight. "I know you're pissed, but I wish you would just talk to me already."

"Why should I be pissed? It was a long time ago, right?"

"Yeah, it was a long time ago," he growled, raking his fingers through his thick copper-colored hair. As he got older, it was getting darker, which I found interesting. "But you're thinking about it and you're thinking really hard, and if you would just come out with whatever the hell is going on in your head, that would be good."

I wasn't ready to put my thoughts into words yet.

"Jory," Sam said softly.

But it would sound like an accusation, and I needed it to not be.

"I lied, yeah?"

He had.

"Why would I do that?"

I could remember the discussion so clearly. I'd questioned him in that diner about how many guys he had slept with while we had been apart. The inquiry had begun with me asking about women and then, when he replied that there had been none, moved on to men. That had been seven years ago.

"Jory?"

I looked out the window instead of at him.

"What would you have done if I told you that night that I had slept with four guys but the fifth guy… that one I liked?"

I closed my eyes. Hearing it now was painful. Hearing it then… I would have run.

"It only lasted three months."

Part of me really wanted to hear the story and part of me didn't.

"I was hurt, and he took a bullet out of me and stitched me up and gave me a shot. When I saw him a week later in a bar, I bought him a drink to say thank you."

I could see how that would have progressed.

"I was really drunk, things weren't going well… one year had rolled by already and we weren't any closer…." He trailed off.

The rain was sluicing down the glass in rivulets.

"It got late and he offered to let me sleep it off at his place because it was close by."

My body flushed hot and then went cold.

"When we got there, when the door closed, he wanted something more, and I… you get it. I don't need to tell you."

I did.

"It was nice to have the normalcy in the middle of all the crazy, to have a small place where I could go to just breathe."

"It was a sanctuary," I said, holding my breath.

"No," he said, his voice low and gravelly. "It was just not blood on the pavement and ten-year-old boys killing each other in the street and girls who should be planning sleepovers turning tricks and shooting up… it was just not horrible."

"I thought you were in the jungle."

"I was everywhere, J."

"I see."

He pulled over, put the SUV in park, hit the hazards, and turned to face me. Not that I saw him, but I could hear the leather seat creak.

"We should get home, Sam."

"Look at me."

I rolled my head sideways.

He reached out and took hold of my chin; his fingers slid over my skin, his thumb tracing my bottom lip. "Our home, yours and mine, that's my sanctuary. What I had with Kevin... I mean, I was in the middle of a big fuckin' mess in a foreign country, and I was tired and lonely, but still, it's no excuse for what I did."

"What did you do?"

"For just a minute, just like a second, I stopped thinking."

I didn't understand. "Sam?"

He brought his left hand up to join the right, framing my face, smoothing his thumbs over my cheekbones. "I felt so bad for using Kevin... I was such a shit to him. I fucked him, I ate his food, I slept in his bed, and I treated him like a whore."

I leaned out of his hands and he let them drop away.

"That was how it went, and then when I realized what I was doing, I tried to apologize to him and end it, and—"

"He didn't want to," I cut him off.

"No." His voice rumbled out of his chest. "He didn't."

"Because what you thought was bad was his wet dream."

"I wouldn't go—"

"He liked you in pieces that he got to put back together, he liked being the guy who submitted to you, liked being the one you held down and ordered around. He wanted you to stay in his bed."

"Yeah." He cleared his throat.

"And?"

"And what?"

"I want to hear the end, Sam."

"And I want you in my lap."

It took me a second because he had changed topics so quickly. "What?"

"If I'm baring my soul any more, I want you in my lap."

I shook my head. "No, I can't do—"

"Fine, it ended," he said, and turned to grab hold of his seatbelt.

I opened my door.

"What're you doing?" he barked, lunging fast but not quick enough as the door swung wide.

I turned to look at him. "I'm not sitting in your lap. This is not a tantrum I'm throwing, and you don't get to treat me like a drama queen or a petulant child. This is you caught in a lie of your own making. Finish the story or I will get out and walk home and you can go back to work and pick me up later when it's time to go to your mother's."

His eyes locked on mine.

"Your choice."

"You're madder than I thought."

"I'm not mad," I assured him.

"Hurt, then."

He wasn't getting an answer. I just waited.

"Close the door," he breathed.

Leaning out, I grabbed the handle and pulled it shut before turning back to him. I was startled by the look on his face.

"You don't get to leave me," he whispered, and his eyes were cold and dark like water under ice. The transformation was scary.

"Sam?"

His eyes were narrow slits. "I forbid it."

Forbid? "Sam, what're you—"

"We weren't together, you were fucking any guy who asked, and—"

"Sam, don't go all defensive and shitty, all right? I'm not hurt because you slept with someone, I'm hurt because you lied about being in a relationship with—"

"It was nothing! It was shit!" he yelled at me, and I heard the pain and the frustration and, most of all, his fear. "You—it meant... I only ever wanted—"

"Stop." I put up my hands before I moved quickly, unbuckling my belt, climbing over the console between us, and scrambling into his lap, my knees on either side of his hips.

"Christ," he growled, hands on my thighs, grabbing hold, fingers digging into my muscles as he jerked me forward so my ass settled over his groin, the bulge in his dress pants sliding over my crease. "Don't leave me."

I pushed forward, against him, rubbing, grinding. "Why? Because you want to keep fucking me?"

"Well yeah, that too." He scowled, taking my face in his hands and pushing my hair out of my eyes. "I knew the difference then, I know the difference now. You're it, you're home for me. If it's not you, it won't be anybody. I can't settle, it's all or nothing."

I sighed, looking at him. "I know."

He brightened, and I saw it, and it was really so dear. "I love you so much it hurts."

And I knew that too. There were too many years between us for me to have doubts about that. But he had lied, and that wasn't like him. "Why were you so scared that night that you would lie?"

"You."

"Me?"

"Yeah. It was brand new, you trusting me again, and if I fucked it up and you sent me away... what the hell was I supposed to do, J?"

I stared into his eyes.

"There was no way I was losing you then, and there's no way I'm letting this come between us now. I'm sorry I lied about Kevin Dwyer. It was stupid, I should have just said. But you were a scared rabbit back then."

"Not anymore?"

"No," he sighed. "You haven't been that guy in a long time."

I leaned forward and wrapped my arms around his neck, hugging tight, shoving my nose against the side of his neck, inhaling him.

"Oh please," he murmured, one hand cradling the back of my head, gently knotting in my hair, the other on the small of my back, holding me close. "I am sorry for never telling you about Kevin Dwyer, but it was a long time ago and doesn't mean shit, I swear to God."

I tightened my arms, pressed closer, and heard him exhale into my shoulder. He needed to know everything was okay; it was imperative that his home was in order. He needed it so he could do his job out in the world. "He's a very handsome man."

He grunted, not paying attention, tipping my head back to kiss the base of my throat. "There's this one freckle right here that drives me crazy."

"I said," I repeated, "he's a very handsome man."

"We both know that you're the only thing I see."

And it was true. I had been surprised and that was all. "Let's go home, Marshal; maybe I have time to do you before my husband shows up to take me to my mother-in-law's for dinner."

"Oh yes, please," he whispered before he kissed me harder and held on tighter.

SAM turned onto our street and then took the left into the driveway along the right side of the house. It ran along the fence separating our property from the Petersons', where the circus had come to town.

There were at least ten squad cars on the street and another two and an ambulance in the driveway. I didn't get to make an inquiry; I was shoved through the back door of my house into the kitchen and told to lock the door behind me. I bolted to the window and watched Sam walk back down the driveway to the street. I could see through the chain-link fence into the Petersons' front lawn; saw all the neighbors standing across the street and a lot of policemen traipsing through the yard. I wanted to go outside, but that would be a bad idea, so I walked to the front door to see if the mail was splattered by the front door.

My whole life I'd had a mailbox; only since we'd moved into this house did I have a mail slot that everything got shoved through. As I expected, my stupid cat, Chilly—all white except for his nose and the tips of his ears, which were black—was lying on his back on the mail, feet up in the air. Why he did it every single day, I had no idea. Sam thought maybe it was something new coming into the house on a daily basis that didn't smell like him. It was just weird.

"What are you doing?" I asked my feline friend.

I got the talking he always did with me, a soft chuffing, before he rolled to his feet to prance over and greet me. He was a "second-chance pet," which meant that when we adopted him from the humane society, he was alone on one side of the cat enclosure. He was in one of the stacked metal cages instead of the Plexiglas area where all the others were. I had walked over to him and he had shoved his little paw through the bars and put it on the top of my head. Right that second, I was a goner.

"Second chance" meant that he had been adopted and brought back. Twice. Apparently he was manic. It was a match made in heaven!

I had had specific directions. Sam had said to go to the humane society and get a long-haired, declawed older cat that would be mellow with the kids. He liked long-haired cats because that's what he had been raised with. His mother always had Persians or Himalayans, so he knew how to care for them, the brushing that was needed, and figured that would be good for the kids, to teach them responsibility. A Maine coon, he had told me, was also perfectly acceptable.

It really was an easy request if he'd have sent the right guy. I wasn't him.

When I brought Chilly home, he peed on himself in the carrier because he was scared. I felt so sorry for him but even though I wanted him to make a good impression, I just couldn't bring myself to add to his terror by bathing him. So, unfortunately, the cat Sam saw for the first time reeked of urine, still had claws, and possessed a sort of crazed look in his eyes. It was not the best first impression that was ever made.

Dylan saved me by coming over with some kitty bath wash that you didn't need water for, but afterward Chilly smelled more like linen-scented piss than anything else. Sam was not impressed.

We had one of those Chia Pets that you buy at Walmart, because Kola had wanted one. It was basically a head, Mr. Grass Head, and Chilly took one look at that thing and decided that it needed to be batted off the Kola and Hannah's desk and dumped onto the floor.

Chilly got stuck between the window ledge and the chair, wedged so that his legs crossed and he looked like Tom Hanks in *The Money Pit*, when he's stuck in the floor in a carpet.

He got up on his back legs and attacked Hannah's stuffed bunny, Bunny (so original), and made her shriek.

He deflated Kola's Spider-Man ball with his claws and knocked down the fan in the kitchen. All of it done within the first hour of him living with us.

Hannah decided she wanted a puppy. Kola thought we should set him free. Sam told me if I took him back maybe I could get a refund.

I told them all if I took him back, he was going to die.

Hannah, still consoling and comforting her bunny, called Chilly. He sprinted over, flipped a somersault for her, grabbed the bunny, bit it, rabbit-kicked it, and then leaped up and tore off in another direction.

"I hope he doesn't suffer when they gas him," Sam cackled.

"Honey," I whined.

"He looks like a snow demon," Kola told me.

"The snow is cold," Hannah informed me.

"Yep, it's chilly," Kola agreed with his sister.

"Chilly!" Hannah squealed, clapping her hands.

"Chilly the cat." Kola nodded, beaming up at me. "Chilly! Chilly!"

And the damn cat came and he brought one of Kola's green Nerf Blaster balls with him.

"Look, he can fetch!" My son was so happy.

"Little shit," Sam muttered under his breath, because he knew as well as I did that it was a done deal at that point.

I had concerns—like the way the cat just ran, for no apparent reason, from one end of the house to the other—but over that, Sam just raised an eyebrow.

"He's a spaz, just like you."

I scowled at the marshal.

The appointment had been made to have the cat declawed, but the night before the surgery, Sam had come home with an assortment of scratching posts and an enormous house thing for Chilly to climb and sit on.

I had just waited as Sam put everything down in the living room.

He cleared his throat. "We'll try this first."

Apparently whatever the marshal had read on the Internet about declawing, he didn't like. So Chilly, who it turned out really liked his plethora of alternatives to shredding the couch, got to keep the weapons he was born with.

Kola adored him, and Hannah kept calling for him to do whatever trick he was doing again and again and he got so wound up that I thought he would ricochet off the walls. She chanted his name, bounced on her toes, and squealed. My girl was in love.

My boy was in love too. He taught Chilly to fetch on purpose and not by accident.

Hannah taught Chilly that batting things off the counter—spoons, forks, broccoli, pretzels, even yogurt very carefully spooned out—would get him lots of petting as a reward. When she was sticky, inevitably so was the cat, and I ended up having to clean them both. Chilly never pulled away or leaned out of reach; instead, he allowed grubby hands to stroke him in whatever condition they were in.

The kids loved to carry him, put him in backpacks with his head sticking out, and walk him on the leash, which Sam thought was the height of absurdity—who walked a cat, for crissakes—and sleep with him. The fact that he would sleep stretched out beside them in their beds was hysterical. And the part where my kids would contort themselves into absurd positions because they didn't want to wake him was even funnier. Heaven forbid we disturb the cat. He was a member of our family, and even Sam was pleased when he was greeted by all of us at the door when he came home at night. Chilly would scold him if he didn't get his own pat of affection, so Sam and he had their own routine. Sam would walk to the couch, where the cat would run to meet him and leap onto the arm so that my husband could bend down and Chilly could lift up and they could touch noses. I had taken a picture of it once just to show Sam's mother, and I was supposed to have deleted it afterward. I still had it.

"Why do you have to scent mark the mail?" I asked the cat, who was purring loudly under my ministrations.

As I gathered the scattered correspondence, the doorbell rang. When I answered it, the man there showed me his badge. It was a marshal badge, like Sam's.

"Good afternoon," he greeted me. "May I speak to Supervisor—"

"Deputy White?" Sam said, walking up beside me, standing close.

The man held a manila envelope out for Sam. "These came for you, and I remember you saying if anything came from Phoenix that you were to get it right away."

"Thank you," he said, opening it up.

The marshal shoved his hands down into his pockets but didn't say anything.

I was uncomfortable just looking at him and leaned ever so slightly to get Sam's attention.

He turned to me, and I made my eyes big, and because it was Sam and he knew me, his eyes flicked over to the marshal on my porch. "Something you wanna say?"

The younger man cleared his throat. "I just—we... if you need us while you're out there on vacation... not that you would, but if you do... we're on a plane in an hour, day or night. Just so you know."

He squinted at White. "No one but you, Sanchez, Kowalski, Ryan, and Dorsey know where I'm going, right?"

"That's correct, sir."

Sam nodded. "Good. So just if anything—"

"We're your team, yeah?" He looked Sam in the eye. "Whatever you need, just call."

"Understood."

White took a breath. "Do you really?"

"Yes."

"'Cause you know if one of those marshals from Nevada wasn't right, then maybe—"

"I'm going to a family reunion in Phoenix—in Scottsdale, actually, so why are you—"

"We've only ever lost one witness on your watch," he said. "And we all know you never got over it. So when we see you—you, Sam Kage—not using regular channels to have stuff delivered, we know something's up."

Sam was silent.

"And you know us; none of us would say shit to anybody about what you're doing or where you're going, but we want you to know that we're ready to move if you need us."

"I'm not supposed to use you guys to follow up on leads, for hunches and wild goose chases. That's a misappropriation of—"

"Cut the shit. We—"

"Take another tone with me, Marshal."

White sighed deeply. "Come on, boss. I just mean that if it turns out that those marshals from Vegas were dirty, even one of them… and the witness is in Phoenix now and something goes wrong… we'll be there, all five of us. Just call. Promise to call. That last one was—"

"I got it," Sam cut him off.

Chandler White—I remembered his first name after a minute— narrowed his eyes and looked at me before realization dawned and he smiled wide. "Oh, okay. Didn't tell your better half about the thing with Rico, huh?"

Sam growled at him, pointed at the street, and told him that he was excused.

"Yeah but—" his smile got goofy—"maybe I should stick around and fill Mr. Harcourt in on the details of that shoot-out if you're not gonna promise to—"

"I'll call," he barked at his marshal before he grabbed my arm, yanked me back, and slammed the door in White's face.

I was going to say something, but I could hear White laughing from outside, and I had bigger fish to fry anyway. I rounded on Sam.

"No," he groaned, turning away from me, crossing the floor, and dropping the envelope on the coffee table before falling facedown onto the soft cushions of our brown corduroy couch.

"Sam!" I yelled, charging after him. "What the hell was he talking about?"

He mumbled something into the couch cushions.

"Samuel Thomas Kage!"

His moan was pure agony before he rolled his head to the side. "I'm fine; you can see I'm fine. What does it matter?"

I flicked him on the forehead and he chuckled instead of yelling. "Shit."

"Sam!"

Another groan before he smiled. I only saw the curl of his lip on the left side, but it made my stomach flutter anyway.

"It all makes sense now."

"Oh God, what does?" he whined.

"Two weeks ago when you crawled home at like one in the morning, said you had a shitty day, took a shower, and passed out naked in bed."

"Yeah? What about it?"

"You were almost killed that day, weren't you."

He grunted before he stood up.

"What are you doing?"

"I'll be right back." He grinned before he leaned in and kissed me.

I watched him go up the stairs and threw up my hands.

When the doorbell rang again, I went to answer it. This time the badge that greeted me was a detective one.

"Mr. Harcourt?"

"Detective."

He was trying to look around me. "Is Marshal Kage here?"

"Yes, hold on. Would you like to come in?"

"Thank you." He smiled at me before pointing to my eye. "You all right there?"

"I scuffled with a crazy driver earlier. You know how that road rage can be."

He nodded like I was maybe not right in the head.

I walked to the stairs, yelled up at Sam that he had a visitor, and went to wash the breakfast dishes that were piled in the sink.

Sam came down a minute later, barefoot, in jeans frayed along the cuffs and a pocket T-shirt. I looked at him long enough to admire the way the denim hugged his firm, round ass and clung to his long, muscular legs. The stretch of the cotton around his biceps, the contrast of the white shirt to his golden skin and his fuzzy arms, was also not to be missed.

In minutes he walked the detective to the door and turned the dead bolt behind him.

"What did he want?" I called over to him.

"To talk about the Petersons," he said as he walked up behind me.

"Yeah, I don't care about that," I assured him. "I want to know what the hell happened with you and Rico, and—"

"Your wish is my command," he cut me off, his lips on the side of my neck sending a jolt of pure heat ricocheting from my stomach to my heart to my dick.

"Sam." I jerked under the hands now holding on to my hips. "I wanna talk to you."

He tipped my head sideways, baring the skin where neck and shoulder met.

"Sam," I whimpered, pushing back into him, rubbing my ass over his groin.

His warm breath touched my skin before his teeth. Gently, slowly, he bit down, and I shuddered from head to toe.

"I—you," I mumbled as his tongue slid up the side of my neck to behind my ear.

A rumbling growl came from his chest, and I lost it. There was no way not to succumb to the sounds he made, the heat rolling off him, and his big hard body.

I shut off the water, turned with some difficulty because he was pressing against me, and jumped him.

He caught me easily, stepping back so my legs could wrap around his hips, my arms encircling his neck. He fused his lips with mine, blanking every thought I had, only want remaining, only need.

As he carried me from the kitchen to the living room, I writhed in his grip, grinding my groin into his, loving the way his hands were digging into my ass, squeezing hard. His breath caught over the sensation.

"You like touching me," I told him.

"Always have," he husked as he leaned in and kissed me again.

His tongue invaded, taking, ravaging. He sucked and nibbled, and I lost track of everything except pushing against him, rubbing my hard, aching cock into his washboard abs and whining my desire in the back of my throat.

Down under him on the couch I went, and our lips never parted even as my hands went frantically to my belt and he yanked and pulled on my button-down.

I bowed up off the couch when he yanked off my Dockers, felt the cool air on my leaking shaft as he freed it from my briefs and it bounced free. His lips lifted away then, and I would have protested, but they engulfed the head of my cock in the same moment.

"Oh fuck, Sam!" I rasped, arching up, burying myself in the back of his throat, which opened to receive me. The motion was fluid after so long, his technique seamless, the pull back, the swirl of his tongue, and the fierce, hard suction.

The hands on my ass were insistent, and I knew what he had gone upstairs for when I heard the pop of the cap on the lube just before a finger slid between my cheeks.

"Oh God, just fuck me already!" I yelled at him, squirming, wiggling, trying to get his finger in deeper while sliding in and out of his hot mouth.

Two fingers breached my entrance, pressing forward as my muscles began to relax and open for him.

"You're so tight," he whispered as my cock slid from between his lips. "And you're all slicked up for me."

I could feel my ass grasping his fingers, three now, pushing in and out, deeper and deeper, and finally curling forward over my prostate. "Sam!"

"Yes, baby?" he asked, his voice raw and strained with desire.

"What are you waiting for?"

"I never want to hurt you, you know that."

I almost cried. "Sam!"

He moved so fast—pulled his fingers from my ass, rolled forward, and flung my legs over his shoulders. I felt the enormous flared head push against my opening.

My heels were on his back, and I leveraged myself up, lifting, aligning myself for his downward plunge.

He tried to ease in, to make the press slow, but I was dying, my body shaking, ready to explode, so I met him as he thrust forward, and stole his well-meaning restraint.

"Fuck!" I screamed when he buried himself to his balls in my ass.

"Jory."

Never, ever, did it stop feeling good, did it stop being what I wanted and needed and craved. I was stretched and filled, and when he eased out to ram back inside, then again and again, the hammering became all there was.

I was solely focused on my anatomy, on where we were connected, joined, and the throbbing pleasure drowned everything else: the burn, the pinch, and my aching muscles. Only his long, hard, thick cock grinding over my prostate mattered, only his hands clenched on my hips, only his mouth as he bent and sucked and bit my nipples.

"I'm gonna come," I whined. "I don't wanna come."

"You feel so fuckin' good." His voice was so low, more a growl than anything else, and I felt his angle change as his rhythm faltered. "Oh fuck, Jory, I want you to come. I love how your body feels when you do it, how you clench around me…."

When he fisted my cock, stroking, tugging, dragging his thumb through dripping precome, I begged him for harder, faster, and deeper.

"Now," he snarled at me, and as his shaft, swollen thick and rock hard in my ass, pegged my gland, I cried his name.

"Oh." He jerked inside me as my orgasm roared through me, my muscles contracting around his shaft, squeezing, I was sure, to the point of pain. "Fuck, that's amazing, you tighten up so hard, so fast… the heat and the pressure… fuck!"

I was coming and that's all there was: the release, the euphoria as I spurted over the rippling muscles of his abdomen.

"Jory!" he gasped before he emptied himself inside me, flooding my clasping channel, his hands keeping a death grip on my thighs as he held me against him even as he straightened. He rose to his knees, and hauled me up off the couch so I was plastered to his skin.

We stayed there, heaving for breath, both of us shivering with aftershocks, until slowly, carefully, Sam slid me back down under him and then eased free. I felt hot liquid dripping from my ass, rolling down my inner thighs, before his T-shirt was there, wiping and cleaning.

"This room smells like sweat and come," he grumbled, bending to kiss me hard and claiming. He sucked on my tongue a moment before pulling back, the look on his face the same as it always was after sex: smug and satisfied. "And you look all used up."

"You still have to tell me what happened with Rico," I informed him, bursting his postcoital happiness bubble.

He groaned and stood up, and only then did I notice that his jeans were pushed only to his knees.

"Really, you didn't even get naked?"

"I was in a hurry," he grumbled at me, but couldn't hold on to it.

"What?"

He smiled suddenly, his eyes heating fast. "I never get tired of seeing you all marked up and flushed after sex. It's so fuckin' hot."

I stood up in front of him, head tipped back because, as close as I was standing to him, I had no choice. It was amazing how big he was and how small and fragile I felt every time we stood together. The man was a mountain of hard muscle, and I was not.

"Love?"

"I need you to talk to me."

"I promise, right after you get out of the shower."

I opened my mouth to argue, but his hands encircled my hips and he tugged me close. He bent his forehead to mine and closed his eyes.

"Sam?"

"I'm so lucky you love me, that the kids love me, that the stupid cat loves me. My life is perfect, and I won't do anything to jeopardize that."

"I know."

"I didn't love Kevin Dwyer. That's why it ended. I've only ever loved you."

We were standing together, quietly breathing, and I felt the calm wash over me.

"Lemme look at whatever is in the envelope that White dropped off, and then I can explain everything, okay?"

I nodded, and he kissed my nose before I eased out of his grip and darted naked through the living room to the stairs.

"Hey!"

I turned at the landing. "What?"

"You look good running around bare-assed."

"That's charming, thank you," I teased him before I ran up to the second floor.

I could hear him laughing.

THREE

I CAME down a half an hour later in jeans and a lightweight black turtleneck sweater. Sam had changed and his hair was wet, so he'd obviously used either the kids' bathroom or our guest one while I was using ours. He was back in the same jeans but the T-shirt was gone, thankfully, replaced by a long-sleeved one. As always, I admired the lines of the man, and he was not so deep in thought that he didn't look up and smile at me when I neared him.

"You'll be happy to know I have on clean underwear."

I chuckled. "Thank you for letting me know."

"Here, come sit."

I planted myself on the coffee table in front of him, and he passed me a file folder that I didn't open. "First Rico."

He shook his head. "That's nothing. This is the story."

"Sam." I was insistent.

He rolled his eyes and leaned back on the couch, knees spread, fingers laced behind his head, and looked at me.

"You promised."

"Fine. What do you want to know?"

"Just start at the beginning."

He took a breath. "Okay, so we got word on an escaped fugitive, and we went to apprehend him."

"You make it sound so simple."

"It was simple."

"Obviously not."

He leaned forward, his eyes on mine. "All we had to do was go in and bring the guy out."

"But?"

"But…." He paused, taking my hand in his. "Our intel turned out to be crap, and there were more guys in the house than we expected."

"And?" It was like pulling teeth.

"And they grabbed Rico and had me at a disadvantage."

I could barely breathe. "What happened?"

His smile was wide; the laugh lines at the corners of his eyes got so deep. "What would you like to know, J, because obviously I'm fine."

"How are you fine?"

"Just am."

"No, I mean, what did you have to do to remain fine?"

"I killed the men who were going to kill Rico and me. It's just how it went down."

I lunged at him and heard the deep exhale before I kissed him, opened for him, and whimpered in the back of my throat.

His tongue slipped over mine, coaxing, stroking, the tangling slow and sensual. I wrapped my arms around his neck, and he took me into his lap, into his arms, and I was pressed to his muscular chest and held tight. Sam was so dominant that whenever I submitted, he had to show me that he was there, powerful and strong, ready to take care of me in any way I needed. He was hardwired that way.

When we parted, he eased only far enough away so that he could look deeply into my eyes.

"I will always come home, do you understand?"

I nodded.

"You're mine, my kids are mine, and nothing and no one will keep me from you guys. Ever."

"Make sure."

"I will."

I shivered hard. "I can't lose you."

"No," he whispered.

I untangled myself, moved back onto the coffee table, and picked the folder up again so I wouldn't sit on it. "So both you and Rico got out of that situation okay."

"Yes." He smiled at me, putting his hand on my knee.

"You should tell me this stuff."

"I'll try, but it's hard. When I get done with a day like that, all I want to do is come home, take a shower, and crawl into bed with you."

"Naked." I smiled at him.

"Oh hell yeah, the naked's the most important part."

"Okay." I took a breath. "I freaked because you didn't tell me."

"You freaked because you were scared. You can't be scared if you know how the story ends. You can't."

I thought he knew me. "You could have died."

"But I didn't."

"But you could have," I insisted. "Sam. You could have."

He shook his head. "This is why I don't tell you when I almost get shot."

"If I have to find out any more secrets today… oh no wait, there's one more, isn't there?"

He groaned.

I pointed at the folder. "Go ahead."

"I'd rather tell you about the Petersons," he chuckled and hooked a hand around the back of my neck so he could haul me close to kiss me again.

But I really needed to talk to him, so I squirmed free, shoving him back.

"What're you doing?"

"This is serious."

His eyes met mine and I held his gaze.

After a minute he sighed deeply and fell back against the couch.

"Sam?"

"I know. I know this is serious."

"And?"

"And so I promise to just talk to you and not paw you like some hormonal teenager." He smiled at me. "I won't grab you and kiss you stupid."

"Sam—"

"No, I know. Normally I like to mix me talking to you about work with blow jobs and my hand down the front of your jeans or kissing you until my balls ache. I promise we'll skip that today."

"Yeah?"

"Don't sound so happy about it."

"No, it's not that, I just—this is important right?"

"It is," he agreed.

"Good. Now, about the folder."

"All right," he said, leaning forward. "Do you remember last year a couple of my guys went to Vegas to pick up a witness?"

"Yeah. There was trouble with that, though, wasn't there?"

"Uh-huh. They were compromised at the first safe house before they could get on a plane."

"That's right." I put my hand on his knee as I thought for a second, as always liking the closeness. "What was that guy's name... uhm, something Turner?"

"Very good." He grinned at me. "Yeah, Andrew Turner."

"What about him?"

"This is him," he said and opened the folder so I could see all the eight-by-ten glossy black-and-white photos of a handsome middle-aged man with dark hair and eyes. "This is Turner."

I committed the face to memory.

"So they had the marshals there looking, plus Vegas PD, but he was in the wind."

"I remember. You were upset because they blamed your guys."

"But that never made any sense, because Kowalski and Ryan lost him, yes, but they were already at the safe house, and there's no way that just happens."

"You lost me."

"Well, people just don't find safe houses, it's not possible. Someone had to have tipped off the guys who took the witness, and the only people who knew the location were the Vegas marshals and my guys."

"So it was for sure an inside job."

"Absolutely."

"And who thought this, that it was an inside job? Just you and your team?"

"Oh no, everybody thought so at the time. My boss, my boss's boss... they could never prove it, but there's no other explanation. Either all the marshals in Vegas were dirty or just one, but somebody sold us out."

"But nobody knows who."

"Right. Without the witness testifying about how he was removed, we have no case against anyone."

"But something new has happened."

"Yeah." He nodded. "When Turner first went missing, I sent his picture out to every informant I have across the country. People I put into the system, old contacts from when I was with Chicago PD, and just friends, ya know?"

"Sure."

"Well, so two days ago, I got a hit."

"Somebody saw Mr. Turner?"

"Yeah, a guy I know in Phoenix recognized Turner from the picture I sent out and shot me a text on my phone that's not registered to Marshal Kage or Sam Kage."

"Why is that important?"

"Because no one in the department monitors that phone."

"You have three phones?"

"Yes, J." He smiled at me.

"Man, how easy would it be for you to have an affair, huh?"

He squinted at me. "Really? That's where your brain goes?"

"Sorry." I smiled sheepishly. "But so, when I send texts to you… with pictures… they could look at that?"

"In theory, yes. But if anyone gets shocked over our private texts… fuck 'em."

"Oh God," I groaned.

"Are you blushing?"

"Sam!"

"You are," he chuckled. "That's adorable."

"Don't—get away from me!" I yelled, swatting his hands away. "Answer the question!"

He cleared his throat. "Okay, so I got a text message and a picture of Turner that my contact took."

"Oh shit."

"Oh shit is right."

"And so what does that mean?"

"That means," he said, leaning forward, hands on my knees, "that I have to go to Phoenix and find my missing witness."

"Okay."

"Because if the witness that was taken from my team is actually alive and well and living there," he went on, "I need to find him and bring him in so we can have a talk and clear things up."

"Like figuring out who took him and why."

"Yeah, the why is important," Sam assured me. "I mean, I've checked the Turner case a million times to try and figure out why anyone would go to all that trouble to tamper with the Marshals' Office for such a small-time bust."

"So you're thinking what?"

"I'm thinking that Andrew Turner knows something about somebody that has shit to do with the case he was actually involved in. I think there's another story."

"So he's blackmailing somebody scary?" I asked.

"I would think so. I mean, for sure somebody bigger than his old boss in Vegas, yeah. It's the only thing that makes sense."

"The boss in Vegas, did anyone ever question him?" I was trying to put pieces together in my head.

"He turned up dead two weeks after Turner went missing."

"So technically, there's no one that Turner would be running from?"

"Except that he's still considered an escaped witness until he turns himself in and clears everything up," Sam explained, his voice low and gravelly. "His new identity never went live, so he's still running around being Andrew Turner. If anyone discovers his identity, runs him through the system, his exact whereabouts will become clear and marshals will show up wherever he is."

"Wow."

"I know."

"So you think that he's living happily ever after in Phoenix on whoever's bankroll, blackmailing them?"

"That's my guess, yeah."

"God, that takes balls."

"Yes it does," he agreed.

"Okay, so, what's your plan? When we're in Phoenix, you're gonna pop in on your buddy Mr. Turner and bring him back?"

"If my information is right, then basically… yes."

"Is it dangerous?" I was checking because that fast I was worried.

"I won't know until I get there." He sighed, taking hold of my hand.

It was funny, because everyone who knew Sam—his parents, siblings, friends, people he worked with—they all saw a different man than the one who sat in front of me now. Only with me and the kids did he hug and kiss and take comfort in the simple act of touching.

"Jory?"

"So if it comes out that one or all of the marshals in Vegas are dirty, what happens then?"

"It's federal prison for them."

"Don't you think they might want to hurt you to keep that from happening?"

"In theory."

"No, not in theory, in real life."

"Except that I don't think all of those marshals were dirty. Maybe one, but not all."

"But if the one dirty one finds out you're onto him, he'll try and stop you."

"Possibly." He shrugged.

"Possibly? Sam?"

"If my whereabouts are being monitored, then yes," he agreed. "But that's why I have the third cell phone that no one knows about, that's not connected to me in any way."

"There are an awful lot of questions that need answering."

"Yeah, I know."

"And so?" I pressed him.

"So I have a video conference in an hour with my boss, and I'm gonna tell him what I'm gonna do, and he's gonna advise me, and we'll go from there."

"You trust your boss, Sam?"

He nodded. "I do."

"Okay, so, when we're in Phoenix at the reunion, will you be working?"

"I don't know yet. If they want me to approach Turner, then yes. If not, then no."

"When will you know?"

"I have no idea, but as soon as I get word, I'll tell you."

"All right."

"Don't look so sad," he said softly, putting a hand on my cheek. "I'll be around."

"And you won't be in any danger."

"I can't promise that. You know better."

I nodded. "Okay."

He gave me a gentle pat and then got up, took his wallet out of his back pocket, and removed the card that the officer had given him at the hospital.

"So it turns out you're gonna have to deal with your van just like you wanted to. I can drop you off on the way or you can get a cab. What do you wanna do?"

"I'll cab it," I said after I looked at the card and saw the address. "Your office is in the complete opposite direction."

"Okay."

"I'll meet you at your folks' place at six."

"Sounds like a plan." He smiled at me before he bent to kiss me.

Alone in the house ten minutes later, I called him quickly because I had forgotten to ask about the Petersons.

"Yeah," he chuckled evilly on the other end. "The bad guy in that scenario is Mrs. Peterson. She was the one having the affair, and that baby she's carrying now is not Mr. Peterson's, since he had a vasectomy after the birth of their second child."

"Holy shit."

"Yeah."

"Is he in trouble?"

"Nope. He gets to keep his kids and she is going to live with her boyfriend in Parkridge."

"So she's just leaving her kids?"

"Yep."

"And Mr. Peterson?"

"His mother's moving in."

"Aww, man."

"You and Mrs. Martinez and all the other harpies on the block better go make nice. Make the man a casserole, J. Invite him over for dinner. You owe him."

"I thought—"

He grunted, cutting me off. "You're a crappy judge of character, you know."

I did know. "I'm not a harpy."

"No you're not, I apologize. You're much too cute."

I growled, and his rumbling laughter sounded good.

"Once the cops are all gone—"

"Why were there cops to begin with?"

"Mrs. Peterson's boyfriend came over to get her, and he wanted to take the other kids too."

"Mr. Peterson wasn't letting his kids go with them, I'm guessing."

"Hell no. I wouldn't have either. A man doesn't let anyone take his children from him, especially not a cheating piece of crap."

"I'll remember that if I ever have an affair."

His grunt made me smile. "Never happen, J. You're addicted to me."

Yes, I was.

"I'm the only man for you."

"You're very conceited."

"I am very loved." He sighed.

"Yes you are."

I hung up on his very smug male grunt.

When my phone rang minutes later, I was surprised to see Aaron Sutter's number. There was a time, before we reconnected, when we were just exes, that I would have never thought he would ever be in the friend column. But it turned out that he wanted me in his life and I wanted him in mine, so we had both worked at it. I was glad, he was worth it.

"Hey," I greeted him. "What's up?"

"Where are you?"

"I'm at home, why?"

"I just fired the people who were in charge of my art auction at Darwin Manor next month, and I wanted to know if you and Dylan and Fal wanted it before I went out and shopped around for bids."

"I told you to give us that even when you were first talking about it."

"Yes, but it seemed too big for your little company."

I hung up on him.

He called back twenty seconds later. "What the hell was that about?"

"Little company?" I was indignant.

"Jory—"

"I hate it when you talk down to me." I said, trying not to snarl.

"I hate it when you hang up on me!"

"So?"

He growled on his end.

"So?"

"Fine," he snapped at me. "The account is yours, but if you screw—"

"I'm sorry. When, precisely, have I ever not come through for you?"

"Shit."

"I'll need the deposit transferred tomorrow and all the specifications for the event." I was using my Stepford wife voice just to piss him off, the perky one.

"Fine." He grunted.

"Good."

There was a silence, our usual one where we both decided to climb down off our high horses.

"So are you hungry?" he finally said. "You wanna eat lunch?"

"I can't, I wish I could. I gotta go down to look at my van and get a rental."

"Why are you renting anything?"

So I explained about the man freaking out from road rage earlier and how I got knocked out in the stupidest maneuver ever, and then explained the most important part about Kevin Dwyer.

"You want me to come get you?"

"No, that's okay, I—"

"I don't mind," he told me. "And this way I can check out Dwyer on my way over."

"What do you mean?" He had my interest.

"Well, we can do some background research."

"Like Google him?"

"More than that. I have people that that's all they do."

"Yeah, okay, come get me."

"Be right there."

It took him half an hour to reach me, but I did some last-minute packing with all four suitcases on the bed in the guest room: mine, Sam's, and one for each of the kids. Sam had said that my clothes and his could go in together, but I had shoes to pack, and jackets, and…. He gave up and packed a duffel bag, since I was taking a garment bag for his suit and mine.

In Aaron's immaculately kept vintage Lincoln Town Car, I greeted his driver, Miguel, who had worked for him for years.

"Nice to see you, Mr. Harcourt," he smiled as he closed the door behind me.

"Are you still driving this thing, Miguel?" I asked as he got in.

"We keep upgrading it, don't let the outside fool you."

"Oh no, I get that I'm in Batman's car."

He chuckled as Aaron patted my leg in hello and passed me his iPad. There was *Kevin Dwyer, MD,* and all his stats.

"This is just—"

"Scroll to page two," he said drolly. "Where are we going?"

I passed him the card, which he read to Miguel before the two of them started discussing rental places. Miguel didn't like where my car was and suggested to Aaron that we move it to a place he knew. That was as much as I listened to, since I was reading.

Apparently Sam had been under surveillance when he was in Columbia, and those pictures, classified though they were, were not off-limits to the people who worked for Aaron Sutter.

Sam looked younger but mostly the same, and Kevin Dwyer looked even better, which was amazing. It was hard to see the way he smiled at Sam in the pictures, touched him, and how close they walked together. The thing that kept me from losing it, though, was the look in Sam's eyes. The smile did not reach them. The instant I recognized that, realized that I was looking at a lack of caring, I was filled with very unbecoming pride. Clearly whatever Kevin Dwyer had thought there was between them was not the case. Sam Kage had never been in love with him and I knew what I was talking about. I could say for certain what love looked like on the man.

"You look happy."

I grunted at Aaron and then looked over Kevin's relationship history since Sam. Surprisingly there wasn't one. It was as though he'd poofed out of existence before he popped back up in Chicago six months ago.

"That's weird, huh?"

"The way he just disappeared after Sam left Columbia?"

"Yeah."

"I thought that was strange too, but I have good people and asked them to dig."

"Yeah?"

"Yeah, and if we find anything, I'll let you know."

"Okay." I exhaled.

"All better now?"

I nodded and passed the iPad back to him. "Thank you. It's cheating, what I just did, but thanks anyway."

"There should be benefits to being friends with the rich, yes?"

I nodded and leaned into him, bumping his shoulder. "You're the best."

"I keep telling you that."

I laughed at him as we came to a stop. "Yeah, right. You don't want me anymore, Sutter. I have baggage now, little people and a cat."

"I like both of your children, and I suspect if I got Kola a race car and Hannah a pony they would love me too. Your cat just needs to be shot up with tranquilizers to mellow him out."

"You want to medicate my cat." I smiled as I got out, Miguel holding the door for me. Aaron followed.

"Yes," he said smugly, buttoning his suit jacket before pulling on his topcoat and scarf. "Shall we?"

I realized I had no idea where we were. It looked like a car dealership, not a rental place. "What's going on?"

"We're getting you a new van."

"But I like mine. I just need a rental."

"You like your Nissan thing."

"Yes, I love it."

He grunted, and the glass doors of what I could see was a Mercedes-Benz dealership slid open.

"Oh for crissakes, Aaron, I just need a rental."

But there was a team of people in front of us, a man and three women, and when one of the three asked for my driver's license, I got out my wallet and passed it to her. Really, fighting with Aaron—especially in front of other people—was useless unless I was prepared to bolt, which I didn't do anymore.

"I'm hungry," I told him twenty minutes later.

"We'll go get beef sandwiches at Al's after this, all right?" He offered it like I was five instead of thirty-five.

I looked over at Miguel. "You want that?"

"My favorite," he assured me. "Now pay attention. The lady asked you what color?"

"Black," I told her.

"How about metallic slate instead?" She tipped her head and smiled at me.

I groaned.

Driving the new Mercedes-Benz R-Class minivan out of the dealership, I was hazy on whether it was a rental or not. It seemed to be all paid for and registered in my name, but I was told very firmly that I could return it at any time during the month. I had a printout of an insurance card in the glove compartment, and Miguel had left to go to wherever my Nissan was to get everything from it and meet us at Al's. I hadn't been worried—Sam had a set of car seats in his enormous SUV that we would take with us instead of the set from my van—but now I would have both.

The food had just gotten to the table when Miguel joined us at Al's. He had me give my keys to two guys who came to the table, and my guess was that, while we ate, they moved everything.

"It must be nice to have staff," I told Aaron.

"Pretty much, yeah." He smirked at me.

I let it go, asked him how much the van was, and he answered me with his mouth full of spicy beef sandwich. "I love the peppers," he told me when he swallowed.

"Aaron."

He knocked his knee against mine under the table. "You know, Jory, the back of your van was completely crushed in."

I looked at Miguel. "It was?"

He made a noise as he was chewing. "Yeah. Somebody plowed into you from behind, huh?"

I didn't remember that.

"You know a Mercedes is built like a tank, yeah? The kids would be safe."

When I looked back at Aaron, he waggled his eyebrows at me.

"I can buy my own new minivan if I need to with the insurance money. As soon as I get it, this one goes back."

"Whatever you want," he agreed.

Once I was back in the van, I realized that everything was there: the carved, ivory-colored agate butterfly that hung from the mirror, the car seats, Kola's gi, two sets of roller skates, a cat carrier, a first aid kit, and all my coupons from the glove compartment.

"And you didn't have AAA, but you do now. I had the number and your ID downloaded into your phone," Aaron said from where he was leaning into my open window.

"I don't need you to take care of me."

"I know."

I squinted at him. "Did you just buy me a van, or is this a rental?"

"I bought you a van."

My sigh was long. "I'm going to take it back as soon as I get my insurance money and get a new van."

"Like I said, if you decide that's best, that's fine with me."

"It's not fine with you."

"No, it's not, but I've never had any luck giving you gifts."

"I can't fall in love with it. I can't afford it."

"You can give me what you get for your van from the insurance company and we can call it even."

"But it wouldn't be."

"But it could be," he said, his eyes locked on mine. "For once."

"Aaron—"

"If the roles were reversed, would you buy me a new van? I mean if I had the kids and had a strict monthly budget, would you do it for me?"

"Well yeah, but—"

"Do what you want," he said, about to lean free.

I grabbed hold of his forearm. "Don't be a dick."

"Then let me do something for you," he grumbled at me. "I have a lot of money, and I do for my family and friends. I don't expect you to put out just because I—"

"Okay," I laughed at him.

"Okay, like, okay?"

"Okay like I'll drive it for a month and see what's what."

"It's got an awesome safety rating."

"The car costs more than I made last year."

"No, probably right about the same."

"Aaron—"

"You have never, ever, let me do a thing for you in over nine, almost ten years of friendship. Maybe just this once, since it's not just for you and the insurance will pay for a third of it easily…."

"I'll see what Sam says."

"Good." He smiled at me. "Now so you know, everything's done. The registration will come in the mail, but you have copies in the glove compartment in that zippered pouch, okay?"

"And the insurance?"

"Is there."

"You transferred my insurance from my old van to this new one?"

"Not exactly."

I squinted at him. "What does that mean?"

"Just… call me when you get back from your reunion thing next week, and in the meantime, I'll send all the information for the art auction over to Dylan and Fal."

"Okay, step back."

He moved, and I got out and lunged at him. "Thank you."

He groaned like he was annoyed. "This display of appreciation is so—"

"Needed," I told him as I hugged him tight.

FOUR

I PARKED out front of Sam's parents' house, and since he had no idea what I was driving, I was certain Sam wouldn't know I was there. Aaron had said he'd call him, and so for once I wasn't going to try to manage their friendship, or whatever it was called when an ex and the love of your life tried to be friends because the person they both cared about was in the middle.

After walking around the house to the backyard, I went in through the door that opened into the kitchen. The pot roast smelled fantastic, and there were dinner rolls cooling on the stove. Moving through the room, I walked to the swinging door and out into the dining room. I could hear the music from the living room and went to see.

I found Hannah entertaining everyone as she danced with Sam's sister Rachel's now-teenage daughters. The thing was, Whitney Houston was belting out "It's Not Right, But It's Okay," and Hannah was way too familiar with that tune not to sing it along with her. It was on my iPod, which I usually played when I dropped my kids off in the morning or picked them up. The best part, though, was not that she knew all the words, which she actually didn't, but that she was the only one keeping the beat as she danced. She was jumping and moving her hands, the cardiovascular workout daunting. Her head was tipping back and forth, she waggled her finger, and she stopped when the music did. She could not have been any cuter, and when she sang the chorus, everyone howled. Picking it right back up, she started bouncing again, and her cousins gave up, unable to match her style or her energy. When the song ended and everyone clapped, she shrieked with happiness before bolting over to her grandmother and hurling herself into Regina's arms.

"That was so good, pumpkin," she cooed over my kid.

"I'm the best dancer in my class."

"I'm sure you are," she laughed, still not seeing me.

"I'm sure she is," some guy I didn't know snickered under his breath. "Having two daddies, how could she not be?"

I was in the doorway and off to the side, out of view, not really in the room, but even from where I was, I felt the chill in the air.

"What?" Regina's voice cracked like a whip as she turned to the man. "What did you say?"

"Michael." The voice of Thomas Kage, Sam's father, boomed through the space. "Your friend—what was the name again?"

"Noah."

"Yes, Noah—he can't stay for dinner. Take him out of my house."

Like a dog. Take him out.

"Uncle Michael."

He was distracted by my daughter, but it was hard for him to look away from his father.

"Uncle Michael."

"Yes, B?" he answered, finally giving her his attention.

"Where's Auntie Bev? I miss her," she said, inquiring as to the whereabouts of Michael's glamorous wife.

How or why, I had no idea, but Hannah and her aunt got along famously. It was odd because most children were too messy, too sticky, or too loud for Beverly Kage. She liked everything just so, from her makeup to her nails to the handbag she carried. But all that fell by the wayside when it came to Hannah. She doted on her niece, allowed herself to be hugged, even if something that was on Hannah would rub off on her. The whole thing had made Regina rethink her impression from earlier in her son and daughter-in-law's marriage, that motherhood and Beverly were not suited. Regina had hope when she saw Beverly with my daughter.

"She had a meeting tonight, B, but she'll be on the plane with you tomorrow."

"Okay." She beamed at him.

"Hey," I heard Sam call as he came through the front door. "Anybody home?"

"Daddy!" Hannah squealed and tore across the room to him, leaping like a spider monkey toward him, arms and legs outstretched.

He caught her effortlessly and lifted her up high so she could do the airplane pose as she giggled like crazy.

"Sam," Regina called to him as she rose and stalked across the room.

"Wait," Noah recanted, turning to Michael. "I'm so—I didn't mean any—"

"Let's just go," Sam's brother sighed, turning as I stepped into the room. "Jory."

All eyes on me.

Silence.

It only took Sam a minute. "What's going on?" he asked.

Hannah was held now against his chest, one little arm around his neck and her other hand fiddling with the collar of his leather jacket. "That man thinks that because I have two daddies that's why I dance good."

Before I had kids, I had no idea that children had selective supersonic hearing. I always assumed that they heard based on the regular laws of physics. But it wasn't true. If you said something stupid—as Michael's guest just had—if you mentioned dessert but didn't mean to, or if you swore as you stubbed your toe, all these things would carry instantly to their small ears. However, requests to pick up their rooms, directions to brush their teeth, and inquiries as to who had thrown the ball that knocked over the vase in the living room— normally these questions had to be shouted before being heard. So I was not surprised in the least that my daughter had heard every word that was uttered under Michael's friend's breath, even over the pop classic.

Noah, however, was stunned. I was guessing he was not a parent, or he might have known better.

Sam's eyes went cold and hard the instant Hannah uttered the words.

"But it's not true." She beamed at him. "'Cause Kola can't dance, and he has you and Pa too. So that's not right, is it, Daddy?"

"No, B, that's not right."

You could hear the antique mantel clock ticking.

"Pa!" she shrieked when she realized I was there.

"Hi, B." I waved at her.

She gave a violent dolphin twist, and Sam put her down. In an instant she was across the room to me. I bent and grabbed her, and when I lifted her up, her head went down on my shoulder, her little arms around my neck as she snuggled. I rubbed her back and heard her sigh.

"I'm really so sorry," the friend said to me, stepping close. "I didn't mean anything."

"Sure." I smiled at him before turning to Thomas. "We could just let it go, couldn't we?"

Sam's father studied my face. We both knew I was asking permission for Noah to stay. If Thomas Kage gave an order, everybody had to listen.

"I'm okay. Are you okay?"

He grunted, gave me a quick nod, and I looked to Regina.

"I'm starving and that pot roast smells amazing. Did you make the red potatoes?"

"I did." She hesitated for a minute before moving fast, hands on my face when she reached me. Then she kissed my cheek. "And I made the monkey bread you like, along with the rolls."

"Heaven."

Her brows furrowed as she studied me. "Were you in a fight?"

I shrugged. "It's nothing, it doesn't even hurt."

From the look on her face, I could tell she was not convinced.

"Sam," I called over to him, needing the backup.

"He's okay, Mom," he vouched for me. "I promise."

She lit up with relief; it was easy to see that she loved me. "I have your itinerary."

"Which is why Sam and I came, for dinner and to get that."

Jen, Sam's sister, made a kissing noise as Regina told everyone to get to the table.

"You're just jealous," I hissed at her.

"Of what? You having to kiss my mother's ass?" she whispered back, making her eyes huge for me. "You think?"

I laughed at her, and she smirked as Rachel walked over and rubbed Hannah's head. "Your daughter is an angel."

"Yeah I know." I smiled at Rachel. "Where's my boy?"

"In the playroom with Peter and Riley." She yawned. "My kids love watching their cousins."

"And even if they didn't, you'd make them do it anyway."

"Yeah. So?"

"You're so bad. Do they want to go to the reunion at this point?" I asked her.

She shook her head. "No, but I guilted them into it. I told them if they didn't go then they obviously loved their stepmother more than their mother."

"Rachel," I scolded her.

"What? Dean decides to divorce me and marry a woman in her midtwenties and I'm supposed to be the grown-up? Did I tell you she's pregnant?"

"Oh shit," I said before I thought about it.

"Daddy! Pa said a bad word!"

"You're such a narc," I told my daughter, pinching her butt through her leggings and underwear. It was nice that even at night now she wore panties—her potty training was finally and completely done.

We still had the occasional accident, but that was to be expected, especially if she was overtired.

"Daddy!"

I heard Kola before I saw him, and he was charging though the living room to reach Sam. He dived at him, and Sam caught him the same way he had Hannah. He didn't lift him, though, because Kola was too old for that now. He had announced that since he would be seven soon—four months away—he had to get used to doing grown-up things. I loved it when his brows furrowed and he got serious.

Once we were all sitting down, after grace was spoken, Sam asked his son to tell Uncle Michael about the report he'd given last Friday.

"Oh." Kola's face lit up. "I did my report on the weapons that a US Marshal carries."

Noah blanched.

I kicked Sam under the table. His smile in return was evil.

"Marshals carry a Glock 22 as their main gun, and a backup one that they get to pick."

"Why are we talking about guns at the dinner table?" Regina asked.

"Shhh," Thomas hushed his wife. "Kola's talking about his report."

"Oh, Kola's talking about more than his report," Jen assured everyone.

Michael's eyes flicked to Sam. "Is that right?"

"Yes," Kola told him. "Do you want to know what Daddy has?"

"I can't wait to hear."

"Daddy has a ten millimeter Smith & Wesson that's this big," he said, the space between his hands far too wide. "And if you got shot with it, it would make your whole head explode."

"Ewww." Riley, Rachel's daughter, made a face. "That's disgusting."

"That's so awesome," Peter, Rachel's son, chimed in, which was the first time I had heard him engaged in any conversation in quite a while. Both kids, now teenagers, were taking their parents' divorce and their father's recent nuptials very hard.

"But guns are only to be used after you are trained to fire one," Kola cautioned us all. "A gun is not a toy."

"That's right," Sam agreed.

"I would love to learn how to use one correctly," Peter said hopefully.

"Maybe I can take you out to the gun range sometime if you want, Pete," Sam offered.

"No, Sam," Rachel said firmly. "I don't want Peter to learn that guns are—"

"Learning to respect a firearm is the first step to the prevention of accidents," Sam assured her. "Now that you live alone, what is your protection in case of a break-in?"

"I have a bat, Sam," she said, and I could tell how close she was to exploding. They had been waging this debate since Dean moved out. He wanted her to have a gun, and she was having no part of it.

I was actually with her. I hated guns. Sam being in law enforcement was the only reason there were three under my roof.

Sam slept with a Sig Sauer in the nightstand drawer on his side, and every morning he replaced it in the combination safe built into the wall in our closet. It was a whole ritual when he came home at night. Kiss the kids, kiss me, pet the cat, and put his two work guns away in the safe. And then, before bed, he'd go back to the safe and remove the Sig and place it at the front of the drawer before he got into bed.

There had not been a gun in the nightstand when it had just been him and me; he'd never slept with a gun close except for a long time ago, when I was being hunted by a serial killer. But once he had his life how he wanted it, had his own family, a house, and became a father, things changed. Now there was not just me right there beside him, the only thing to protect; now there was his son and his daughter and the cat sleeping in one of his children's beds. He needed the certainty that he could guard us all, and the gun gave him that.

I hated having a gun that was not locked away at night. I was not crazy about a gun period, but the man was a US Marshal. There was no way around it. But the firearm in the nightstand had been a problem. I told him one of those badass ASP batons would be better. He disagreed. A handgun wielded by someone trained to use it was the best defense.

"Sam, I don't want to—"

"Mom, can I go to the gun range with Uncle Sammy? Please?"

The eyes she turned on Sam were hard. He looked bored, not flustered even one little bit.

"Sure," she said softly.

"Thanks." Peter smiled at her, and for a second I saw how happy she was to be getting anything but snarling anger or cold apathy from her kid.

It went in waves. Sometimes it was Dean's fault and the kids hated him and loved her, and sometimes it was her fault and the reverse was true. I felt so bad for her and wished for the hundredth time that Dean had not been out looking for a new woman and had instead invested time finding fresh ways to love the one he had.

"I'd love to go to the gun range too," Doug, Jen's husband, chimed in. He was Jen's second husband, her first one having left her for his accountant. They had not had any children together, but Doug had three—Ben, Todd, and Melissa—from a previous marriage of his own, and along with Jen's daughters—Ally and Carla—they had five children they shared with exes. The choice to have no more kids had been made because Doug wanted to travel and take the kids they already had to see the world. Jen had agreed, and they had taken their tribe on many adventures. I was looking forward to going out of the country with my own brood someday, it just hadn't happened yet.

"You got a gun?" Rachel asked her sister.

"Yes," she told her. "Doug thought it was a good idea."

"What'd you get?" Sam asked Doug.

"The Sig SP, like you suggested. You were right. I tried the Glock and the sort of stiff mechanics of it, I didn't like at all. The smoothness of the Sig was much better."

Sam was nodding. "Yes."

"So why do you guys still carry the Glocks, then?"

"Really?" Regina said. "This is dinner conversation?"

"Mother," Jen shushed her. "Doug's asking a question."

And heaven forbid we interrupt! It was sweet how Jen catered to him, but after seven years, you'd think she would be over the honeymoon stage already.

Rachel rolled her eyes, and her daughter, Riley, caught the look and giggled. It was nice to see, and when Rachel's eyes flicked to mine, I saw the happiness there.

"The good thing about a Glock," Sam began, "is that even though it jams sometimes, it never needs to be taken apart, you don't have to clean it or oil it, and you can fall into water wearing it and it will still fire."

"Okay, that's cool," Peter chimed in.

"Yeah, see." Sam shrugged. "So the good outweighs the bad, but I just don't like it. That's why I have the Sig for home protection. If I aim at something, I wanna hit it."

And the last part he said while looking at Noah, and I thought the poor guy was gonna throw up right there.

I put my hand on Sam's thigh under the table and patted gently.

"My daddy was a Marine," Kola told the stranger. "He was a sniper. Do you know what that is?"

"Yes," Regina asked the guest, "do you know what that is?"

Poor bastard, but really, what had he been thinking with that comment? Gay equaled good dresser, good dancer, and good decorator? Really? I was sure that Michael had mentioned it in passing to his friend, like "I have two sisters and one brother, one of my sisters is divorced, the other's married, and my brother's gay." It would have been nothing, a throwaway comment that his buddy had pulled out for no good reason. But it was offensive, and Sam had been annoyed and then made sure the guy knew it. Sam and subtlety had never met.

"Yeah," Sam told Doug. "I'll take both you and Pete out. It would be my pleasure."

"Great." Doug smiled at him. "I can't wait."

"Pass the potatoes," Ally, Jen's daughter, asked her mother. "And I wanna learn to shoot too, okay, Mom? I'm thinking about joining ROTC next year in high school."

"Oh, that's great," Sam told her.

She beamed back at him, and Kola told her that since Sam was an expert marksman—he had explained in his report how Sam had to take a test every six months to keep that status current—there was nobody better for her to learn to shoot from.

"So you see," Regina commented, arching one eyebrow at Michael, "dancing is not the only thing Hannah's fathers know how to do well."

Michael threw up his hands in defeat. I doubted his friend, whom I didn't even get a proper introduction to, would be back.

EVERYONE came outside after dinner, before dessert, to look at the new minivan. Sam explained that the old one was done and would be sold as salvage, and Hannah was sad that she didn't get to say good-bye to it. He told them that this one was a steal and looked over at me.

"Are you mad?"

"It's really safe," he told me. "And we'll send the insurance money to Aaron when we get it."

"He called me because he needed a favor, and I explained about the van, and—"

"I already heard all this." He smiled, hand on the back of my neck, pulling me close, and pressing his lips to my forehead.

"How?"

"He called me," Sam said, curling a piece of hair behind my ear. I had cut it short for a long time but was back to wearing it long, my dirty-blond hair now falling to my shoulders.

"He did?"

"Yeah, he's getting smarter in his old age about talking to me, including me. I mean, I know how he works. I know he just does things. I get it."

"He just sees it as helping."

"I know. If we end up keeping it, we'll give him the insurance money and make up the difference. We don't take charity."

"I told him that's what you'd do. What I would do too."

"It's better not to argue with him, just go along. When he gets a cashier's check, he won't have a choice but to cash it."

"He'll just overpay me for the job we're doing for him," I sighed.

"Whatever, that's between his company and yours. That has nothing to do with me or my kids. So I'm good."

"He's gonna be pissed," I chuckled.

"He's lucky I'm not," he said, smoothing a hand down my back, pressing me close. "Because he doesn't provide for you or my kids, only I do."

"I know."

"He can't ever cross the line again, J. You understand?"

I did.

"I already told him." Sam coughed.

"Yeah?"

"Yeah."

"And what did he say?" I was interested.

"He said okay. We'll see if he can do it."

I bit my bottom lip.

"What?"

"I, uhm, cheated."

Sam let out a breath. "He showed you whatever he had about me and Kevin Dwyer."

I was stunned. "How did you know?"

"I know you and I know what he wants, and whatever he can do to help you helps him."

"Sam, he—"

"Oh I'm not saying that Aaron Sutter has been anything but civil to me and not a complete gentleman with you for the past four years, but one of these days, he's gonna slip up."

"He's not in love with me anymore, Sam. Not really."

"If I died tomorrow, J, he'd be the first guy there to offer condolences."

"Well then, you better stay alive so the kids and I don't fall into his clutches."

"That's my plan," he said, dipping his head so he could gently bite down on my earlobe. "It's always been my plan."

He was very pleased with the goose bumps that covered my skin.

FIVE

HANNAH did not want to walk into the security scanner alone. It was the new one where you stand and lift your arms, and she was having nothing to do with it. She even watched Sam do it first and then Kola, but still, it looked weird to her.

"It only beeps if you have any dog hair on you," I said, using the last trick in my arsenal. That quickly, I had all her attention.

"I have a cat."

"I know, so you'll be okay."

"I want to call Chilly at Auntie Dylan's house when we get our shoes back."

"Okay."

And with that, she walked through.

I followed her and got picked for the routine search thing and taken to the side and wanded. The woman swiping me for metal told me how cute my kids were. I thanked her, then she thanked me and I was back to my family, pulling on my harness boots. I had to get water to put in the kids' bottles, plus more snacks for the plane. Sam thought that the feast I had schlepped with us was enough, but I explained that it couldn't possibly be.

"Daddy, we only have Goldfish and pretzels and grapes and apples and graham crackers and yogurt, cheese and crackers, and pudding."

Sam gave me a look.

"We don't have any gum, and Pa said we have to chew it or our ears will explode."

"Does blood come out when your ears blow up?"

Kola nodded.

"Eww." Hannah's face scrunched up as she covered her ears.

"That was a good idea to tell them?" Sam asked me.

"Well, they're gonna chew the gum now, right?"

"I want the mint Trident."

"I like the fruit one," Hannah told her brother. "The mint one is hot."

"Not the cinnamon one, stupid."

"Don't call your sister stupid," I told him. "That's a bad word."

"But Riley says it about Pete."

"Well, they're stupid for saying that," I said.

"Does earwax come out of your ears before the blood?"

"I dunno." Kola thought about that. "Probably."

She nodded.

"Can we go?" Sam asked me irritably. He was already grouchy.

At the store to buy the water, Hannah wanted a stuffed animal, Kola wanted a key chain, and Sam bought three different kinds of gum, water, and magazines for me. I had given both kids Dramamine before we left home, and had it in my laptop bag for the return trip. I grabbed some antacids for Sam's dad, in case he forgot, and a deck of playing cards, because sometimes you just wanted to do something mindless and talk to someone else.

Once we were at the gate, I called Dylan so Hannah could talk to Chilly. Afterward I thanked her again for keeping the snow demon, since I didn't want to put him in a kennel and Dane and Aja's two Dalmatians didn't much like cats. By the time the airline personnel called for people with small children to go on after the first-class passengers, the rest of the family still wasn't there. I wasn't worried, but I was surprised since Regina was normally right on time.

We had nothing to go in any of the overhead bins, and it was nice because we had space in front of both kids' seats for stuff as well. By the time everyone else started showing up around us—Michael and Beverly, Rachel and her kids, Jen and Doug and their kids—it was getting close to departure time. When Regina and Thomas finally showed up, I saw how flustered she was.

"What happened?" Jen called over to her mother.

"I don't know, there was trouble with our tickets. They had an itinerary but no flight number."

"How is that possible?"

"I have no idea," she breathed out and then tried to take her seat.

The man who was sitting on the aisle was supposed to be sitting by the window, simple as that. He had read the little seating icon thing wrong—everyone knew the curve represented the window, but he read that as the aisle. Thomas had to sit on the aisle because if his claustrophobia started to kick in, he needed to be able to get up. People thought it was a prostate thing, but it was all about feeling confined. Unfortunately, it turned out the other passenger was drunk. I got how the flight crew had missed it, because he was quiet the whole time, but once he got belligerent, he got loud, and from the slurring words, you understood that he was sloshed. He was so out of it that he started swearing and then stood up and pushed Thomas.

It was a ballsy thing to do, because Thomas Kage was a big man. Both Sam and Michael had inherited their height and broad shoulders and heavy muscles from the man, so for the guy to go straight to physicality before anything else was gutsy. There was a flight attendant right there, and Beverly, who had been one herself, immediately stood and explained what had happened.

My seat was next to the aisle; the guy had started out beside me, stood up, gotten in Thomas's face, and then shoved him down into the seat. I got up to help Thomas because Regina yelled and Doug and Michael were stuck on the other side. The attendant came up behind the drunk man, explained that he was to be escorted off the plane, and he lost it. He shoved her, which meant he was so going to be taken off the plane in handcuffs, and I reached for her. She grabbed hold of my arm so she didn't fall down.

"Thank you," she said quickly before turning and bolting down the aisle, calling for security.

When I moved to reach Thomas, who had banged his head hard on the overhead bin, the drunk guy barred my way.

"Please move," I asked.

Instead, he came at me.

"Pa!" Hannah shrieked.

I never liked her to be scared.

"I'm gonna get Daddy," Kola yelled, and I saw him scramble out of his seat.

Sam had gone to the bathroom; that was where Kola went, I was certain. But I wasn't worried about him. He couldn't go far. I was more worried about the man looming in front of me.

"Just sit down." I tried to sound soothing. "You're drunk."

"Fuck you!"

Thomas would have kept him off me as soon as he got up, I had no doubt, as would the other passengers who were moving in the aisle, but Kola had gone to fetch his father, and Sam had run.

He came over the seats, stepping on the armrests. He had to duck down, and really, for a man Sam's size, it was impressive. And so fast. The guy was on his feet one minute; the next on the floor, face pressed to the carpet, his neck under Sam's boot. Before the flight attendant could even get back, before anyone else came to my aid, my man was there. When the air marshal arrived, Sam had his badge out for him before he could even get a word out.

The applause was instant.

"What the hell?" Sam barked at me.

"I—"

"Daddy, that man pushed Papa and wanted to hurt Pa," Hannah told her father.

The guy groaned from the floor as Sam looked down at him.

"Oh God, somebody hurry and get him off the plane," I almost whined. The guy was dead if they didn't move.

Policemen came and took the guy off. They exchanged cards with Sam. All in all, the delay only cost us maybe twenty minutes. What was nice was that Sam was golden after that, and since the kids and I were in his reflected glow, we got the star treatment as well.

Thomas was very impressed with his son and had Regina trade places with Sam for a while so they could talk. I gave Thomas the antacids I got for him, and he gave me a pat on the cheek for being such a good boy. Having never had a father of my own, I was always thrilled when I made him happy. Kola showed his grandmother how to play *Fruit Ninja* on my iPad and read her all the fun facts. Hannah leaned against me, using Kola's DS since they had switched diversions two hours into the four-hour flight.

I had passed the cards to Jen and Rachel, who ended up sitting together, with Doug passed out beside his wife. We were a low-key group, and when we landed in Phoenix at eleven in the morning, Kola thought that was the coolest thing ever.

"We time traveled," he told me.

I agreed that we had.

Even though we had sat in economy plus class on the 747 because Sam's legs were just too long for us to sit in coach, he was still complaining when we walked to the baggage terminal.

"You should have asked the pilot for an upgrade for the ride home," I teased him.

"You're funny," he groused at me.

But I knew that. It was a gift.

KOLA was sick of sitting by the time the shuttle got us from the airport to the hotel in Scottsdale. The driver talked as he drove, explaining about the two hundred acres the boutique hotel sat on, the amenities, the dessert bar that the kids would enjoy, the waterslides, the pools, the horseback riding, and so on. Even the drive in to the hotel was amazing. The grounds were gorgeous, beautifully landscaped, and a staff member greeted us and walked us to the front desk.

Hannah loved the fountain in the lobby; looking at it reminded Kola that he had to pee. And then Hannah had to go too. I excused us and went to take my kids to find a bathroom. Another nice person walked us there, and once you went inside, there were individual rooms with sinks inside the bathroom, plus a place to sit down and relax when you came out. I had never seen five different kinds of hand soap and lotions and towels and pitchers of ice water with lemon in a bathroom before in my life. I had a feeling that we were swimming in the deep end of money. I wondered briefly how much we were shelling out for the weekend. Sam and I normally did our finances together, but Sam's father was taking care of this and then we were paying him when we got back. I started to worry because we had to make payments for the school as well, and between this and our regular bills, I saw dipping into savings in our future.

I was okay to take money out, but we needed a new water heater, and we were paying Aaron back for a minivan that was more than we would have spent, and we didn't have to pay him back, but it would be weird if we didn't—

"Pa?"

Hannah was finished, smiling, looking up at me like she was worried.

"This is nicer than my first apartment," I told her.

"You lived in a potty?"

"Yeah."

She found that hysterical. After we all washed our hands and Hannah used the rose soap and the aloe-and-clover-scented lotion, we made our way back to the front desk.

Apparently we had suites and not rooms, and my anxiety rose as we traveled up the elevators. While I appreciated the suite, because sleeping in the same room with my kids meant that I would be celibate Thursday through Saturday, the cost looked staggering.

"It'll be okay," Sam whispered close to my ear.

"We need a new water heater," I reminded him.

"I know," he said, pressing a kiss to the side of my neck.

As the elevator slid open and we got out with Jen and Doug and their two kids, Regina reminded us to all meet in the lobby in twenty minutes so we could be in time for the reunion to kick off on the west lawn.

"Absolutely." Jen gave her mother the thumbs-up before the doors swooshed closed. "Ohmygod, I need a drink."

"It's not even noon," Doug chuckled.

She pointed back at the elevator. "We can go right back down to the bar."

"We'll get mai tais right after we unpack," I promised her.

"Oh God, thank you." She beamed at me.

Our suite was fantastic. It had a living room and two bedrooms—one for the kids with two beds in it and the other with a king-size bed for me and Sam. There were two bathrooms, a guest toilet, and both bedrooms had their own balconies. It was easily 1,800 square feet, 1,300 square feet bigger than my first apartment. There was Italian marble and a gorgeous view, fresh-cut flowers—birds of paradise and dragon lilies—on the table, and a fruit basket.

I took Kola and Hannah to their room and showed them how to unpack while Sam took care of our stuff in the other room. Once I had the kids situated, I led them back to our room.

We all lay down on the bed and watched Sam work.

"Daddy?"

"Yes, B?"

"Do we hafta go to church on Sunday when we get home?"

"No, we'll miss church."

"But I was gonna ask Miss Ginny about Cain again."

He turned from hanging up his suit beside mine to look at her. "What about him?"

"Well, last week I asked Miss Ginny who Cain had babies with when he had to go away, and she said she'd tell me this week."

"Why did you have to wait a whole week?"

"Because she was gonna look it up," Kola chimed in. "I told her it was the evolution people, but she didn't like that answer."

Sam squinted and looked at his son. "The evolution people?"

He nodded. "In school we learned about Neanderthal man and Cro-Magnon man, and so I told Miss Ginny that even though Adam and Eve and Cain and Abel lived in the Garden of Eden, that outside there, evolution was going on."

"I see."

"And I told her that's where Cain got his wife from."

"But she said you were wrong."

"Yeah, so I told her she needed to show me."

Sam sighed. "You know, some things you have to take on faith, buddy."

"Like God."

"Yes, like God."

"Yeah, but maybe God made the evolution people too, to see which one would work out better. Maybe the evolution people didn't kill their brothers."

"I would never kill Kola," Hannah told Sam. "Maybe I'm a—" She looked over at her brother. "—emolution people?"

"Evolution."

"Evolution," she parroted.

Sam looked at me.

"What?"

"Can you help me with this so we can go downstairs? I'm starving."

"Me too!" Hannah said. "I want ice cream."

"I want Honey Comb," Kola informed me.

"You can have something much better than that."

"Like what?"

"Like fruit and an omelet or—"

The retching noise he made cut me off.

Back down in the lobby, everyone else was there so we could walk to the west lawn. It turned out to be a lot closer than we thought, and there were white tents set up everywhere with a banner that read *Miller/Kage Family Reunion.*

Thomas's oldest brother, Frank, who had planned the whole thing and was much wealthier than his other three brothers and two sisters, came barreling up to us to say hello. A representative from the hotel went to the podium on the dais and welcomed the families to a great time in the valley of the sun. It was assigned seating, because people were supposed to mix up and mingle and not just stick to their own family clusters. I walked around looking for our names until I found them at a table with an older couple and two beautiful women who had to be their daughters.

Once we sat, I introduced myself, Kola, and Hannah to Jim and his wife, Anita, and their two daughters, Renee and Joyce. When I saw Sam cutting across the tent—he had been waylaid a couple of times by his cousin Levi and others—I waved so he'd see where we were.

When he joined us, of course, the women sat up straight and leaned forward, both very happy to meet him. I understood. If a big, strapping, virile alpha male was your wet dream, you needed to look no further than Sam Kage. The dimples were on display, as was the stubble over his square jaw and under his lip; he had laugh lines in the corners of his eyes and bulging muscles. Power rippled off the man, combined with dominance and strength. I would have creamed my jeans too if he weren't already mine.

"So how are we related?" Sam smiled at Anita, the mother.

"We're not really." She smiled at him. "Frank married my mother, Donna, after his first wife passed away, and she already had me and my brother Paul."

"Got it. Is your mother here?"

"Yes, she's at the table with Frank and a lot of other people I don't know."

"This is huge." Sam grinned as Hannah reached up and touched his chin. "Yes, B?"

"Daddy, I'm hungry."

"I know, love. We just have to wait until they call our section to go up."

"Where's your Mommy, bunny?" Anita's daughter Renee asked Hannah.

Now, maybe she asked because there were two more free chairs at our table—it was supposed to seat ten. Maybe she thought Sam and I were cousins and we were waiting for our wives since we were both wearing wedding rings. Who knew? It still happened sometimes when we went out, and normally I wouldn't have cared, but this was a family reunion, and I wanted people to know that the big guy was with me. I opened my mouth to set her straight.

"I don't have a Mommy, I have Pa and Daddy. Do you have a mommy and daddy?" Hannah chimed in cheerfully, taking advantage of the moment between the end of her question and me deciding what to say to take control of the conversation.

Renee flushed beet red and her eyes got huge. "Yes, I—"

"Do you have a big house, 'cause I do, and I have a cat named Chilly. Do you have a cat?"

"No, I—"

"Chilly's all white except he has black on his ears and his nose and his paws. I can draw you a picture of him if you want. Do you have dog since you don't have a cat?"

"No, I—"

"Kola was born in Neverland, but not like where Peter Pan lives. It's a different place," she said authoritatively. "Do you know where that is? I know where that is. I know where Uglay is too. That's where I was born. Do you know why I have a Daddy and a Pa? Because where Kola was born, Pa means Daddy. So that's why Pa is Pa."

"I—"

"Where's your mommy?"

"R-r-right… there…," she stammered, pointing at her mother.

"You're her mommy?" Hannah asked Anita brightly.

"Yes, darling."

"How come she doesn't have a cat?" My daughter was very concerned about this development.

"She's allergic to them."

The piece of information floored my daughter. Hannah scrunched up her nose like that was the worst thing she'd ever heard in her whole life before she whispered for Sam. "Daddy."

"Yes, B?" He chuckled.

"She's allergic so she can't come to our house."

"Okay."

"Tell her, 'kay?"

"I will."

Hannah's eyes flicked to the woman suspiciously.

Renee leaned forward, eyes on me. "Forgive me, I meant no offense."

"Yeah, open mouth, insert foot, Renee." Her sister rolled her eyes before she turned and smiled at me. "So, Jory, what do you do?"

I explained about my graphic design business and then asked her what it was that she did. Interesting to learn that she was a public defender in Miami, where she lived. Of course, Sam telling her he was a US Marshal was the high point. Big, beautiful man and he worked a sexy-sounding job on top of it? Game over.

Once we were called up, I walked with Hannah and Sam with Kola. We were on opposite sides of the buffet table, so of course Kola and Hannah talked over it.

"How do you think you get allergic to a cat?" Hannah asked her brother when she was sure Renee couldn't overhear her. I had wondered why she had hung back enough to let a few people in front of us.

"I think it's made up." He was adamant. "How do you get allergic to a cat? You're not supposed to put them in your mouth, Daddy said."

Hannah's mouth made a perfect little *O*. "That's right, huh?"

"Yep," he insisted. "It's not a real thing."

"Yes it is," I assured him. "People are allergic to cat dander."

"What's dander?"

"Like dandruff."

"What's that?" Hannah wanted to know.

"It's like little pieces of skin, and sometimes it's itchy."

"Ewww." She made a face. "Chilly doesn't have that."

I sighed. "Some people are allergic to their hair too."

"How?" Kola wanted to know.

"It makes them sneeze."

"Is this in a book?" he wanted to know. Lately everything I said was questioned in this manner.

"Yes, and you can look it up on the Internet too."

He looked skeptical.

"So is she allergic to all cats?" Hannah wanted to know.

"I suspect so."

"Like lions? She would be allergic to Simba?"

"Simba's not a real lion," Kola reminded her. "He's a cartoon."

"But if he was a real lion he would make her sneeze, huh?"

Both faces turned up to me, waiting.

"I think it's just house cats, but we'll have to look it up when we get back to the room."

My answer seemed to placate them.

"Kola, look." Hanna pointed at some kind of casserole. "That looks like monkey brains."

"Or like a horse blew up." He retched, which made the woman behind us gasp.

"Guys," I cautioned them.

"Remember that time Chilly barfed up that hairball with the jelly beans?"

"Eww, the red ones!"

She dissolved into her husky laughter.

He gagged again, which sent his sister into hysterics.

Sam had to apologize to the people behind us and I noticed that no one even picked up the spoon to put any of the red glop on their plates.

"Daddy," Kola began as we moved down the side of the buffet table. "When I get big, I'm gonna be a marshal too."

"Is that right?"

"Yeah. I'm not gonna shoot people, though."

"No? What're you gonna do?"

"I'm just gonna make them sit in a room and talk to Hannah," he announced with diabolical intent, his voice rising at the end.

"Kola!"

He started laughing, and she picked up a roll.

"Hannah Kage, don't you dare throw that roll," I threatened her.

"Kola is made of boogers!"

"Well, Hannah is made of poop!"

"Guys," Sam was chuckling so his warning lacked any real power. Stern he was not.

Once we were sitting, Hannah asked me why a lady hit a girl when we were in line.

"That was her daughter," I explained.

"So why did she hit her?"

"She probably did something her mother didn't like."

"So she was bad?"

"Kids aren't bad. Sometimes they do things that make their parents upset, but it's not bad. It's just that the behavior is misguided."

She looked at me like I was from another planet.

I made a noise. "Fine, yeah, she was bad."

"How come you don't hit me when I'm bad?"

"I don't think hitting accomplishes anything."

"Me neither." She nodded, patting my arm.

I started laughing, and when Kola waggled his eyebrows at me, I lost it.

Sam just shook his head.

THE day was a whirlwind. There were so many activities and sign-ups, and Sam's father wanted both his sons with him. I left to take the kids to the playground, let them run around like crazy people for two hours, and then took them for a walk around the lagoon. Hannah started getting whiney and grouchy, and when I picked her up and carried her, she fell asleep in seconds. We went back to the room, and I had Kola do the homework his teacher had given us, and put Hannah down on the couch so she would be out with us instead of in the bedroom alone.

I got a call around two that reminded us we had horseback rides scheduled for three. Apparently we were already signed up to do lots of things.

We didn't see Sam again until after five. We had already showered and changed when he came through the front door. "Hello!"

"In here!"

He found all three of us under the covers, watching a movie on my bed with the remainders of room service around us.

"We have to go to dinner, guys. Are you ready?"

Kola moaned and burrowed into my side, his arm on my stomach as he hid his face.

"What happened?" Sam looked at me.

"Kola got horse sick," I said with as much of a straight face as I could manage.

Hannah pretended to puke for Sam, just in case he was confused. "He threw up all over the saddle, Daddy."

Kola said something no one could understand into my T-shirt.

"Tell me." Sam smiled.

"Well, it was all fine until—"

"He has it on video," Hannah informed her father.

"Which I think might have been the problem," I sighed. "You know when you're looking through that viewfinder too long... I think he got motion sickness."

"Poor guy," Sam empathized, moving over to Kola's side.

His son rolled over and, when Sam bent, wrapped his arms around his father's neck.

"Maybe I should order room service too, huh, and stay here with you guys."

Kola nodded.

"No, you gotta be with your family, Sam. You—"

"I am with my family," he assured me, reaching out to take my hand. "And my boy needs me."

"You wanna see the video, Daddy?" Hannah was trying to be helpful.

"Don't look at the barf," Kola cautioned.

"Maybe later."

I covered my face with a pillow so there was no snickering.

When the phone in the room rang twenty minutes later, Sam answered and shook his head, obviously ready to tell whoever was on the other end of the line no. I waved, getting his attention, and told him to go ahead and go.

He covered the receiver with his hand. "Jory, I need to stay here."

"It's a reunion," I reminded him.

His heavy sigh made me smile before he agreed to go.

When he left, Kola snuggled up on my right, Hannah on my left, and we all got warm and toasty watching *Homeward Bound* in the air-conditioned room. I wasn't sure what time Sam got in because I fell asleep.

SIX

BASICALLY the adult events and the kid events were separate. I understood it perfectly; you couldn't really mix them. So while the grown-ups ate and drank and went hot air ballooning and golfing and did yoga and hiked and sat under tents in the gardens, the children, and the guardians of the children, did completely separate activities.

Kola and Hannah loved the paddleboats. We went bike riding together; I took them to the pool, and the waterslide was a huge hit. I was lucky—we did the program at the YMCA every summer, and since Dane and Aja had a pool in the penthouse apartment they lived in—they had ditched the house in Oak Park after Robert was born—we always had a place to swim. So my kids didn't need the floaties or the swim rings in all assorted shapes and sizes. The only other boy who kept up with mine was a little towheaded kid who was having the best time swimming under ten feet of water with Kola. Hannah couldn't go down quite that far, but she could swim under the water in the shallow end. They both had their goggles on, and when Kola swam over to me, his friend followed.

"Pa, this is Theo."

"Hi." I smiled at him.

He smiled back.

"Are your folks out here, Theo?"

"My dad is. My mom is home with my stepdad and the new baby."

"I see."

"Theo."

We all looked up, and the man who joined us looked a lot like his son except taller, broader, and tanner. He was very handsome, and I was certain that I was not the only one at the pool who noticed the fuzzy chest, long legs, and toned musculature. He must have worked very hard at the gym for that kind of definition.

"Sorry." He grimaced at me.

"Nothing to be sorry for," I said, moving towels, my cell phone, and the video camera off the chair beside me. "Here, sit, I've got the shade here."

"You sure?" The smile was shy and sweet.

"Please."

He took a seat, and we all met: Kola; Hannah, who was in my lap, drinking a juice box and eating Parmesan-flavored Goldfish; and him and his son. It was nice to sit and talk, watch the kids, and drink iced tea.

His name was Milton Kage, and he was a professor of biology who lived in Houston. He and his wife had divorced two years ago after an eight-year marriage. Theo was seven and had been the reason they stuck it out for as long as they had.

"He's gorgeous," I told Milt.

"Thank you, I think so. Yours too."

I smiled at him.

"Is your wife busy doing some fun family bonding thing?" he teased me.

"My husband," I corrected. "I hope that doesn't bother you."

He took a breath. "No, actually. That was the reason for the divorce."

I nodded. "Did you cheat?"

"I didn't." He grinned back. "She did with the man she married."

I shrugged. "Sounds like it worked out for the best."

"It did. I can't find the man of my dreams being married to a woman."

"No," I chuckled. "Not so much."

He laughed, and the sound was good. When Kola and Theo were pruney, Milton asked me if we'd like to go to lunch with them. The cheering answered his question.

Lunch was nice. It was always good to go with other parents who got that sitting outside was better than sitting inside, that getting finger food was always best, and that if something spilled, it was not the end of the world.

We all went back to our rooms to shower and change and then met back downstairs for the jeep tour guide. It turned out we could all go together, and the kids had a great squealing time bouncing all over the trail. Going up and over rocks bounced us easily a foot up off our seats. Our tour guide, Robbie, was funny and well informed about all the flora and fauna. He was very cute and very gay and recognizing another bottom when he saw one—wanted nothing to do with me and did everything but put his hand in Milton's lap. As we were standing looking out at the valley, I leaned close and told Milt that I would watch his kid for him if he wanted to ask the guy out for a drink.

"My folks are with us"—he grinned at me—"and I'd much rather have conversation than a fifteen-minute fuck in the room of the apartment he's sharing with three roommates."

"Hey, that was me," I laughed.

"Yeah, me too, but I shared a room, so I had to have sex in the back of my Explorer."

Just imagining the fumbling made me dissolve into peals of laughter.

When we got back—Milton with Robbie's number stuffed into the back pocket of his jeans—we stopped for water, then took the kids to the playground.

Milton wanted to know all about me, about Sam, and about how long we'd been together.

"A marshal? Are you screwing with me?"

"No, why?"

"What is that, cop fantasy on crack?"

My eyes narrowed. "Oh, Milt, honey… are you a badge bunny?"

He spit out his water. "A what?"

I arched an eyebrow for his benefit. "Do cops make your balls ache?"

He nodded vigorously.

I put my head back and laughed like I hadn't in days.

"Come on, Jory," he chuckled, arm on the back of the bench we were sitting on. "The whole perfect V those guys have when they're in their uniforms… I have this one who goes to my gym, and when he changes and comes out—God."

"You should ask him out." I waggled my eyebrows at him.

"And if he shoots me?" He gestured at his son. "Then you've got a fatherless kid there."

"You've never smiled at him?"

"No, I just ogle from afar."

"Gutless."

"Cautious." He smiled at me. "Jesus, how old are you?"

"Me?"

"Yeah."

"Thirty-five, why?"

He shook his head. "You look maybe twenty-five."

"Good genes," I teased him, tugging on the denim I was wearing.

"You're hysterical."

"Seriously, though," I sighed. "The cop, he's hot, huh?"

"You would drool."

I doubted that, I only drooled over one man.

"Oh God, Jory, he's so gorgeous."

"And really, you've never checked him out and let him see you?"

"Yeah, I have."

"And?"

"And I don't know. I mean, we're talking a tall blond god with blue-green eyes and a body that just…."

"Tell me."

He looked at me. "The deal is I'm verse, right? So it's either…."

"What? Spit it out."

"It's either big gorgeous mountains of men or guys like you."

"Oh, I see."

"You have to know that you're just gorgeous. That boy today had nothing on you."

"Thank you," I said softly. "But Milton, you shouldn't be having any trouble yourself."

His smile curled his lip. "So I've been told."

I bumped him with my shoulder.

"You sure you don't wanna be the guy I pick up tonight?"

"Too late," I teased him. "Already friends."

"Friends are good too." He smiled.

"Yes, they are."

AT DINNER, the rule was that you could not sit with your spouse, but anyone else was fair game. Married people, any kind of couples, were supposed to scatter. So since Sam had not come back to the room by the time we were supposed to go to dinner, I took Hannah and Kola with me to join Milton. His mother, Denise, was lovely, so charming, and she thought my kids were amazing. Since I agreed wholeheartedly, we got along famously.

Milton was entertaining the table with tales of the exam he had given his classes right before he came on the trip. Listening to him talk about some of the answers he got was hysterical.

"Did you know that birds have fur?"

"They did not write that." I defended the obviously clueless underclassmen he taught.

"As God is my witness." He grinned. "I had this one answer to a question on convergence—"

"Explain to Jory what that is," Denise interrupted her son.

"Mom, I'm sure Jory is well aware of what convergence is," he said as he looked at me.

"I'm not, though," I told him. "Please explain."

He smiled at me. "Convergence is when distantly related species have similar forms because they live in the same environment."

"Oh, okay, so you were looking for examples of this."

"Yes."

"And you were what, unclear?"

"No, I was crystal clear. I told them that they didn't have to use the examples I gave in class, that they could come up with their own."

"Come up with or make up?"

"See, yeah, right there." He spread his hands to illustrate the fact that he just didn't get it. "That's what happened. I said *come up* and they heard *made up*."

"Did you get unicorns for an answer?" I teased him.

"No, but I did get fish and mermaids."

I started chuckling.

"This is college, you understand." He sounded pained. "I mean, come on."

"That makes no sense." Kola was frowning.

"No, it doesn't." Milton smiled over at Kola. "What would you have said?"

He thought a minute. "Dolphins and sharks."

His face broke into a wide smile. "You see, that's a great answer, Kola. What made you think of that?"

"Well, they both have the same kind of bodies."

"Very good." His eyes lit up as he leaned on the table. "What's an example of an amphibian?"

"A frog."

Milton looked at me. "On the test I just gave, I got 'bat' to that question."

"Oh you did not." I laughed at him.

"And did you know that Procter & Gamble discovered the DNA molecule?"

"I thought it was Abercrombie & Fitch," I baited him.

"Oh you're hysterical," he said, smiling, before his face slowly started to change.

"What's wrong?"

"I don't—there's a guy coming over here, and he looks upset, and he's really… big."

I turned and saw Sam moving through the sea of tables. He looked dangerous, and the way his clothes clung to him made him seem like a mountain of hard muscle. His stare, currently focused on me, could and did frighten people who didn't know him, as it looked cold and dead. But I knew better, I knew the intensity of the gaze was just him zeroed in on one particular thing.

Hannah's greeting, high pitched and excited, always tempered the impression he made on strangers. How scary could he be if he knelt to receive the little girl who had hopped off her chair to run to him? And they had their *Dirty Dancing* ritual—he lifted her and she did the airplane pose.

There was applause, and she scrunched up her shoulders and waved. She was so cute; sometimes it took all that I had not to eat her.

Sam moved like he always did, fluidly, his innate power so easy to see. When he returned Hannah to her chair, he put a hand on the back of mine before he leaned down close. I was surprised when he kissed my cheek, as the action was more than he was normally comfortable with in public.

"Hi," I greeted him, my hand going to his shoulder. "How was your day?"

He ran his stubble-covered cheek up the side of my neck to behind my ear. "I missed you."

It was just a simple statement, but because of his closeness, the soft, husky growl, and the warm breath on my skin, it felt so very intimate. I caught my breath.

"Did you miss me or did you replace me?" He was teasing, mostly.

"Stupid man," I breathed as I tilted my head back to look up into the dark smoky-blue eyes. "Let me introduce you."

I saw his jaw clench and knew why. My soft voice, hooded gaze, and the lazy smile I gave him all reminded him of sex, and that fast, he was mine. He tumbled into my web so easily.

"Sam, this is Milton Kage; his mother, Denise; and his son, Theo. Everyone, this is Sam."

Milton stood to offer him his hand. "Heard a lot about you today, Marshal. Your family doesn't talk about much else."

And that fast he was on the receiving end of happy, smiling Sam Kage. "Pleasure."

After Sam shook hands with everyone, he hugged Kola and then returned to me, his hand, whether he knew it or not, settling on the base of my throat.

"I'm sending Riley and Peter up to babysit so you can meet me in the bar overlooking the mountains. They have a blue margarita that apparently, Jen says, you would like."

"Okay." I smiled up at him. "What time will you be there?"

"I have to go with my dad and Michael to meet some people, so, eight?"

"Eight is perfect." I sighed, unable to help myself.

"It's a date."

"It's drinks," I clarified, "and I'm bringing my wingman."

His eyes flicked over to Milton and then back to me. "You do that."

THE Blue Moon Lounge, with its indigo-illuminated floor, cobalt glassware, and blue Formica, was aptly named. As I sat with Milton at the bar, nursing a blue Hawaiian, because I thought it would be funny, I should have been the picture of ease. I was tense.

Sam was late.

Sam was never late.

If, heaven forbid, the man couldn't avoid being tardy, I could always count on a call letting me know what the problem was. It was unsettling that he was not there.

I tried his cell, and it went immediately to voice mail. My heart was suddenly in my throat.

"Jory, I'm sure it's nothing," Milton told me. "Have another drink."

But it was nine, and then it was ten and now eleven, and Sam didn't answer any of my texts.

"Jory, I'm sure he—"

"No," I told him, excusing myself, abandoning Milton to go back to the room to check to see if Sam was there.

Riley and Peter were watching a movie they probably shouldn't have been, but my kids were asleep, and Riley was watching through her fingers while her brother called her a girl. I checked the phone to see if there were any messages and then left the kids alone and went down to the front desk. They had no messages for me either.

Waiting was never my thing.

As Milton joined me, having come to look for me, I called the WITSEC field office in Chicago. They would know what to do.

After a whirlwind of phone calls, I was alone, and I didn't think I would be.

It turned out that Sam had to be missing a full twenty-four hours before the police in Phoenix would do anything. The deputies at home in Chicago were not aware that Sam was on anything more frightening than a vacation. Even when I spoke to Deputy White, he said that any communication to them would need to come from Sam. If he called them for help, if he got word to them, they would move. Unfortunately my concern over him being gone, and especially for such a short time, was not enough for them to go on. They would not be riding to my rescue.

"But you said all he had to do was call you," I reminded him, somewhat frantically, over the phone.

"Yeah, *him*," White told me for what must have been the fifth time at that point. "I'm sorry, Mr. Harcourt, but you saying he's missing is just not enough of a reason for us to scramble our team. If he were actually in trouble, he'd let us know."

"How?" I was yelling by that time, and there was nothing I could do about it.

"We have our channels. I assure you, he's fine."

I hung up on him so I wouldn't yell. I knew Sam Kage; he didn't. I knew what trouble looked like.

"Jory," Milton said hesitantly as I paced the lobby at midnight, "do you think maybe you're overreacting?"

I reminded myself that he didn't know me or Sam, so ripping his head off was not fair. "No" was all I said as I called one of Sam's oldest friends.

Charles "Chaz" Diaz and Patrick Cantwell were Sam's closest buddies from back when he had been a detective. They had been friends of his first partner, Dominic Kairov, too. But even before it became evident that he was so much more than simply dirty that going into witness protection was Dominic's only option, they had both taken Sam's side in the fallout he'd had with Dominic over Sam being gay. When Sam joined the US Marshals, nothing changed; they all still saw each other constantly. So it made sense when I was freaking out to turn to Pat or Chaz. Since Chaz was before Pat in my phone, he was the one who got woken up.

He answered on the fifth ring. "Whoever the fuck this is, it's two the fuck o'clock in the morning here, just so you fuckin' know."

"Sam's missing," I said instead of hello.

"Jory?" he said and sounded a little clearer, less gravelly, even that fast.

"I can't find him and I'm freaking out. He was supposed to come see me, but he also came here tracking a witness, and maybe that witness—"

"Where are you?"

"I'm in Arizona."

"No, I know that. I mean are you at the hotel or somewhere else?"

"I'm at the hotel, but how did you know Sam and I were in Arizona?"

"Because friends fuckin' talk, Jory, how the fuck ya think?"

All three of them swore too much, that's what I thought.

"So you're at the hotel and Sam's missing."

"Yes."

"How long has he been gone?"

"Three hours."

"And no word from him?"

"No word."

"Shit," he groaned, and his concern sent a surge of gratitude through me. Chaz and Pat knew Sam Kage just like I did. They knew that him being gone without telling anyone where he was going, if he was not specifically undercover, was cause for concern. There was no second-guessing; Chaz was simply right there with me, taking the situation seriously. I would have gushed at him, but I knew, to him, it was unnecessary. It simply was.

"Okay, J, stay on the line," he ordered me before he was gone.

I took the time to text Dane that I needed him to come to Phoenix to pick up the kids. As soon as he woke up and read the message, I was sure I would be getting a call.

"Jory," Milton began, sliding his arm around my shoulder, trying to offer me comfort. It wasn't what I needed.

"J?"

"Chaz," I said, shrugging off Milton's arm as I walked a few feet away from him.

"Okay, so the ping off his phone tells us that his last location was at some place called The Ram, west of Scottsdale where you are, close to Peoria. I punched up the club, and it looks like it has drugs and a whole lot of other shit running through it. Do not go there alone."

"Okay."

"I repeat. Do not go there alone. Wait for me and Pat, we'll be there by—"

"We both know I'm going there like right now."

There was a long-drawn-out sigh. "Yeah, I figured," he grumbled. "So there's a guy I know from our department who's on vacation out there, and Pat called him, and he's gonna pick you up at your hotel and drive you there."

"Who?"

"Duncan Stiel. You remember ever meeting him?"

Vaguely. "I dunno."

"Listen, just…." He took a breath. "Don't go anywhere without him, all right?"

"What is he doing here?" I asked as I started for the front of the hotel. I needed to be where Duncan Stiel could easily find me.

"He's been on vacation. First he was in California for a while, and now he's driving back to Chicago, taking the scenic route home. Sam had called Duncan already about backing him up if he needed help while he was there."

"He did?"

"Course. You know Sam. When have you ever seen him not prepared?"

And it was true, but God, did the man need to learn how to communicate! "Okay."

"So he'll be there soon, but I need you to wait for him, you understand?"

"And you're still coming? You and Pat?"

"Yeah, we'll be there. Pat is seeing what flight we can get on, but just listen to Duncan, all right? He's a good guy, and he'll take care of you."

"Okay."

He cleared his throat. "I don't suppose I could convince you to just stay at your hotel and let Duncan take care of this."

"Yeah, no."

"Shit. I knew I shouldn't have told you the name of the club, but Pat said that if we kept it from you and you ever found out—"

"I'd sic both your wives on you," I told him seriously.

"Yeah, I know, and that's what he said."

There were big-time perks to having such close friends.

"Okay, so Duncan will be there shortly. Listen to him, yeah?"

"Yeah," I agreed quickly. "But how will I know him?"

"He's as big as Sam, blond hair—no, wait, maybe it's brown, I've never really noticed. He's got gray eyes, I think, but ya know—most important he's big, right?"

"Got it."

"Do not—"

"Go without him, yeah, I heard you the first time."

"Good."

"You know Sam won't—"

"Anything happens to you on my watch and Sam Kage will put his foot up my ass, so let's not debate what he will and will not do. Just wait for fuckin' Stiel, all right?"

"I promise."

He took a breath, and I told him I'd see him soon and hung up.

I was outside waiting when Milton found me.

"Jory, where—"

"I'm going to get Sam," I told him.

"Yeah, but who's with your kids?"

"Regina," I told him. "I asked her to go to the room and relieve Rachel's kids of their babysitting duty."

"So where are you going?"

I explained about where Sam's phone was and that it was the best lead I had.

"Jesus, who are you, James Bond?"

"Hardly." I smiled at him.

"But you're so calm about this. I mean, he could be in real trouble, right?"

"Yes."

He gestured at me. "And you're going to do what?"

"Get him out of whatever he's in."

"Yeah, but—"

The car horn startled us both—stunned, more like it.

There, in a Jeep Wrangler that had just pulled up, was Sam.

"What the fuck are you doing?" he roared at me as he got out of the car and came charging across the driveway.

"Me?" I yelled back. "Where the hell have you been?"

"Goddamn, Jory, what the hell are you doing out here?" He was seething, he was loud, and his body language was murderous. He scared the crap out of poor Milton, who scurried backward.

I just put my hands on my hips, planted my feet, and held my ground. When he reached me, I had to tilt my head all the way back to meet his glare. "You better fuckin' call everybody, because I scrambled the damn Marines," I announced angrily, my own volume nothing to scoff at.

"Who the fuck did you call?"

"I called everybody, Sam! I was this close to getting ahold of your FBI buddy Agent Calhoun, even though I fuckin' hate him. But Duncan Stiel is supposed to be meeting me here in—"

"Duncan? How the fuck do you know about—"

"Because I called Chaz and he called Pat and Pat called him!"

"Jory, do the words 'secret meeting' mean—"

"You were supposed to meet me for drinks!"

"I know that! That's why I sent you a text when I—"

"I got no text, Sam! I got shit!"

He pulled his phone from his back pocket as mine started ringing.

"Fuck," I swore when I answered it, turning away from Sam. "I'm sorry. Never mind."

"You're sorry?" my brother Dane rasped at me. "Never mind?"

"No, I—"

"You will be at the hotel when I arrive."

"No, Dane, you don't have to—"

"I will hear about whatever you have gotten yourself into then."

He hung up, and when I tried him back, he didn't answer.

"Fuck!" I yelled.

"Jory!"

I whirled on Sam, and his scowl could have peeled paint off the walls.

"So I sent the text to the house," he said matter-of-factly and not sounding repentant even one bit.

"And then you put your phone on silent." I smirked at him.

"Yes," he said through gritted teeth.

I growled at him.

"Okay, so I'm a dick and I messed up, but—"

"Tell it to Duncan. He's on his way."

"Shit," he groaned, taking a step toward me.

I took one back. "You better take a fucking shower because you smell like really gross perfume and cigarette smoke, and you have lipstick on your jaw."

He let his head loll back on his shoulders in the "Lord, give me strength" posture that I really hated.

"That's bullshit, Sam!" I railed at him. "You scared the shit out of me, and you know better, and you were obviously not very concerned that I was worried, or you would have done a better job communicating with me!"

"You should trust me to take care of myself," he thundered. "I've been taking care of myself a whole helluva lot longer than you've been taking care of me!"

I could feel my face get hot, felt a tremble run through me. "Is that so?"

"Yeah," he said flatly. "Between the two of us, J, I am so not the one who needs saving. You get in more trouble than ten people combined!"

I was nodding fast, so pissed but just letting him get it all out, vent.

"Now if you'll excuse me, I have to get everyone to stand down from the clusterfuck that you created."

I pivoted and stalked back into the lobby.

"Jory!" Milton called my name as he ran to catch up with me and joined me in the elevator.

I was silent as we rode up together.

"Are you okay?"

"I will be," I assured him.

"I guess being married to a marshal can be hard sometimes, huh?"

Yes, it could.

I RELIEVED Regina, sent her back to her room, and watched her from my door until she went inside and I heard the door lock behind her. I bothered only with taking off my shoes before I crawled into bed between Kola and Hannah, who were as usual, sleeping together. I needed to calm down before I did anything else, but at the moment I thought I would lie there all night, fuming.

The anger didn't last; I was much too relieved. The man had reappeared, unscathed, and I was so very thankful. Not that he wasn't in trouble. He'd texted the wrong phone after all and not even bothered to check, but… he'd tried to do the right thing. His intention had been good. Of course I was still going to rip him a new one, especially because the display downstairs hadn't been fair, but I could possibly let him live until the morning.

Maybe.

I let out a deep breath, releasing the last of the tension, until I saw something move on the balcony.

Shadows didn't shift without cause. There was no wind, and it was a cloudless night, so there was really only one conclusion to draw. With my kids on either side of me, I was suddenly freezing, my whole body flushed with cold. I had never been so terrified in my whole life. Fear for my children was like nothing I had ever imagined.

Slowly, carefully, I muted the phone so the buttons would make no sound, keeping it tilted so the light would not be a dead giveaway, and then sent Sam the 911 call for help—or for us, what translated to it. I texted his name to him and then put down my phone and tried to breathe.

Trying to think of what I would do, I narrowed my eyes even as I heard the glass door open and saw a man step inside the room.

"I know you're not asleep, Mr. Harcourt."

I didn't move.

"Please don't make me hurt your—"

"Freeze!" Sam yelled as he kicked the door open and charged into the room.

It was so fast. Kola and Hannah both screamed as they were woken up and saw the man aim his gun at us in the light that had spilled in from the outer room with Sam.

Everything happened at once. I grabbed both kids and shoved their faces against my chest so neither of them saw their father fire the gun. The sound of the shot was loud in the small room, but it was instantaneous and followed by silence. My children's crying lasted longer, but I was thankful that they needed comfort, needed me, because if they didn't, if I had been allowed even a moment to think—I would have come apart myself.

SAM gave Duncan's gun back to him when he joined Sam over the dead man. I had taken the kids into our room, put them under the covers after they both went to the bathroom, and was thankful when they dropped off after Sam came in and kissed them good night. We shared a look, and then he left to join Duncan. I had left the kids and was back in the living room of the suite when I heard another gunshot.

"Sorry," Duncan said as he came in from the kids' room where the dead man was.

I went back to look in on the kids in our room, to make sure that they had not been roused from sleep for the second time that night and was thankful when I opened the door to find them both still passed out.

Returning again to the living room, I found Sam there with Duncan.

"What's going on?" I asked both men.

"I needed to have gun residue on my hands," he told me, replacing the weapon that Sam had used in the holster under his leather jacket. "Ah, shit."

"What?" Sam asked.

"I need to go back to my car and get another bullet for this gun, and you need to call this in while I'm gone."

Sam nodded. "They'll take that off you. You got a spare?"

"Oh sure, I have two. You want one?"

"Yeah, I better," Sam told him. "Where did you discharge the gun?"

"In the tree," Duncan told him. "They won't be looking, since I'm taking responsibility, but I gotta go get the bullet."

"Lucky the walls are nice and thick in here."

"Yeah, it's a nice hotel you've brought your bullshit to, Kage."

Sam flipped him off as Duncan left quickly.

When we were alone, Sam turned to me. "You did very well."

I was silent.

"You protected the kids, and you didn't get yourself hurt in the process."

My eyes went down to my socked feet.

"I was mad, I was pissed, you scared the fuck out of me because you would have been eaten alive if you stepped foot in that damn bar. You can't be the one riding to my rescue, J. You have to depend on other people now. You have kids."

"So do you," I breathed out.

He stepped in close to me, and his hands went to my face, gently, tenderly, and when he lifted my head so I would look at him, I saw how scared he was.

"Sam?"

He took a shaky breath as my hands closed over his wrists. "I didn't think I'd get here in time. I thought... and you and Kola and Hannah...." He squinted, but I saw how red his eyes suddenly were. "I can't lose any of you, it would kill me. Just... I'd be done."

"I feel the same about you."

I was grabbed so tight, crushed against the mountain of muscle that was Sam Kage. He didn't even let me go when he called the police.

Sam held my hand when Duncan came back, and I met him again.

He was tall, the same six four that Sam was, and built with a similarly powerful physique, but whereas Sam moved fluidly, Duncan Stiel moved like a bull. I remembered him once I was looking at the short dark-blond hair and dark-gray eyes. They were not Dane's gray, not charcoal and flecked with silver, but more gunmetal, and ringed in black. We had met once, before Sam had left the Chicago PD.

Duncan, it turned out, was gay as well. You could have knocked me over with a feather when Sam whispered that news as I watched Duncan hand over his gun to the Scottsdale PD. They were all over the hotel room and in the hall, but since it was close to one in the morning, there weren't many people out there anyway.

As I stood beside Sam—he was still holding my hand—he quietly related Duncan's story to me. It was a sad one, about how he couldn't come out, not at work, not to his family, how his last relationship with an English professor had ended because Duncan was in the closet, and how he was currently cruising bars and picking up one-night stands. I felt bad for him, but by the same token, Sam Kage had come out to everyone he knew, both personally and professionally. It had been hard for him, and friends had been lost along the way, but for him, it was all he could do. Sam was not the kind of man who lived closeted for anyone, and the fact that Duncan was made me respect him less. But as Sam quietly cautioned me, I had no right to judge Duncan Stiel. Never had I been in either his or Sam's situation.

I nodded as Sam's hand closed around the back of my neck. "Go check on the kids. We'll have detectives here when you get back."

After quietly opening the door and closing it, I found my two little people snuggled under the blankets together in our bed. It was cute how both Hannah's arms were wrapped around her brother's one. He didn't seem to mind, as his chin was resting on top of her head.

I had checked the room once already but did it again just because I had seen way too many horror movies in my life. The closet was empty but for clothes, I had locked the balcony door and wedged a chair against it for good measure. The only way in or out was the door I had just come through. They were safe, and I had even checked the ceiling and the bathroom for ninjas. You never knew.

When I returned, my living room was, in fact, now filled with detectives in suits as well as the uniformed officers who had been there when I left. I was immediately asked if I could answer questions.

So I stood there and lied, explaining how Detective Stiel had kicked the door down, yelled out for the man to freeze, and when he didn't, he had fired and killed the intruder.

It all made perfect sense.

The police detectives—there were too many to even consider remembering names—liked that my story matched Sam's and Sam's version matched Duncan's. It was ruled a robbery attempt gone wrong, as there could be no other reason for the break-in. Sam had no open cases, and he and Detective Stiel were just catching up, having drinks together away from the hotel, when they had returned and then come running after I had texted Sam. There were no holes, and until they found out the identity of the man, there was nothing to go on.

Duncan left, agreeing to return in the morning for breakfast so Sam could talk to him. I thanked him profusely, shook his hand—and I saw it, the wistful look in his eyes as they ran over me and then the things in the room: shoes, stuffed animals, and action figures. It was very easy to see that the man needed a mate and a family. Sam's life looked really good to him.

When the door closed and Sam and I were alone, I opened my mouth to give him a piece of my mind. He kissed me before I could get a word out.

It was rough, the mauling he gave me, opening my mouth, his tongue tasting and tangling. He pressed me to him, devouring me until I had to tear free before my head exploded from lack of oxygen.

"Sam," I gasped.

He knotted his hand in my hair and shoved my head back so he could bend to my throat, suck the skin into his hot mouth, and nibble down to my collarbone. The hickeys would be dark against my gold skin in the morning. Just the thought of him marking me brought a guttural moan from deep in my chest.

As I stood there, shivering and panting, he lifted me with strong arms corded with muscle, arms that I loved to be in, and walked backward, carrying me, suckling my neck as I tilted my head sideways so he could reach as much of me as he wanted.

"Sorry, I'm sorry," he chanted as he licked up behind my ear, his big hands digging into my ass as he shoved me roughly up against the wall, pinning me there, recapturing my lips, and kissing me again, hard and deep.

He smelled dangerous, the mixture from the bar still clinging to him, smoke and acrid perfume, but there was sweat in there too, and the taste of scotch on his tongue. I tried to wiggle closer, undulating in his grip, rubbing my now leaking cock against the rock-hard abs.

My legs tightened around his narrow hips as he levered off the wall, turned, and manhandled me down onto the couch.

"Don't fuckin' move."

I did as I was told, and he was back in minutes from our bedroom with the extra sheets from the closet. He also had the bottle of lube from where I had stashed it in the armoire.

He spread a sheet on the couch and then put another one over him, draping himself—as he was now gloriously naked—from head to toe.

"What are—"

"The kids could wake up and come out."

The man was always thinking.

"And what are you planning?"

He grabbed me—which answered my question—and dragged me to the floor, flipped me over on my stomach, and told me to get on my knees.

I hurried, shucking out of my belt and dress pants and briefs as fast as I could.

The swipe of lube over my crease made me catch my breath, and the feel of his hairy thighs pressing against the backs of mine brought on the whimpering. "Oh, Sam."

"Forgive me, I was an idiot. Of course you would worry, I was just mad."

We could talk about it later. "Yes."

The first slick finger breached me, and I put my head back and moaned. He was pushing in and out, curling forward before pulling out only to add the second finger as he licked up my spine. I was panting, mouth open, pushing back as hard as he was pushing in. He rubbed and scissored, working my muscles, opening them, relaxing me like he wanted.

"I want to suck your cock," he told me, his voice scratchy and low.

"No," I barely got out. "You fuck me. Hard."

His moan was strangled and needy, and the sound, all dark and growly, sent a flush of fresh arousal over my skin.

"Sam… please."

His hot, wet mouth made me shiver as he kissed up the side of my throat. The bite on my shoulder made me jerk under him, and when I felt the flared head of his cock against my entrance, the pleading began.

Slowly, pushing insistently forward, inch by inch, he pressed inside me. My muscles were still resistant even though I was slick with lube, and I could feel every bit of the stretch as he filled my clenching channel.

"Oh fuck." His voice cracked as he slid home, buried to his balls, his hands gripping my hips too tight not to leave fingernail marks and bruises.

I shivered under him; the feel of him fully seated inside me was almost more than I could bear.

"You're so hot," he whispered. "And tight, and I so wanna—"

"Yes."

"Then you grab ahold of yourself, 'cause I can't even think."

I closed my hand around my own shaft as he pulled out and then thrust back inside me.

The cry I let out was too loud.

That quickly, Sam slapped a hand over my mouth and came down on top of me with his full weight, crushing me under him to the carpeted floor, now covered by a thin sheet.

My dripping erection was forgotten, trapped as he lay on top of me and ground his massive cock into me, pushing deep with each swivel of his hips, the movement sensual and drugging, not the pounding thrusts he normally delivered.

I was panting against his hand, and he finally laced his fingers over the top of my head, using that leverage to plunge deeper and longer. His weight, his smell, the sound of skin slapping against skin, the heat rolling off him, the absolute, utter dominance—it was all too much for me, and I bit down on my own forearm so I wouldn't scream when my entire body seized at once and I came so hard I almost blacked out.

My muscles fisted around his cock, tightening so fast that he let out his own garbled shout as he lifted me up with him and then sat down on the couch.

I cried out as I was impaled on his long, thick shaft. My back to his chest, I let my head hit his shoulder and lean against his as he grabbed my ass and pounded up into me.

There was still come dripping down my dick as I felt my ass flooded with liquid heat and Sam suddenly froze under me, his entire body tensing as he pulsed within me. As usual, the man's orgasm had rendered him incapable of any thought or movement. I was exactly the same.

All I could do was let the aftershocks vibrate through me. Sam put one of his big hands on my throat, making sure I didn't try to rise. The other slid through the thick semen on my stomach, spreading it and rubbing it into my skin.

We sat there quietly, the sheet covering me from the waist down and Sam still seated within me.

"I take back every word I said. No one takes care of me like you do, and you know that."

"Yes," I sighed. "I do know that."

"You scared me because if I hadn't gotten back at that exact moment, you would have gone to that dive bar with Duncan, and there's no way he would have been able to protect you."

"He's a big guy, Sam."

"He's not as invested in you as I am."

No, he wasn't. "So what the hell is going on?"

"Well, someone doesn't want me digging into this witness situation, that's for certain."

"When will you know who that guy was?"

"In the morning. After I put you to bed, I'm gonna wake up my guys at home."

"I want you to come to bed with—"

"No," he said, lifting me easily, sliding me off the end of his softening cock with a warm gush of fluid.

"Sam—"

"It'll fall on the sheet, J."

For a minute I was lost. "What?"

"You're worried about my getting jizz all over the—"

"I don't give a crap about that," I said quickly. "I just want you in bed with me."

"Uh-uh, you go take a quick shower and get in bed. I'll be in to tuck you in."

"Sam—"

"Jory, there's a police outline in the room that our kids were in. You and Kola and Hannah are going home tomorrow."

"Sam—"

"I mean, you called Dane, right?"

I groaned.

He cackled. "You'll be lucky if he spares you the yelling."

Crap. "Why did I do that?"

"Because after me, it's Dane, and you couldn't get me."

"But I can't ever unring the bell, you know?"

He was laughing. "Yeah, I know."

SEVEN

I WAS sitting in the lobby the next morning with Kola and Hannah, both of them entertained for the moment and quiet. She was coloring and he was playing something on his DS.

"Jory?"

I looked up and found Milton standing over me.

"Hey," I greeted him. "Sorry about last night. It just got weird."

"You and Sam, that's kind of volatile, huh?"

Not how he thought. We were only explosive in bed. I shrugged.

He gestured at Kola and Hannah. "Why are you guys all packed up? Are you leaving?"

"Yeah," I told him. "We're going home a day early. Sam needs it that way."

"So he says jump and you say how high?"

"Not quite," I chuckled, because what would Sam actually pay to make that the case?

"Then why are you going?"

"Because we're not safe and Sam needs us to be so he can concentrate on what he needs to."

"Ohmygod, Jory, what—"

"Jory?"

Regina and Thomas were cutting across the lobby toward me, and when they got there, with the others in tow, the whole Kage clan that was mine, I tried to force a smile for Regina.

"Honey, where are you going?"

"Home," I explained, soothing her at the same time. "But just a day early. We'll be there when you guys get in."

"But why?"

"I'll let Sam tell you."

"Tell me what?" she asked.

I looked over at her son, saw him standing where he had been for the last twenty minutes, with Duncan, two Scottsdale detectives, three of the guys from his field office in Chicago, and two marshals who had flown in from Langley. One of them was Sam's boss, Clint Farmer, and he was standing shoulder to shoulder with Sam. The other guy I didn't know, but he was listening intently even as he was on his cell at the same time. It didn't look good to me—it looked like extended time away from home.

"Jory?"

"Sorry." I forced a smile. "We just need to go home, Regina. Apparently we'll be under police protection, with one officer in the house at all times and a patrol car outside until the man that Sam is looking for is found."

"Oh my goodness." She was scared. "Sweetheart, we should all go then. You should move in with us until this whole thing goes away."

"No, I—"

"And we can help you with the kids."

"I don't need help," I explained. "And home is better for them so they don't have their routine upset."

"Jory," Michael began, "don't you think that it would be better if you—"

"Oh… my," Milton breathed out, clearly and utterly floored by whatever he was seeing.

"Uncle Dane!"

I looked up—we all did—and there, crossing the lobby of the hotel, was Dane Harcourt. People stopped and stared. It was a known reaction.

The first thing you noticed about my brother was his towering height. He was six five, so you couldn't miss him. Next it was the stare, normally a slight squint, just enough to pinch his brows together and to convey his irritation with the world at large. The length of his stride and the way he moved commanded interest. There was an energy you could feel, and looking at him was a pleasure. I was not alone in my assessment that Dane could still, even in his late forties, begin a lucrative modeling career. Yes, he was a wealthy architect, but he could grace fashion magazines all over the world. The glossy black hair and charcoal-gray eyes with flecks of silver in them, chiseled features, and swimmer's build made the man a standout in any room he was ever in. As he walked across the lobby of the hotel, all eyes were on him.

I had thought, as Dane aged, that his appeal would wane. But even now, with the white at his temples and the laugh lines in the corners of his eyes much heavier, he was stunning. Women flirted harder, men were drawn faster, and Dane, being Dane, just scowled. He was private; he had a small circle of friends and his family, which included me and Sam and our kids, who were precious to him, and that was all. Dane didn't invite new friendships. When he was younger, he'd been more patient, more able to forgive things, but now, with his focus on his wife and children, he'd didn't have the time or energy to devote to newness. You could be an acquaintance of his, but really, he was done making lifelong friends.

"Jory, who's that?" Milton was breathless.

"My brother," I said as Hannah wiggled down off the chair and ran, arms flailing like she was running from a fire, to greet her uncle.

He went down on one knee, and everyone saw it then: the smile, so rare, so unguarded, that it took your breath away.

Hannah hit him hard. She is not a gentle flower, my girl, more like a projectile missile, and she wrapped her little arms around his neck. He hugged her tight, rubbed her back, and then, when she wanted and only then, did he let her go so they could talk. Kola was right behind her, but he leaned into Dane's arm, and they hugged gentler.

When Dane stood, he had a kid in each arm and, seeing me, began walking over.

"Is he gay too?"

"No," I told the very hopeful man lusting after my brother. "He has a wife and two kids."

"That doesn't mean—"

"It does for Dane," I assured him. "The man is madly in love with all of them."

"Got it," Milton said as Dane stepped into my personal space.

"Tell me now," my brother demanded instead of greeting me.

We always talked as though our conversations were on a continual loop. "I thought Sam was missing but he's not," I said, pointing to where he was standing. "But he wants us to go home where we're safe. There was a man in our room last night."

His grunt was very soft.

"So we'll go home with you."

"Of course you will."

Like there would have been a choice. "You know I'm thirty-five, right?"

"Mmm-hmm."

I rolled my eyes.

"Where are your things?"

I tipped my head at the pile of bags in pink, lime green, and black. There were blankets and toys and a little pink ribbon-yarn poncho.

"Call Sam over. We're leaving."

"Kola, go get Daddy," I directed my son.

He ran over, stood beside Sam, put his hand in his, and waited until Sam acknowledged him. When Sam looked up and saw Dane, he excused himself and walked back toward us, hand in hand with his son.

Regina was upset and so was Thomas. Sam's sisters and Michael were all, I could tell, a little annoyed with me. They were talking over each other to assure me that the kids and I could stay. But the thing was, as soon as I thought Sam was in trouble, I had called Dane to come pick up my children so I'd know they would be safe while I looked for him. It was ingrained in me to go to my brother. After Sam, it was Dane. And everyone wanted to know why I didn't have any faith in them. Why did I need Dane when Sam's whole family was there? Didn't I trust them?

It was hard to explain. It wasn't that I didn't trust them, and it wasn't that I didn't think they cared as much about my kids as any of the others, but these were *my* kids, and my brother and his wife were who they were going to if anything ever happened to me and Sam. And now because Sam couldn't be there, he wanted Dane to take us home and help watch over us. It was how we were: we both believed in my brother.

Into the many raised voices stepped Sam, who only got loud because he had never been one to have a discussion when someone questioned a decision he had made. He wanted me and the kids to go home with Dane. His parents, his sisters and his brother were questioning if that was best. Sam's temper could easily have gotten the better of him, since he was on edge to begin with. He didn't want to deal with questions; he had to find a witness, and that witness was either trying to kill Sam himself or the man who had hidden the witness was trying to kill Sam to keep him from said witness. Either way, it was out in the open now, and there were several agencies ready to work together to figure out what the hell was going on. Sam wanted to be doing that, wanted to be concentrating on that. He needed me and the kids gone so he could focus all his energy there and be in hunter and not protector mode. His family was only pissing him off.

I saw his jaw clench and would have said something, but at that point Dane quietly lifted his hands to get everyone's attention. I usually had to jump up and down or stand on my head to get the silence that was his in only moments.

It was one of Dane's many strengths: the ability to spread calm, to be a rock in any kind of crisis. He explained gently, calmly, employing the voice he used in contract disputes with builders, how Sam was concerned for everyone's safety. He told them that Sam was worried about putting any more of his family in danger, and that this way everyone else could stay and finish up the reunion and maybe have some semblance of normalcy. They all looked at Sam, who was glowering at that point.

"Get them out of here, Dane."

And Dane passed Hannah to her father so the good-byes could commence.

Hannah cried because she wasn't at home. In her own house, Hannah said good-bye to her daddy every morning. The idea of getting on a plane without him was not appealing, and she clung and howled, which I could tell just from looking at him tore Sam up.

I took her, and she sobbed into my shoulder, her being overly tired not helping one little bit.

Sam went down on one knee, and Kola stepped close and fiddled with Sam's collar and the buttons on his dress shirt. "Do you have your gun, Dad?"

"Dad" was newly shortened from "Daddy."

"Yes, I do."

"So you'll be safe, huh?"

"Yes, I will. You need to take care of Hannah and Pa and Chilly for me, okay?"

He nodded, and Sam pulled him close and hugged him tight. Kola looked miserable, but he turned and pressed his face into my stomach and leaned.

Sam stood up, took my chin in his hand, and stared down into my eyes. "I'll be home shortly."

"Okay," was all I said.

He looked at Dane, who nodded.

Sam walked away and didn't turn back around.

Dane reached down and swept Kola up into his arms, and I saw a man grabbing all our things from the chairs where we had left them.

"Is that your driver, Uncle Dane?" Kola asked him.

"He is today, love."

Milton stopped me. "Jory, it was great to meet you. This is my card with my e-mail address."

"Thanks," I said softly, wrung out all of a sudden.

"You know"—he smiled at Dane—"you and your brother look nothing alike."

"Oh no?" Dane glowered at him. "Everyone thinks but for the hair color that we could be twins."

"Don't be an ass," I said under my breath.

"Come now," Dane said sharply.

Kola put his head down on his uncle's shoulder, and I followed my brother out of the hotel. I didn't look over at Sam.

KOLA and Hannah thought that first class was the coolest thing ever. They had their own video monitors, the flight attendants brought warm cookies and milk, and they got to pick what they wanted for lunch. They sat in front of Dane and me, and we talked about everything on the way home. I explained about the witness and what had happened and how there had been a man in our room. Dane listened and nodded, taking it all in.

I really wasn't surprised when we weren't driven home.

The loft in River North was one of Dane's many investments. He had places in the Gold Coast area as well, which was considered very trendy and up and coming. Dane bought real estate, fixed it up, sometimes did the interior design himself and sometimes hired someone. This one had been done by someone else, as exposed brick, exposed pipes in the ceiling, and all-wood floors were not Dane's aesthetic. If you were going for an urban feel, a concrete floor was more him, or wrought iron or tile. It was nice, though: two huge bedrooms, two bathrooms, one guest washroom with just a toilet and a sink, an office, a kitchen, a great room, and a sort of reading nook area. The patio was small but secure with no access other than through the loft. It was smaller than our house but still, for me and the kids, enormous. Chilly was already asleep on the rug in front of the fireplace when we got there.

I groaned and let my head roll sideways to look up at Dane.

"The kids have to share a room, but for the short time that you'll be here, that should be fine. Their room is at the back end; you and Sam have the first one closest to the front door. I had most of your clothes brought over, but honestly, who needs that many shoes?"

"This isn't—"

"There's a doorman out front and two security guards that check people in and out. You need to give them a list of who gets access to the apartment. I gave them Sam's name already. There are four apartments per floor. On this one, the eighteenth, you have Mrs. Garcia and her son Ramon in 1801, the Patels in 1803, and Gabe Fukushima and his partner, James Garrett, in 1804. The walls are thick; you shouldn't hear anyone, the garbage chute is out the door to your left, and your minivan is on the basement level in stall B44. Any other questions?"

"We'd be fine at home."

"Next Friday you plan to have my kids with you, right?"

"Yes."

He squinted at me. "I don't feel comfortable with you alone in your house without Sam. The idea of you putting not only your kids but mine in danger as well… Jory, use your head. You lock that front door, you set the alarm, which is zero-zero-seven plus the number one when you disarm it and zero-zero-seven plus two when you arm it—then I know you'll be safe and sound in here."

"Double O seven? Really?"

He just looked at me.

"Dane—"

"No." He shook his head. "Not on my watch. Never. If Sam was there with you, if you weren't in mortal danger… fine. But someone tried to shoot you and your kids in a hotel. Absolutely not."

I squinted at him. "Is this why you and Aja moved into that building downtown? Were you worried about your safety in Oak Park?"

"Oh no, Oak Park is gorgeous and safe. It was just even that small commute to her work and my office and the kids' school got to be tedious. This way I can drop them off, Aja can pick them up, and we can both actually make it home to eat dinner together as a family and not have to sit in traffic for an hour, hour and a half."

"Did you sell it yet? The Oak Park house?"

"No." He squinted at me. "Sam asked me not to."

I was surprised. "Sam asked?"

He grunted. "Yes, he apparently really loves it and the backyard and the front yard and the neighborhood and the whole area. He's thinking about putting in an offer on it."

"But?"

"But he doesn't trust me."

"What does that mean?"

"That means that he thinks I'll tamper with the appraisal to sell it to him for cheaper than it is."

"And you would." I smiled at him.

"I would give it to you if he weren't so exasperatingly stubborn."

"Maybe Aja wouldn't want you to do that. Her brother and his wife are expecting a child, maybe he'd like you to give it to—"

"Alex moved to Delaware."

"Yes, I know, but—"

"He married a woman from Delaware."

I growled at him.

"He lives in Delaware now," he said pointedly, like I was stupid.

"You know what I mean. If Alex had a house here, or Carmen, maybe they—"

"Carmen is a journalist, technically now a foreign correspondent with *ABC News*. She lives in New York and Paris and—"

"Yeah, I know, but—"

"Aja's parents have no interest in returning to Chicago even to visit. It's—I'm quoting her father now—stupid cold. He's done bundling up. He wants to golf and wear Crocs."

"You're making that last part up. The man was a judge, for crissakes."

"I have a picture on my phone if you'd like to see. Aja was mortified and sent it to me on her last visit when I was stuck here for that convention."

"Oh God."

"The fact is that you and Sam are who Aja and I have. Aja would love to see you both in our old house and would love to have it be yours. She doesn't want to sell her baby to strangers, but neither does she want to continue holding on to a property that we have to pay to keep up."

"And so?"

"So I'm tampering with the inspection report as we speak."

"Dane, you can't do that. He'll find out."

"It will take at least six months for him to find out, and by then we'll have closed on it and he'll be wrapped up in a mortgage he can't get out of."

"So you're trying to trap Sam into buying the house."

"Precisely."

"I could just talk to him."

"And ruin the surprise and take away his happiness? Would you do that?"

"I really don't like you right now."

"I'm well aware."

I sighed deeply. "So, me and the kids are stuck here until Sam gets back."

"Yes."

"Did you bring my laptop?"

"Yes."

"Kola's karate gi?"

"Yes."

I had to think. "Hannah's Barbie Dreamhouse?"

"Yes." He smiled at me.

"Chilly's dishes and his litter box and his toys and his cat tower and—"

"Yes. May I ask why he had stainless steel bowls instead of the kind that feed and water him automatically?"

"Because automatic doesn't teach kids any responsibility."

"Is that right?"

"Yes, that's right."

"And setting the feeder, filling it, this teaches nothing?"

"You know what I mean."

He grunted and gave me a pat on the arm before he headed for the door.

"You always take care of me. Thank you."

"That is what family is for."

I nodded as he reached the front door.

"Come let me out. Remember: when you're home, when you leave, make sure the alarm is engaged."

"Yes."

"At night before you go to bed—"

"I got it," I said as I reached him.

"When you're home, you press the occupied button and the alarm will shut off for movement and only alert you if a door or window is opened."

"Okay."

"When you leave, when you go to bed, you arm it for movement."

"Yes, General."

"Funny."

"I try."

"Tomorrow is Sunday."

"Announcing the obvious." I snickered. "You haven't done that in years."

"Very droll."

I shrugged.

"On Monday Aja expects you for dinner and drinks at our place at seven."

"Why?"

"She's having a dinner party for her friend, Randall Erickson, who just moved back into town."

I studied his face. "Who is he? Old boyfriend?"

Dane scoffed. "No, actually, he's a friend from college, and I got the feeling he was gay, though I didn't pry."

"You wouldn't even let Aja's exes in your house, would you?"

"Aja does as she pleases, it's *our* house, and she invites who she wants."

"And you wouldn't care?"

"No, I wouldn't."

It made sense that he wouldn't. Dane did not suffer the normal feelings of inadequacy or have the bouts of uncertainty that most people did. He knew exactly who he was, knew his pros outweighed his cons, and had been told, on more than one occasion by more than one woman, that if he should ever find himself single again to please, please call. But I knew Aja, and she and Dane were in it for the long haul.

I always enjoyed watching them in any social situation. They would check on each other across rooms; Dane would smile and give her a head tip; she would blow him a kiss or crook her finger at him. When they stood together, normally she held his hand, and if not, his arm was around her. They sat together always unless there were place cards, and even then, they would be up and down because one of them had thought of something to tell the other. People stopped seating them apart because it was simply too distracting. They finished one another's sentences; she laughed at his jokes, which were horrible; and he was always on time because, as he said, her time was precious to him, so why would he make her wait?

"Jory."

"Sorry. What?"

"I took the liberty of having Pedro speak to Dylan about babysitting your kids for you when he picked up your cat, and she agreed."

Pedro Blue was Dane's assistant—had been for going on four years at this point. I was proud of myself because I was the one who had chosen him and he was still there and had become invaluable to my brother. Pedro had recently gotten married in New York, and the honeymoon to Paris that Dane had sent them on had probably cemented his and Dane's relationship for life. Pedro had gushed over the phone to me the last time we had talked.

"And how was their honeymoon?"

"I didn't ask." He squinted at me.

"You didn't have to ask him how many times a day he got laid, but you could have inquired if he liked the Louvre."

He grunted.

"I'll be at the party. Go away so I can get my kids settled."

"Okay." He smiled at me. "Drinks are at seven, yes?"

"Yes."

I got a shoulder squeeze and that was it. Dane didn't do demonstrations of affection other than with his wife, his kids, my kids, or Aja's mother, who hugged and kissed him a lot. By all accounts, Dane's parents had been very kind, warm people, but they were not the sort that he saw every night or even every week. His father was a real estate developer, his mother a socialite, and though they cared for him deeply, they were not hands-on. When his parents were there, the three of them laughed and got along wonderfully, but Dane could turn that devotion off and on like a faucet. Because his parents had wanted him to learn that relationships between employer and employee were transient and not to be counted on, his early life had been filled with rotating staff. No one was allowed to become permanent. Butlers, maids, gardeners, chauffeurs, and a never-ending stream of nannies had filled his formative years. I was certain that the way he used to change out women was a direct reflection of the nurturing, care-giving women in his life having been swapped out so frequently. Dane did not maintain long-term relationships with anyone but people he chose himself: his friends and then, finally, me.

I had been Dane's assistant for five years before being fired and then told that he was basically adopting me as the little brother he'd never had. I changed my last name—Keyes—to Harcourt, and then there were two of us. Dane had been adopted as an infant; he then turned around and adopted me. It had always made great sense to me and, I knew, to him. And no one ever questioned that we didn't look alike, that he was tall and godlike and I was short and not. I suspected that when Dane looked at people who thought to ask and the gray eyes were on them, the gaze solid and unwavering, the idea of questioning the man about anything in his life became moot. Best not to challenge him. Better to simply smile and nod.

As I held the door open for him and he reminded me, again, about the alarm, I was going to give him some smartass remark about the size of my brain being bigger then a poodle's so that I could, actually, retain information when he reached out and put a hand on my cheek.

"What?"

"Nothing," he said softly before he turned and walked away.

"You could just say you love me and you worry about me!" I called after him, chuckling.

He didn't even glance over his shoulder, and that was endearing for reasons that most people wouldn't get. But I understood him so well. Dane demonstrated how he felt about you; he was not big on declarations of devotion. Anyone could say they loved you, Dane showed it, and I had always been an action over words kind of guy—except where Sam was concerned. From him I needed both.

I called Kola and Hannah out of the bedroom, and they were excited about the Wii in their room and the PlayStation and the ginormous television set.

"Ginormous?" I repeated.

Kola nodded.

"When's Daddy coming?" Hannah wanted to know, because she was so Sam's girl, his champion, his cheerleader, and his biggest fan.

"Probably not until next week, B."

She began the blinking that normally happened before she started to cry, so I grabbed her and pulled her onto my lap for a cuddle.

"Pa, I wanna play hide-and-seek."

"Okay, and after should we order pizza and watch a movie?"

"Pizza!" Kola chanted.

"I wanna watch *The Wizard of Oz*!"

"Not again." He changed instantly to whining. "You just wanna see the melting part anyway."

Hannah looked thoughtful. "I should take my water gun in my backpack to shoot at Ms. Brady and check if she's a witch."

Kola's face lit up. "That's a really good idea," he said as though he was surprised his sister had come up with it. "You could just shoot anyone who was mean to you."

Her eyes got huge.

"No," I told her, then looked at him. "And no. We don't go around hosing people down with water guns. It's rude."

"But what if a person is a witch?" Kola wanted to know.

"How do you know they're a witch?"

"You won't unless you shoot 'em with water." He was appealing to my logic.

"Which is rude," I repeated. I got a D in Logic in college.

Kola threw up his hands in defeat.

"And besides, there are good witches and bad witches, just like in the movie. What if you melt a good one?"

He considered that. "I don't think good witches melt from water."

"I don't think so either," Hannah agreed with him.

"Well, we'll have to look it up."

That seemed to appease them for a moment and I had a thought. "Do you even have your water gun here?"

Hannah nodded. "Yeah, Uncle Dane brought it for me."

For what reason? Why in the world would my brother have taken the time to pack her Super Soaker? The man was so odd sometimes.

"What did you say about the zombies?" Hannah said to her brother as she cuddled with me. They had obviously been engaged in some sort of discussion while I was talking with Dane.

"When?"

"I asked you if they could push buttons."

He shook his head. "Oh, yeah and no, they can't, only on accident."

She nodded. "What about climbing ladders?"

"No, they have stiff legs. You hafta bend your knees."

She nodded, clearly accepting his expert testimony on this subject.

"Pa?"

"Yes, my son," I said seriously.

"If dinosaurs turned into birds and apes turned into humans, what did fish turn into?"

I really needed Sam home; he could do this for hours, speculation and hypothesis. I was no good at it. "I dunno, what do you think?"

Kola looked at his sister to make sure her voice was heard and included. He never answered one of his own questions without her getting to chime in.

"Big fish?" Hannah offered.

He shook his head, pensive. "Sharks?"

"You said there were sharks already," she reminded him.

"Yeah, so." He looked at me. "Pa?"

"Fish came on land and turned into dinosaurs," I told him. "I think. Or something like that. You should have asked Milton while we were in Arizona."

"Oh yeah, huh."

"You could e-mail him."

He nodded. "I think you're right though, 'cause in my book the sailback one was a fish and then a lizard then a dinosaur."

"There, you see?" I felt validated because my six-year-old agreed with me.

"Okay, so then fish don't count."

"Meaning?"

"They just stayed fish," he concluded.

"That's right," Hannah nodded, putting that part of the discussion to bed.

"Then what about bugs?"

"Like what did bugs turn into?"

"Yeah."

"Robots?" I offered after a second. "Transformers?"

He started giggling. "I don't think you get evolution, Pa."

No, probably not, but he hugged me so tight and kissed my cheek, so really, I didn't care.

EIGHT

SAM'S family came home on Sunday, and since I knew they would all be exhausted from the trip, I invited them all over to the loft for a quick dinner before they went home. Regina was so thankful, and said the antipasto salad I made, along with lasagna and garlic bread was a blessing.

When Chaz and Pat showed up with wine, I fed them too, and they got to add to what I was telling my mother-in-law, my father-in-law, and Sam's siblings. Everyone loved the hideout, as they called it, and over dinner and after, we all talked about Sam's case and the missing witness and the handsome man—Rachel's words—who had left with Sam.

"He's not handsome," Pat assured her. "He's a—"

"Kids," I cut him off.

"Jerk," Pat finished, passing judgment on Detective Stiel.

"He is handsome, though." I smiled knowingly, thinking of the detective's impressive build, sharply cut features, and gunmetal-gray eyes. The man was gorgeous, actually, and I would have been impressed if an even more beautiful man didn't sleep in my bed.

When Sam had called the evening before to say good night to the kids, it had been quick. But he had called back right before I went to bed to rumble in my ear that he missed me and he loved me and to please keep his side of the bed warm.

"Dane moved us."

"I know, he told me. I liked his idea better, and the Chicago PD really appreciated not parking a patrol car in front of our house indefinitely."

"I bet."

"Hey, tomorrow Chaz and Pat are gonna come check up on you, okay?"

"Yes, dear."

Heavy sigh. "I really do."

"What?" I fished.

"Love you."

"I know, Sam."

"'Kay, good. It's good you know."

My whine was soft, but he still heard it.

"I'll be home soon, baby."

I could only nod.

The second night, that Sunday after the talk, after everyone went home, after I set the alarm and did the dishes and put the kids to bed, I waited for another phone call. But all I got was a text message to say that he loved me and that he was going out of cell range and wasn't sure when he would be in touch. I figured I had to prepare myself for the silence.

THE following morning I got to work fast. It was easy to just zip down to my office from where the hideout was. Dane was right; there was something to be said for a quick commute. I greeted Dylan with her six-shot vanilla latte, gave Fallon his scone, and was about to sit down at my desk when I got a call from Hannah and Kola's school. True to her word, Hannah had packed a water gun—the same Super Soaker her uncle had made sure to bring from our house—and tested her theory on witches and melting. Kola was in trouble as well. He had apparently taken exception to being told that his set painting for the school Thanksgiving opera was not good. We were working on him accepting constructive criticism, but at present he didn't like to lose—his tantrums gave new meaning to the words "poor sport"—or be told something he was doing wasn't right. Questioning him to try to bring him to the right conclusion was also on his list of pet peeves. The thing was, he was a sweet kid, loving and considerate, but he was turning into a real brat. But only sometimes. Playing anything with him was getting harder. I, of course, gave him chance after chance, and Sam just stopped whatever they were doing as soon as he showed even a hint of a tantrum. We had to come to some agreement until he either grew out of it or we changed the behavior. Sam had suggested we beat him, and I had just shaken my head. I knew he was kidding, but I really did want to wring Kola's little neck sometimes when he was crying and stomping his foot.

At the school, Hannah was sorry about the water gun; Miss Chun, her teacher, was biting her bottom lip every five seconds so she wouldn't laugh; the principal, Mrs. Petrovich, had her closed fist pressed over her mouth so she wouldn't laugh. The only one who was annoyed at all was, of course, Ms. Brady, their music teacher. So not amused with being soaked with a water cannon.

"I am so sorry, Ms. Brady. It will never happen again."

Miss Chun nodded and squinted before turning around fast to hide her face.

Mrs. Petrovich let out one snicker, looking very pained, and then gestured for Ms. Brady to go ahead out. Hannah was sent to sit in the hall, and as soon as the door closed behind her, both women dissolved into fits of rolling laughter.

"You guys aren't helping," I scolded them.

"It's not even the first time it happened," the principal told me as tears ran from her eyes. "I had a kid two years ago wearing a lei made of garlic because he thought she was a vampire!"

Miss Chun was wheezing.

"Three years ago, three kids kept spilling water on her to see if she'd sizzle."

I squinted at them. "Maybe it's time to look at what she's doing around here, education wise."

"Oh no, she's a very good teacher, it's just that—"

"She's a witch!" Miss Chun announced, falling down onto the couch, just done.

I threw up my hands and went to go find Kola.

His teacher, Mr. Michaels, who was just as cute as he could be, was sitting with Kola in the front row of the auditorium, watching the other kids paint and hammer and hang lights. There were a lot of parents there, and I got many waves as I came down the aisle.

Kola saw me, got up, and ran to meet me. He threw his arms around my waist and buried his face in my stomach.

"What happened?" I asked him.

"I didn't do it this time, Pa. Ollie did."

"Tell me," I said, leaning him back as I went down on one knee so I could see his eyes. His face was streaked with tears and his eyes were red.

"Ollie wanted to use the hammer, but it was my turn, but he went and told his dad that it was his turn, and Mr. Parker didn't even ask Mr. Michaels, he just came and took the hammer away from me."

"Okay. What happened then?"

"Then I got upset and said it wasn't fair, and Mr. Michaels brought me down here even though I told him that Mr. Parker bent my finger when he took the hammer away."

"What finger, buddy?"

The ring finger of his left hand, his writing hand, was huge. It was red and swollen and at least three times its normal size.

My eyes flicked to Mr. Michaels.

"Mr. Harcourt?"

"Did it escape you that his finger might be broken?"

He was up out of his chair and over to us in seconds. "He didn't show it to me and—" He turned his head and yelled up to the stage. "Mr. Parker, could you come down here, please!"

A big man I didn't know—obviously a new parent who had just enrolled his child, as I had never seen Oliver before—came down off the stage and lumbered over to us.

"Chet?" He addressed Mr. Michaels by his first name—not the way we were asked to address the teachers at school.

"Did you peel Kola's fingers off the hammer when you took it from him?"

He shrugged. "Sure, he didn't want to let it go and it wasn't his turn."

"As I told you, it actually was his turn, but that's not the issue. Did you hurt him when you took it from him?"

"Nah." He shook his head, reaching out to tousle Kola's hair.

I knocked the hand away. "Don't touch him."

"Okay, sorry." He put up both his hands. "But I didn't hurt him."

I gestured at his hand. "I think you broke his finger."

"I did not. I didn't apply that much pressure."

The man was big, though. He was not as powerfully built as Sam—there were no cording muscles—but he was certainly strong enough to hurt a little boy.

I looked back at Mr. Michaels. "You'll both be hearing from my lawyer because you"—I pointed at Mr. Parker—"should never be touching any other kids but your own, and you"—my gaze fell on Mr. Michaels—"should have been there to protect him."

I turned, pulled my phone at the same time, and called Aja. She had been the principal of a public high school; she would know what to do.

"Hi, honey, you're not calling to cancel on my—"

"If a man just broke Kola's finger at school, what can I do?"

"I'm sorry, what?"

I repeated what had happened, and she gave me a barrage of quick questions.

"I'm on my way to the hospital now."

"Which one? Saint Joe?"

"Yeah."

"Okay, I'll call Rick. Either he or someone else will be right there."

"Thanks."

"Baby, do you need me there? Dane?"

"No, I'm fine." I took a breath, because who I needed was Sam.

"All right."

I hung up, held the door of the auditorium open, and had Kola and Hannah walk out before me.

"So we have to go to the hospital now, okay?"

Kola nodded and leaned into me, head on my hip. "I didn't throw a fit that time, Pa, I promise."

"I believe you, buddy, and I'm glad that you know when you do it and I'm glad that you're working on it. We just have to—"

"Mr. Harcourt!"

Turning, I saw Mr. Parker charging down the hallway after me. I shoved Kola and Hannah behind me.

"You don't threaten me! It was an accident," he yelled as he reached me.

"It wasn't," I corrected him, standing my ground. "You hurt him on purpose, and there's no excuse for that. Like I said, you can talk to my lawyer."

"Listen, you little faggot," he sneered, driving his fingers into my collarbone. "You're not gonna make any trouble for me. That pissant kid of yours—"

"Mr. Parker!" Mr. Michaels yelled—terrified, I could tell—as he came hurrying down the hall to us.

"No! This is bullshit! I—"

"Step back," I told him, my voice cold and hard. "I'm feeling threatened, Mr. Parker, and I don't like it. I don't want you within a hundred feet of either of my kids. So step… back."

His eyes locked on mine.

He glared, but really, compared to others I'd known, the man was not scary at all. A few days ago a man had pointed a gun at me; a man without one was not about to inspire any terror.

After a minute, he took a step back. I whirled around, grabbed Kola's right hand and Hannah's left, and walked toward the front of the school. Mrs. Petrovich tried to stop me to talk, but I was too upset and walked straight to my minivan and put them in. As I was driving out of the parking lot, I glanced in the rearview mirror and saw all three of them—the teacher, the principal, and the parent—on the front steps.

At the hospital, I went to the emergency room, and within minutes, we were in a room. An adult could wait for hours, but not little kids. Hannah sat on the bed beside her brother playing *LocoRoco2* on her PSP. She loved it—she sang along to songs that I didn't think were actually in any real language, and it was mindless. Her brother watched her, doing his damnedest not to get sucked into what he called a baby game but was really not.

I was not pleased that Dr. Varma thought his finger was broken, not just sprained.

"But we'll take an X-ray to be certain." He smiled at Kola, holding his good hand in his. "So you'll be here just a little bit, buddy, okay?"

Kola nodded.

"Okay." He looked up at me. "How did this happen?"

Once I told him, he said that the police would have to be notified.

"I'll call them," I told him.

He nodded and said that he would give a statement. While we waited for Kola to go down for an X-ray, I called Pat.

Hannah and I went with Kola when they came to take him, because my kids didn't go places without me. I didn't take my eyes off them. I had been called a nervous mother many a time, but it didn't matter. It was why they didn't spend the night over at the houses of people I didn't know, or walk to the park without me, or talk to strangers. And it was funny how many times Kola or Hannah came up to me after school with some kid I'd never met in my life, and said that so-and-so's mother said it was fine if he or she came over to our house.

The parents had never even met me, and we had never spoken, but they were sure, since our kids went to the same school together, that it was safe to send them home with me. It was mind-boggling. I had to know people before I trusted them with my kids.

One time Kola called me from his friend Owen's house because Owen's mother, Georgette, had left and Owen's uncle was there watching them. The uncle, Georgette's little brother, was seventeen. He had taken Owen and Kola to the store, where they had gone to pick up cigarettes and beer and some beef jerky. Owen lived downtown, which meant my little boy, without close adult supervision, had walked through not the greatest neighborhood to wherever the drug store was. I thought I was going to pass out.

I had called Sam, completely unglued, because his office was closer and in traffic it would have taken me more than an hour to reach our son. He had left work and gone right over and collected Kola. In the process of picking him up, Sam had apparently scared the holy crap out of the brother after confiscating both the beer and the cigarettes.

Georgette called me later that night to apologize, and I invited her for coffee after school the following day. She was surprised when I brought her back home with me, sat her down in my breakfast nook while the kids played upstairs, and made her a latte with my espresso machine.

"I love your house," she told me, and I appreciated that, even though it was messy. "It's just me and Owen at my house, and… this is nice."

Working mothers—I understood that they needed help. I offered to take Owen on holidays, like the Fourth of July or the day after Thanksgiving, when she had to work her retail job. Owen was on scholarship at the school; she didn't have the money to just send him there. She was alone; her ex-husband had walked out on her and her son and never looked back. Currently she was in the midst of suing him for child support. When Sam came home and the kids flew through the house to greet him, even Owen shuffling forward to say hi, I watched her eyes fill and her bottom lip tremble. The way Owen looked up at Sam Kage with greedy eyes as Sam tousled the little boy's hair was hard for her to see. And it wasn't me and it wasn't Sam, it was just the illustration of the family in front of her. I was still amazed sometimes that all the things I had thought I would never have were now all mine.

So because of that, because I took nothing for granted, letting my son go down to X-ray alone was not an option. He had to know that I was right there and that I would always be.

When we got back, Chaz and Pat were waiting in the room for me.

The kids were happy to see them, and I noted, as I always did, the differences in the two men: Chaz in his suit and tie, Pat in the sweater under the leather jacket, with jeans and work boots. They could not have looked like more of an odd couple. Chaz was smooth and sophisticated, and Pat was the one who would hold you off your feet against the wall while the good cop asked you questions. They had been partners forever, and neither had any desire to change it. Sam had told me that either one of them could take the captain's exam and move up, but neither of them ever would. Bureaucracy and politics you could keep; they would just do what they did best and solve crimes.

"Hey, J," Chaz greeted me. "Long time no see."

Since it had just been the night before, I got the joke.

"Hey, Steph wants you and Sammy and the kids over at our place as soon as he gets back, okay?" He tipped his head at Pat. "She said she already told E."

"I'm sure she did." Pat smiled back at Chaz because their wives, Stephanie Diaz and Ersi Cantwell, were as thick as thieves. When your husbands were as close as Chaz and Pat were, you prayed you got along. Ersi always said that, in Stephanie, she had been blessed with both a best friend and a sister. What was nice for me was that they had both taken to me as well. I was so very thankful.

"As soon as Sam gets home, we'd love to."

Chaz nodded.

"Okay, so," Pat said, moving over beside Kola, "what happened, Kage?"

Kola loved it when Pat called him "Kage." It made him feel big and strong because it reminded him that he was Sam's son, and that was always good. I was sure during the teenage years it would be a problem, but at six, it was still a source of pride.

"Mr. Parker bent my fingers way back when he took the hammer away from me, and one of them hurts real bad."

Pat's eyes flicked to mine, and they were scary.

"Oh." Chaz shook his head. "You realize you're like the luckiest guy on the planet that Sam's not actually here right now."

"I am aware," I told him.

"Can you show me how he did it?" Pat asked Kola. "I'll be you and you be Mr. Parker."

"Okay." Kola nodded.

To bring the tension down a little, I asked about Chaz's three boys and Pat's four girls. Pat's oldest was graduating from high school in June, and the idea that her college acceptance letters would be coming soon was freaking Pat out. Not that he had to worry—I knew Iris was thinking of the University of Chicago, if not for her first choice, then certainly her second.

Apparently from the grunted replies, the broods of both men were good. What was not, was how Kola had been treated by Mr. Parker.

Pat moved over beside me after Kola showed him what had been done. "I would kill anybody who touched one of my girls like that. I'll talk to the doc and if he says yeah, that the injury is consistent with Kola's story, I'm gonna have this guy picked up. You hear me?"

I nodded.

"Did he threaten you? Kola says you told him to back off."

"He was too close to the kids. If it had been just me, I wouldn't have worried."

He nodded and put a hand on my back lightly. "Kids stay home tomorrow, J, all right?"

"Okay."

Chaz and Pat walked out to go and find the doctor, and Rick Jenner, my friend Aubrey Jenner's husband, walked in, followed by two women.

"Oh." I smiled at him as he walked over to me, hand extended for me to take. "I figured you'd send somebody, I didn't think the managing partner of Riley, Jenner, Knox, and Pomeroy would be the one in my son's hospital room?"

He smiled warmly. "It's actually Jenner Knox now, Mr. Harcourt, and I'm the founding partner; Tobias Knox is the managing partner because I like to golf."

"I hadn't heard. Congratulations, Rick."

"It's because you and the marshal don't come to parties that you're invited to."

"We don't live in your tax bracket, either."

He chuckled. "I'll see you tonight, though, right?"

"I dunno. We'll see how Kola feels."

"No, **Pa**," Kola whined. "I have to go to Auntie Dyl's. She's gonna make s'mores in the oven, Mica said."

Mica, Dylan's son, because he was the oldest of our four kids, often made big plans that his mother had no prior knowledge of. "We'll see how you feel, baby."

"I'll be fine."

"Let me talk to your lawyer, okay?"

He squinted at me. "Isn't he Uncle Dane's friend?"

"Yes, he is," I told my son before turning back to Rick. "Sorry, tell me what to do."

"Well for one, I hope it's broken, because a break will heal faster than a sprain, and what we're going to do is sue that school to the ground."

I shook my head. "Oh no, I just want Mr. Parker not to be able to be near my kid, either of my kids, at all."

"You want him barred from school property?"

"Yes."

He nodded. "Okay, I can do that. But you're sure that's all."

"And he should pay for this doctor visit, don't you think?"

"Again," he sighed, "you're being very nice. If this was me, I'd sue him for everything he's got."

I made a face. "No, you wouldn't."

"Yes, I would, but that's how I am."

"What do you need me to do?"

"I'll have papers delivered by one of these nice people with me; this is Theresa Lin and Nadira Kothari."

I smiled at both women.

"Whoever shows up will go over everything with you, and we'll get the papers signed and filed. Right now, Theresa will head over to the courthouse to get a restraining order filed."

"Okay."

"Okay," he echoed me, patting my shoulder.

I was finally starting to feel a little better.

I CALLED Dylan on the way to the loft and explained that Kola's finger was broken and that I wasn't sure if I should leave him with her. The plaintive whining in the background notwithstanding, she begged me to drop them off.

"It sounded like fun, and you never go out, and it's just to your brother's house and back."

"Yeah, but what if assassins come to your house after—"

"Really? Assassins? Are you sure they're not ninjas?"

"This is serious."

"I get it, but your life always looks like this in one form or another, and I don't think anyone is coming after you or the kids. I don't think Sam would have allowed you to not go into protective custody if that was really the case. Think about it seriously for a minute and think about what you know of your man."

She was right.

"And really, on my street?" She scoffed. "Who has more busybody neighbors than me?"

"Oh yeah, you win," I muttered under my breath.

"Hello! Mrs. Applebaum and her best buddy Mrs. Flores? And Mrs. Wong? Dear God."

"So you're saying that my kids would be safe with you?"

"Auntie Dyl, come get me!" Hannah squealed.

"That's what I'm saying."

"I just feel like Kola needs—"

"I want s'mores!" my son whimpered.

"Dyl—"

"I hear the chanting of the peanut gallery behind you, by the way." She snorted out a laugh. "C'mon, baby, gimme your kids. I promise not to sell them to gypsies."

I started laughing.

"Unless I get a really good price."

"I hope Chilly didn't make you crazy."

"He made the dog insane. I was fine. I have a great picture of him hanging off the end of her nose."

I groaned. Sheila, Dylan's Saint Bernard, was nothing if not long-suffering.

"So?"

"Pretty peas, Pa."

"Please, not peas."

"Pees." She started giggling. "Kola pees!"

"Pa! Hannah said I pee!"

"Fine," I told Dylan. "Make sure the gypsies give you top dollar."

Her snort of laughter made me feel normal for the first time all day.

NINE

I WAS hiding out on the balcony with the others.

"What? What did I say?"

Aubrey Jenner had her hand over her face because wine had come out of her nose when she laughed.

Dane had his head back, and he was counting so he would not crack a smile even as he held on to the concrete railing.

Rick Jenner was standing beside his wife, arms crossed, head down, shaking just enough so you'd know that he was going to lose it at any second.

"Holy fuck." Jude Coughlin, Dane's oldest friend from back in their prep school days, swore as he walked into our circle. "We're all gonna have to stay out here in order to breathe since there's no air left in the entire goddamn apartment!"

Rick started snickering; his wife put her face down on my shoulder.

"Because he sucked it all out!" Jude went on. "Jesus!"

"What are you talking about?" I was indignant. "He has wing tips made out of seagull, for crissakes! That's the important thing."

"It's seal," Aubrey corrected me, obviously trying so hard not succumb. "Right?"

Jude threw up his hands.

"Who makes boots out of seal?" I asked her dramatically. "My God, woman, don't you know anything?"

"Stop," Dane warned slowly, because he too was just about to break down.

"I mean," I went on, "so I like talking about myself, is it my fault that I'm incredibly wealthy, educated, funny, urbane, and gorgeous? Why wouldn't you want to talk about me? What else would you desire to discuss, peasant?"

He started smiling. "Peasant?"

"I have a ring you can kiss."

Jude choked on a laugh.

"I have a house in the Hamptons, a penthouse near the Water Tower, and a Park Avenue residence. You're just jealous. Perhaps if you spent more time managing your stock portfolio and less time masturbating, you would be rich too."

That was it. Rick lost it. His head went back and he howled. Aubrey was laughing so hard she was barely able to breathe; Dane was chuckling and rubbing his eyes because they were watering, and Jude was clutching Dane's shoulder as he joined Rick in raucous laughter.

"I will beat you all dead," Aja announced as she came charging out onto the balcony.

"Not me," Dane said. "You need me."

She growled at him before turning on me.

I made big eyes for her.

"You." She glared.

"What?"

"Oh, that innocent act is crap!"

"Daddy always said 'An ounce of pretension is a worth a pound of manure.'"

"You're gonna make me pee," Aubrey barely got out. "Stop it!"

"*Steel Magnolias*?" Aja was fighting not to smile. "You're quoting movie lines now?"

"He's an ass," I told my sister-in-law, enunciating the word for her. "How were you ever friends with that guy?"

She had to think.

"He probably changed," Dane offered, rubbing his forehead. "Right, love?"

She turned and looked at him, because the endearment the man was not big on using made her bite her bottom lip.

"Yes?"

"He was more grounded." She took a breath. "I think he's trying too hard."

"Oh you think so?" Jude chuckled. "Aja, darling, may I buy you a diamond?"

His comment, his inflection, made me laugh.

She swatted his chest.

Dane intercepted her hand as she pulled it back, and drew her to his side, and she fit, as she always had, under the man's arm. She passed me her wine glass so she could put both hands on Dane as she leaned into him.

"We haven't even had dinner yet," Rick finally said, still with traces of laughter in his voice. "We'll all be held hostage through the meal."

"Oh, those poor people we left him in there with," Aubrey said sadly.

I couldn't hold in the snickering. "If Sam was here, he'd shoot him."

"Which is why Sam's not allowed to bring his firearm to dinner parties," Dane reminded me.

"And that reminds me," I said, leveling a gaze at my brother. "Why in the world did you pack Hannah's Super Soaker to take with us to the apartment?"

He squinted. "Both my boys would want their water guns, why would your daughter not want hers? That makes no sense."

"No," I made a face at him. "A water gun in November makes no sense."

"As though you and logic have ever been formally introduced," he scoffed. "Nine times out of ten your decisions are flawed."

"At least I don't have shoes made out of baby duck."

His snort of laughter got him a pinch from his wife, and I noticed then that her focus was on me. I grinned like a crazy man.

"You."

"Me?"

"You," Aja nodded.

"What?"

"You're so bad."

"Me? He's the one with seagull dress shoes."

"Jory!"

The doorbell rang.

"Maybe that's his missing date." Jude sounded hopeful. "Please, God, deliver us."

"Oh it's not that bad," Aja chided him.

We all looked at her, and Dane kissed her forehead.

Maybe Randall Erickson was a nice guy who was simply very nervous in the company of such a successful group of people. But he went to the bottom of my list when I emerged from the kitchen and saw my partner's ex standing there.

"Everyone, I'd like you to meet Dr. Kevin Dwyer. He—"

"Jory," Kevin greeted me, smiling, and I didn't miss the way his eyes swept by me, searching for my mate.

I was instantly pissed.

"You know Jory?" Randall asked, and he looked concerned.

"Not Jory. We have a mutual acquaintance."

Breathe in, breathe out.

"Oh? Who's that?"

I cleared my throat. "He knows Sam."

"Really," Dane said like that was the most fascinating news ever.

"Really really," I said.

The mock cheerfulness was not lost on him. "I see." He nodded, his eyes meeting mine. "Shall we eat?"

"Yes." I forced a smile for him.

I remembered, as I took a seat at the long table next to Jude, facing Rick, that before I had kids, I was a follower. It was not a revelation; it had come quite some time before, but at times like the present, I could actually see changes in myself. In the past, I had looked to Dane or others to make me comfortable in stressful situations. I had relied on the physical presence of my brother to steer me to the table or talk to me over dinner. But I wasn't that guy anymore. Yes, I still counted on my brother for the big-ticket items, like shelter so hit men couldn't get me and my kids when my other half was missing, but I didn't need him to direct my life anymore and make me feel better in my own skin. I didn't need to call for backup anymore unless there was something external like my kid was hurt and there had to be police or a lawyer. I wasn't a child anymore; I had two of my own.

The meal was fine, nothing really memorable about it. The waitstaff was efficient and courteous. The chef must have been great because everyone remarked about how good the food was, and the wine, from Dane's collection, was apparently a triumph. It all tasted fine to me, but nothing extraordinary. If Sam's father had been there making his world-famous bacon cheeseburgers, then there would have been something to gush about. As it was, I was ready to go home. Even though I loved my brother and his wife, I realized that us mixing socially just didn't work. My idea of a sit-down dinner was Sunday night with Sam's parents or the evenings I had with Dane and Aja and their kids. I was no longer a cocktails and hors d'oeuvres and a four-star meal kind of guy—if I ever was.

When dinner was done, as the staff asked if the guests wanted coffee with their dessert, I stood up and walked to the end of the table and squatted down beside Dane's chair.

"What?" His brows were furrowed.

"No, nothing, just"—my voice dropped low—"I'm worried about Kola, and my brain's not here, and I was really douchey to Randall, and it's not his fault. I normally make allowances for everyone, but I just wanna go."

"Of course, I understand. Sunday, when you bring the kids back, we'll have dinner just us somewhere," he said, his hand dropping gently to my shoulder. "Are you sure you're still up to taking them on Friday?"

"Oh, absolutely. You guys pack overnight clothes for them and I'll grab them after school."

"Thank you." Aja's voice turned me to her as she took hold of my hand.

"Course," I said, kissing her as I stood up before going around the table to Rick.

"Hey, where you going?" Aubrey asked me.

"Home," I sighed, leaning down to kiss her cheek. "I'm worried about Kola."

"Oh honey, Rick told me. You're so good; I'd be on a homicidal shooting spree."

Smiling, I squeezed the hand she offered me and then turned to her husband. "You wanna get up so I can hug you or what?"

He chuckled, rose, and I leaned and he grabbed me. It was not something he and I did, the hugging, but it was warranted.

"I couldn't figure up from down today and I really needed some help. You were great, and Nadira was awesome when she came over and she explained what she was doing and what was going on and what I should expect. Thanks for just stepping in and fixing stuff. That's normally Sam's part."

He gave me a last squeeze, and then I moved back.

"It's no problem," he assured me. "We're friends too, you know?"

"We are," Aubrey chimed in, taking my hand and squeezing it.

"Okay." I agreed before leaving them, heading toward the coat closet beside the front door.

I was pulling on my topcoat when someone called my name.

"Mr. Harcourt."

"Oh, hey." I grinned at Randall when I turned. "Man, I'm sorry I was a dick to you, so not your fault."

"I… pardon?"

I pointed at my nose. "When I was doing you, I did that nasal thing you do when you talk, like a—goose sort of noise. That was bitchy, and—"

"I'm sorry?"

Uh-oh. "Well, when I was telling my friend Dylan about you on the phone," I lied, "I said there was this guy at my brother's party with me that had shoes made out of platypus or something, and I was sure that you had a lot of redeeming qualities but that so far, since you were the only one talking, it was kind of hard to get an idea of what those were."

"You—"

"So she was saying that being gracious was a virtue and that maybe you were nervous, which accounted for the monologue of your charitable… activities." I cleared my throat. "And I got to thinking that maybe we could have lunch far, far in the future."

"I just wanted to ask for some clarification on how you knew Kevin, but… am I understanding that you were making fun of me?"

"Just the"—I pointed at my nose again—"honking thing."

"Mr. Harcourt!"

"It's just Jory," I corrected him. "Dane is the Mister."

"You—I—how dare you insult… why would you—I…."

How did I end up making people sputter like that?

"Oh, I know." I had an idea for a peace offering. "You like rich people. I could invite Aaron Sutter, you know him, everybody knows him, and as long as you talk about stuff that's not, ya know, just you, then we could all hang out and eat some endangered species of pelican or something, huh?"

"Who are you?"

"He's my brother," Dane said from beside me suddenly. "Please go home."

"I was," I defended myself. "He's the one who stopped me."

Dane pointed and I headed toward the door.

"You—he—"

"Come sit down, Randall," Dane placated him as I opened the front door and then closed it behind me. Sometimes it didn't pay to apologize to people.

"HIS shoes were made of seagull?" Kola asked me on the ride home from Dylan's house. "That's gross, Pa."

"Yeah, I know."

At the grocery store, we had to pick up milk and other various items.

"Hannah," I called out in the cereal aisle when she was getting too far away from me, "how far is too far?"

She turned and looked up at me. "If you can't reach out and touch me, I'm too far."

"Right." I extended my hand.

It was funny how she walked backward until my palm touched her back; I thanked her for respecting my wishes.

"Nana says that you thanking me is bad, that I should just do what you say."

"And what do you think?"

"I think she's right, but I like it when you say thank you."

I took Hannah's hand as I watched Kola do some weird contortionist walk. "Why is he doing that?" I asked her.

"He doesn't wanna break your back by stepping on a crack."

"But you don't care if you break my back?"

"I think you'd be broken already if it was a real thing. I think it's like demons."

This was new. "What demons?"

"Suzy said that demons come up from hell through the floor and get you when you sleep."

"Uh-huh."

"But the floor is hard, how could they come through?" My daughter wanted to know.

"It's an excellent point."

"So things like that, I don't think they're real," she said, putting the topic to bed.

"I suspect you're right."

"On Saturday after the movie, can we go to the aquarium?" Her mercurial mind flicked around even faster than mine.

"Why?"

"The dolphins," she said flatly, like what else could it be.

"We can ask everybody else, but I was thinking we'd go to the park."

"Oh, the park is better, never mind. You're very smart." She beamed up at me.

"Thank you."

"Pa," Kola said, obviously having tossed away his concern for my spinal column from the way he had reverted to his normal stride, "who will I marry when I get big?"

"I dunno, it depends on who you fall in love with."

"But will it be a boy or a girl?"

"I have no clue, love. Whoever you want."

He was thinking. "Do I have to go to college? Mica said that his dad said that he had to go to college."

"Yes, you have to go to college."

"Did Daddy go to college?"

"No."

"Then how come I have to?"

"If you want to do a job like your daddy, then you don't have to, but if you want to be a veterinarian and take care of cats like Chilly, then—"

"Yeah, I think I wanna do that."

"Then you have to go to college."

"Okay, then, I'll go to college."

"Think scholarship."

"What?"

"I'll tell you later."

As we waited in line to check out, Hannah, who had gotten tired of walking, was sitting in the top of the cart, humming and swinging her legs. The man behind us chuckled.

I looked at him over my shoulder. If I had to guess, I would have said he was in his midsixties, nice face, handsome man.

He cleared his throat. "Is she humming 'The Girl From Ipanema'?"

"Yes," I groaned. "Oh God, it's my fault. I do it, and now whenever she's bored… you get the idea."

"It's darling." He smiled at me.

I winced. "Her teacher isn't a fan."

He laughed. "I would expect not."

Hannah drew up her shoulders, tipped her head, and aimed all her cuteness at him, and between her little apple cheeks and tiny rosebud mouth and sparkling eyes, he was turned into goo.

"She's a doll."

"And she knows."

"You're gonna need a gun to keep the boys away."

"We've got that covered," I assured him.

Outside in the parking lot, I was handing the light bag to Kola when we all heard crowing.

"What was that?" Hannah asked me.

"Roosters," I told her as we walked, me carrying three reusable bags, Kola one. At the car, we heard it again.

"Pa, it's coming from there," Kola said, pointing to a parked Ford pickup.

"It's not our business. Get in the car," I ordered him, opening the door.

"But what if they're stuck?" Hannah looked up at me, her big brown eyes worried.

"Fine, you two get in the car. I'll see what it is."

With my kids safely ensconced in the car, I checked around and then leaned over into the bed of the pickup and lifted a tarp. There, underneath, were three large wire cages with roosters in them. I had never been a big bird lover; the wings fluttering in my face was just cause for hyperventilation. Clowns, birds, flying cockroaches—which got added to the list when I was in Hawaii—and wasps all gave me the shivers. I was not thrilled to find roosters but that they were there at all seemed odd to me. They looked like they had been trimmed weird; they didn't look like the ones walking around the petting zoo.

"What the hell are you doing?"

I turned and two men were walking toward me fast.

"My kids heard the crowing, and we thought the birds were in trouble."

"Oh," the first guy said, and suddenly I was looking at a badge that he pulled from under his T-shirt. The other man followed suit. I heard the window roll down beside me, and Hannah poked her head out.

"Are the chickens okay, Pa?"

"Yes, B," I assured her.

The policemen, Detectives Gonzales and Everman, explained to the kids as one leaned against the truck and the other on my minivan that they had taken the roosters from bad men who were going to fight them.

"Why do they fight them?" Kola wanted to know.

"People bet on which bird will win."

"How do they know who wins?" Kola was tenacious when it came to something he didn't understand. "Is it like boxing and there's points?"

I had to remind myself to talk to Sam's father about watching the fights with my kid.

"No, they let them go at it until one of them dies."

"Dies?" Kola was horrified.

Hannah, who was tired at that point, burst into tears.

"Really?" I scowled at both detectives, even though Everman was the one who had said it.

Gonzales elbowed his partner in the ribs, looking sheepish. "Sorry."

But I had to comfort my girl and had no time for them anymore.

They left the parking lot first, and I noticed as I took a right out onto the street that we were following them.

The Hummer that flew by me didn't even blip on my radar until it slammed into the side of the pickup and forced it off the road. I was easily a hundred yards behind, but I quickly turned off my lights and pulled over to the side of the road.

"Pa?"

I hushed Kola and called 911 as the officers got out.

There were three men in the Hummer, and they emerged from their vehicle shooting.

"This is 911, what is your emergency?"

"Two-one-one," I said quickly, remembering the codes Sam had told me. "I have two officers in my sight."

Two-one-one: assault on an officer. The operator went from interested to concerned in seconds. She got my location and asked if I was in danger, and since I categorized danger as people shooting directly at me, I said no. Four cars passed on the other side of the road, then three more, and the bad guys must have gotten scared, because they were suddenly in a mad rush to get back in the car. It was over, and the Hummer—squealing tires, hauling ass—was coming back by me. I saw the plate, memorized it, told the kids to get down, and ducked myself. The car flew by, hopefully not noticing us in our Mercedes but certainly unable to get the plate at the speed they were going.

I gave their plate number to the operator and told her I was driving over to check on the officers. She said I would have company in minutes, police and ambulance.

Getting as close as I could with the van, I got out and locked my kids in the car. I was still on the phone with the operator and went to get a close look at the officers. Everman was down, bleeding from his side. Gonzales was under the pickup, lying on his back, and he gasped out that he was hit in the leg and the shoulder.

"Is Lou alive?"

"Yes," I told him. "Are you okay? Help is coming right now."

"Yeah, I'm okay, and thank you."

"Just hold on," I soothed him as I moved back to his partner. I pulled off my coat and then my sweater and the T-shirt underneath. It was cold outside, but I needed to put pressure on the wound and there was no other option. Everman moaned when I pressed the wadded-up cotton to his side.

"Who are you again?" he asked as I put my coat over him and put my balled-up sweater behind his head.

"Do you know Sam Kage?"

He coughed. "He's a marshal, right?"

"Yeah."

"Yeah, I remember. He used to be a helluva homicide detective."

I nodded. "I'm married to him."

"Got it," he said as we both heard the sirens in the distance. "I don't suppose you got the license plate of the—"

"I already called it in," I said and put the phone to his ear.

"Hey," he groaned to the operator, "you have the plate?"

He was talking to her as the ambulance and a fleet of police cars rolled up. I pointed under the truck, then quickly answered questions so the policemen could holster their guns and everyone could go about securing the scene instead of worrying that someone was going to start shooting at them.

Kola and Hannah got to sit in a police car with a very nice young man who gave them the entire rundown of the car. I was standing outside the car, my sweater and topcoat back on, the T-shirt having been sacrificed to the greater good, and relating my statement to two new detectives. Gonzales and Everman were taken to the hospital in separate ambulances, and Chaz and Pat—who showed up somehow—were now standing with me as I was being questioned. The two new guys—there were too many new people in one night to keep track of them—promised that my name would not appear in the paper.

"You should get a commendation, Mr. Harcourt."

But I didn't want a citation for bravery or whatever. I did what anyone who had a mate in law enforcement would have.

"His name can't be leaked," Chaz stressed, and he used his size, his status, his tenure, his record, all of it, just who he was, to intimidate the two younger detectives.

"Ever," Pat chimed in, and as scary as Chaz was, he was still mild in comparison to Patrick Cantwell.

It was fast, the agreement from the junior detectives: they promised no press—none.

I met Gonzales and Everman's captain, Ibrahim Khouri, who looked crisp and polished even though, at ten at night, it was late for him to look so good. He thanked me for coming to the aid of his men and made sure to pass me his card. He was unsure as to why Chaz and Pat were there, and then they started explaining about what had occurred with me earlier in the day—leaving out Sam altogether. Khouri went with Chaz to talk to Kola.

Turning, I saw Kola get out of the car and lay his little hand in the captain's, who was kneeling in the dirt down in front of my little boy so they were at more or less the same level. I would have put money on the fact that Captain Khouri had kids himself.

He nodded as Kola reenacted what had happened. Hannah's face scrunched up as she listened to her brother, and after a minute, she flew across the grass to me.

"You okay, B?" I asked as I picked her up.

"I wanna go home to my house and my room and I want Daddy to come home." She whimpered the last of it.

"I know, B," I soothed her, rubbing her back as her head clunked down on my shoulder. "He'll be home soon. Maybe tonight we'll all sleep in my room, huh?"

She nodded against the side of my neck, and I asked the detective if we were done.

He agreed that we were. He gave me his card and said he'd be in touch, and we were allowed to go home. The captain told me that he would be in touch with Chaz and Pat, and I thanked him before I got both my kids in the car to finally head home.

"Lucky we didn't buy any ice cream," I told them.

And suddenly things were better, normal, because they both thought the idea of a soupy mess in the back of the minivan was hysterical.

THAT night as I lay between my two freshly showered little people, both in pajamas and both snuggled up against me, I tried Sam. It went to voice mail, and because I was never sure about how safe his phone was, I just texted a heart before I turned out the light.

TEN

I WAS not one of those "hit the ground running in the morning" people. I was probably a reincarnated vampire, truth be told. So it was not surprising that I was standing beside the coffeemaker, waiting for it to brew the precious elixir that would keep me vertical, when he walked through the door.

I was stunned.

I had not expected him for weeks. To find Sam Kage, rumpled and with three days' growth of beard, scowling at me was a surprise.

"What the hell is going on?" he roared at me.

I lifted my eyebrows. "Hello to you too."

He growled, dropped his duffel, pulled off his peacoat, and flung it down onto the couch before striding forward.

I moved around the island in the kitchen, which was counter on one side and a bar on the other. The open layout of the loft meant that one room flowed into the next, so I was thankful for the small barrier between us.

"What are you doing?"

"Why are you mad?"

His eyes widened. "Why am I mad? I dunno… lemme think."

I crossed my arms, waiting.

"Kola had his finger broken, you had to protect your children all alone from this psychopath, and you witnessed a hit on two policemen!"

"The dinner party was really the worst part. Your boyfriend was there." I shivered.

He snarled low in the back of his throat and came at me.

I would have run, but it was just too early in the morning. I turned instead, and he charged up to me, grabbed my arms tight, and shook me.

"Why do you keep letting me go?"

"Why do you keep going?" I asked back, knowing from the haunted, raw look in his eyes that I was seeing a man absolutely eaten up with guilt and worry and pain. He was sick that he had not been there for me or Kola or Hannah.

"I always think if I want something done right, that I absolutely must do it myself."

"I know." I smiled as my voice softened, and he let me go, his hands moving to my face, cupping it. "It's okay."

A shuddering gasp went right through him before his jaw clenched.

"You're mad at yourself, not me."

He didn't argue. He didn't have to; I saw it.

"Let it go," I said, wrapping my hands around his wrists. "I'm delirious that you're here."

He nodded, and when I lifted toward him, I heard the catch of breath.

Still.

After so many years, I still made the man breathless.

It was a gift.

He sealed his mouth over mine and wrapped me up in his arms, using all his power to press me against him, our bodies aligned, tongues tangled, our kiss intimate and languid. I belonged to him, and he could hold me for as long as he wanted.

My arms twined around his neck as he lifted me off my feet, hands on my ass. I slid my legs up his thighs to his hips and tightened them. The whine in the back of my throat made him clutch at me, his big, rough hands digging into my skin as he began walking me out of the kitchen and down the hall.

I really wanted to go home. In my house, early-morning sex was taken care of in the laundry room. I had lost count of the times I had been put over the washing machine.

He broke the kiss, panting for breath as I took my own gulp of air before recapturing his mouth. I sucked on his tongue as he staggered forward, carrying me, then stopped suddenly and shoved me hard into the wall.

"Where are our children?" he asked, whispering against my ear, nibbling on the lobe.

"Still... bed... early...." I trailed off, kissing up his throat to his chin and biting gently before trailing my mouth back down, sucking on his skin, moments away from leaving hickeys.

A frustrated sound, first a growl and then a huff of breath before he levered off the wall and continued down the hall. "Where?"

"First door," I directed him. "Lock it when—"

"Yes."

I smiled against his mouth. When we got there, he kicked the door closed behind him, and suddenly his movements were fast, mauling and forceful.

After putting me on my feet, he pulled my T-shirt up over my head and off, then did the same to his, stretching back between his shoulder blades to grab it. I reached for him, gripping his chest, loving the feel of him.

My deep groan of appreciation brought violent motion. The back of my neck was in his iron grip as he spun me around and pushed me forward, my cheek pressed to the cold, solid wood of the door.

"Hands."

Immediately I put them over my head, palms flat. At the same time, I spread my legs.

He knotted his hand tightly in my hair, and the message that I was not to move was clear. I stayed still as he left me, heard the rattle of the drawer in the nightstand behind me and the break of the plastic seal. We had been together so long, no matter where we were, where we stayed, things always found familiar places. He knew where to look for lube.

He pulled the drawstring of my sleep shorts loose, tugged them down, and slid them over my hips and off. When I felt the warm breath on ass, my breath hitched because I knew what was coming. He bit me hard—he would leave an imprint of his teeth, but I didn't care. The licking that followed, the sucking, was worth it.

If we had not been apart, if this were normal morning need, my cheeks would have been spread and his tongue would have pushed inside my puckered hole. But I was being manhandled, would be pinned to the wall and hammered. I could barely wait.

Every muscle in the man's big hard, body was tensed and ready to surge into motion and take me. And I wanted it. I wanted Sam Kage to simply ravish me.

The first lube-slicked finger slid inside me as his mouth closed on the back of my shoulder, where his name was tattooed and had been for years. I had had an artist trace his signature there, just "Sam," and ink it. He never, ever tired of seeing his name on my body. It was where his lips went every single time he took me from behind.

I pushed my ass out for him, and he moaned in appreciation before stroking and slapping it.

"So beautiful, so perfect and round and firm... like a heart... always amazing."

"What?"

"You're so small and yet... you take all of me."

I did and could, and there was a lot of Sam Kage to take. He filled and stretched me as no one ever had.

"Watching"—his voice was a husky groan—"could make me come."

I pushed back on his finger, and he added a second, working the tight rings of muscle, trying to get my body to unclench.

"Fight me," he ordered. "Go ahead and try, because I can't wait."

I heard the jingle of his belt buckle, the zipper, and then the sound of flesh on flesh. Then the greasing of his dick, and I smelled his precome before the touch of the enormous head at my crease. He pressed between my cheeks, letting his cock part them, and the first nudge made me jolt forward.

His angle changed, lowered, and he pushed up and in, shoving deep and hard, the lube letting it happen. Breached muscles rippled around him.

"Oh God," he groaned loudly, angrily, driving, pushing, grinding into me without hesitation. "You just sucked me in; your ass just swallowed me fuckin' whole."

I was sweating but freezing at the same time as he pounded me into the door, ramming hard, not caring about the noise. He released my hands, leaning back so he could watch his dick disappear into my ass again and again. I knew what he was looking at, had been told enough times over the years.

The steel hold on the back of my neck again. His fingers would leave bruises, but I knew he didn't care. Only exerting power and dominance mattered, seeing me take him in, feeling the silky walls around him, knowing I belonged only to him.

I was impaled over and over on his hot, thick length, and then suddenly his left hand slid over mine. Our fingers laced together, splayed flat on the door as his other hand fisted my dripping shaft.

"Come" was the guttural command as he thrust hard, jerking me off as I cried his name. "You feel so good when you give yourself to me."

The rocking motion, the pound and retreat…. My body was seized in friction and heat, the sound and the smell. My orgasm was wrung from me in seconds, and everything clenched at once.

"Oh fuck!" Sam yelled, my muscles clamping down on his dick so tight he couldn't move, held within my spasming channel. "Jory… baby…."

I was trembling. So was he. And then he was spilling inside me and I could feel every pulse, every tremor, and hear his breath in my ear.

He wrapped his arms around me and held me tight, his muscular chest plastered to my back, his mouth open on my shoulder as he just stood there and kissed every piece of skin he could reach.

I wanted to simply dissolve into him, felt like I could if he would just tighten his grip. I opened my mouth to speak.

"I have things to say."

"G'head."

He took a breath and then gently eased himself free of my body before scooping me up and carrying me to the bed. Once there, he left me and went to the bathroom.

I waited, and he returned with a cold bottle of water and a warm washcloth.

"That minifridge in the bathroom is awesome," he said as he opened the bottle and passed it to me. "We need one like that at home."

"Yes," I chuckled and then gasped as he roughly cleaned spunk from between my thighs and ass cheeks, then wiped off my abdomen. It wasn't a perfect job; I was still a little sticky but not nearly as messy. Not that I had ever cared. I loved smelling like Sam, loved having his spend drying on my skin.

"Like you care."

"What?"

"You don't give a damn if I clean you up or not."

I shook my head. The man was getting very good at reading my mind.

He grunted, and I could tell he was pleased before he turned and threw the washcloth back into the bathroom.

"Did you hit the sink?"

"I got close to the sink."

"Good enough," I said, offering him the bottle.

He drained the rest of it, put it on the nightstand, and then came down on top of me, pile driving me into the bed.

It winded me, and I started laughing as he wrapped his arms under and around me, hugging me tight.

I felt it then, the tension in him. Normally after sex, he was loose-limbed and relaxed.

"Say whatever it is," I urged him, because he needed me to hear it.

"Kevin," he whispered as he began nibbling up the side of my neck, "always wanted me to be calm and not yell and not grab him or hold him down."

"Huh."

"He said I was loud and my temper was volatile."

My chuckle was low and dark, and I felt the tremor run through his massive frame.

"He wanted to be on top. He thought if I loved him, I should let him. He said that a true partnership meant that I should open myself to him in every way."

I leaned my head back so I could see into the smoky blue eyes, and I really tried to keep a straight face. "And?"

"And fuck that! You've never said a word to me like that, ever!"

"So…." I started chuckling as I saw the beginnings of a scowl. "He found you scary-loud and he wanted to fuck you."

He growled at me.

The laughter came bubbling up.

"Jory!" he snarled, shoving my legs apart so he could get them where he wanted, wrapped around his hips. "What do you—I—"

"I belong to you, Sam Kage," I cut him off, pulling him down into a kiss.

He devoured me, and I whimpered and whined, tightening my legs, wriggling beneath him, burying my hands in his hair.

"You," he said, his mouth hovering above mine, his tongue sliding over my bottom lip, "are fucking mine, and you're the only person who gets me and lets me be me."

"I know that, which is why you should never, ever leave me. Right?"

"Right," he agreed before he kissed me again.

It built again, that desire, the same one I had felt the first time I had ever seen the man, the one that had kept him returning to me over and over, the push and pull that had flared and burned and now constantly smoldered, ready to catch fire at any given moment.

I ended up in his lap at an angle, my right leg draped over his, my left thigh pressed to the rock hard muscles of his stomach, as he held the same leg tight in his iron grip under the knee. His right arm was around my side, pinching and pulling on my nipple as he suckled on the other and drove up into me.

My head fell back on his shoulder, and I was lost. My vision went white; there was only me coming and the cold sweat and the heaving of his chest against my side.

I called his name over and over, and the kiss, as my head was wrenched sideways, was hot and wet.

"Sam," I managed to get out in a croaking whisper.

"Mine" was the only reply.

I HADN'T realized I was so tired, but when you were the only parent, you sort of slept lighter than usual, knowing that if an intruder broke in, you were the only line of defense.

An hour later, when there was a knock at the door, Sam slid me tenderly from where I was dozing on his chest and eased me down onto the pillow. I heard him pulling on clothes and then the squeal of delight after the click of the lock.

"Daddy!"

"Hi, buddy," he said softly to Kola, quieting him before the door closed and everything was muffled.

A while later there was a hand in my hair, petting, stroking, curling long pieces around my ear, tracing over my eyebrows.

My eyes fluttered open, and I saw my girl looking expectantly at me, chin on one hand as she touched my cheek with the other.

"Hi, B," I whispered.

"Daddy came home."

"Mmm-hmm." I smiled at her.

"Kola told him about his finger."

I didn't even want to deal with that. I was too sleepy.

"I told Daddy that the man pushed you."

He had poked me, not pushed me, but to my daughter it was probably the same thing.

"Daddy's taking us to school now but not to go, just to visit. He said we have to go talk to everybody."

Oh God.

"His friends are here," she said brightly.

Which meant that Chaz and Pat were out in the living room, ready to go kick some ass with Sam. "That's super."

"I told Daddy to call Uncle Dane, and he is."

She was good, my girl. Thorough. "That's good, B."

"Love?"

Hannah turned her head with the call.

"Come out here."

"But Daddy, Pa—"

"It's okay, Pa's sleepy."

She leaned up and kissed me and then scrambled down off the bed. Seconds later I had lips pressed between my shoulder blades.

"I need to get up," I muttered. "I can go with you."

"No," he rumbled and kissed my temple, his hand sliding down my back before his lips followed. "Go back to sleep. I'll bring lunch when I get home."

My eyes were so heavy.

"I promise not to shoot anybody."

I smiled and he turned my head and kissed me.

"Besides, you smell like come and sweat."

I sighed deeply and then Kola was there, kissing my cheek.

"We're going to talk to the principal, Pa."

I bet they were.

An hour later I got up, took a shower, stripped the sheets off the bed, changed them, and added Sam's clothes from his duffel to the load of laundry. The coffee I had made hours ago was cold, so I dumped it and made some tea instead.

I started a fire because I was cold and the gray outside needed warm inside to balance it out. When I heard keys in the lock an hour later, I turned from staring down at the Magnificent Mile to the door.

It was just Sam and the kids, no Chaz or Pat with them. Sam set a large white shopping bag on the kitchen counter. The food smelled amazing even from across the room. I saw Sam's gun box in one hand, along with more clothes on hangers that he had brought from the house in the other.

"We're not going home?" I asked him as Hannah streaked over.

"No," he informed me, walking down the hall toward the bedroom.

"Would you like to elaborate?" I called after him.

"No!"

"I see you picked up your gun!" I yelled, going to my knees in front of my girl so I was ready for my hug.

"Of course!" his voice carried back.

I hugged Hannah as Kola joined us. It looked like his cast had been changed.

"Hey, buddy, what happened there?"

"Daddy took me to the doctor after we saw Mrs. P."

"Oh, I see," I smiled at him, letting Hannah go so I could cuddle my boy. "You like the new color?"

He nodded. "Purple's your favorite, so I got it for you."

"Thank you." I sighed, squeezing him tight, loving the way he leaned and gave me his weight, his head heavy on my shoulder.

"Daddy yelled at Mrs. P," Hannah told me.

"Did he?"

She pursed her lips like I did, and it was funny to see her do it.

"What else?"

"Daddy had Uncle Dane's friend with him when he went to see Mrs. P," Kola reported, leaning out of our hug to look at my face. "They both looked kind of mad."

My eyes fluttered because really, poor Principal Petrovich. Sam Kage and Rick Jenner in the same room—it was too horrible to contemplate.

"Daddy told us that we could go back to school next Monday."

"Good," I said, as I stood up.

"Oliver and his mommy came and saw me and Kola when we were leaving. She said she was really sorry for what Mr. Parker did."

"Well, that's good."

"What's divorced?" Kola asked me, looking worried.

"Divorced means that your parents don't live together anymore," I explained to him.

He took a breath. "Will you ever get a divorce?"

"No divorce," Sam said as he walked back into the room. He was dressed in a white T-shirt and sweatpants, and he was barefoot. I could barely breathe. Even his hanging out at home clothes made me hot. "Right?" he asked, stopping in front of me.

"Right," I agreed as he curled a hand around my neck and eased me forward into a kiss.

The silence surprised me, and it must have been odd for Sam too, because we separated at the same time and looked down at our children.

"Not making you sick today?" I asked them.

Kola shook his head.

"No." Hannah smiled up at us. "It's okay."

Apparently displays of affection were sometimes good.

SAM had Hannah up on his shoulders and I held Kola's hand as we walked to meet Duncan Stiel. When I'd heard that Duncan was going out of town on a task force starting the following day—he was flying out to New York—I had insisted that Sam invite him to dinner. Duncan had agreed, had picked The Char, a steak place he liked, and we had headed out. When we got there, I realized it was a little fancier than I was expecting, but the decor inside—the lighting, the jazz, the murals on the walls—and the smell of good food all gave me a warm feeling. It felt upscale but not too refined for my family.

"Sam?"

When we turned, we found Detective Duncan Stiel waiting for us at the bar.

"Jory?"

And there at the other end, as requested, was Aaron Sutter.

"I'm hungry," Hannah said, putting her chin down on the top of Sam's head.

"What'd you do?" Sam was instantly suspicious.

"I'm sorry, what?" I opened my eyes wide.

But Sam so wasn't buying it.

Well, yes, I was doing a little matchmaking, but really, was that a crime?

The muscles in Sam's jaw started to tick.

"Just hear me out. I had an epiphany."

"Have you lost your fu—"

"There's a kid on your head," I reminded him.

His growl was deep.

"Oooh." Hannah was pleased. "Do it again, Daddy. Your whole body shook."

I was about to be murdered and she wanted the man to keep snarling.

"What's going on?" Duncan asked as Aaron joined us, stepping into the circle we made.

"Hey." I beamed at Duncan. "I hope you don't mind us being six for dinner."

He turned at looked at Aaron. "Oh… no, I just… fine."

Aaron's eyes swept over Duncan Stiel in that appraising way he had where he missed nothing. He took in the wide shoulders and broad chest that tapered to a narrow waist. He saw the long, muscular legs straining against denim. All of the detective was mapped and categorized: the gray eyes, dark-blond hair, and big, capable hands. I saw Aaron take a breath and go still like he never was. He liked smaller men like me, it was true, but I had always suspected that he could do with some manhandling himself. I also had an inkling that Duncan Stiel had a bit of the submissive in him. It was fun to watch Sam's friend take a quick breath and to see mine lick his lips when their eyes locked.

"Oh God," Sam groaned under his breath.

"Duncan, did you reserve us a table?" I asked cheerfully.

"I did," he assured me and pointed toward the back of the restaurant. It was nice when his hand went immediately to Aaron's back to direct him.

I knew right then that Duncan had no clue who Aaron was, and Aaron on the rare occasions when that happened, was absolutely thrilled.

At dinner I watched Duncan order, saw him drape an arm over the back of Aaron's chair, and watched the man I had never seen flustered smile nervously and fiddle with his drink napkin.

Sam was surprised.

Hannah regaled everyone with tales of the waterslide at the resort in Phoenix, and Kola showed off his cast and told the story of what had happened. Aaron asked if I had a lawyer. Duncan asked Sam if he wanted him to go with him to "talk" to Mr. Parker. What was nice was that they both offered so quickly.

When the appetizers came—cheesy bread for the kids, stuffed mushrooms and bruschetta for the adults—Duncan leaned close to Aaron and told him that he was in for a treat because it was so good.

Sam opened his mouth to explain to Duncan who Aaron was and that he probably would not be impressed, but Aaron beat him to the punch.

"I'm sure I'll love it."

Duncan asked if he wanted another drink, and when Aaron thanked him, I saw Aaron shift in his chair and knew what that meant. I dropped my napkin to confirm.

Under the table there were thighs touching, knees pressing, and… *oh yes, Houston, we have liftoff.*

I still had it.

IT WAS fun to turn and watch them, my clueless blind daters, standing together in front of the restaurant, under the awning, as we walked away. Aaron had offered to give Duncan a lift home, and the detective had agreed. I hoped that Sam's buddy would ask mine in when they reached his place, or that Aaron would just have his driver take them home. It didn't matter where they went; I just wanted them together. But I was done—I had put the ball in play, it was in their court now.

The hand on the back of my neck made me smile.

"Bad Jory. Naughty."

"Awww, but they were so cute."

"Can we eat dinner now?" Kola whined. "That meat was gross, the potatoes were disgusting, and I have never seen broccoli that big."

"It was humungalous," Hannah agreed, holding my hand. Kola was on Sam's back now. "They were like trees, Pa."

"Fine," I relented. "I'll make peanut butter and jelly sandwiches when we get home."

"Can I have one too?" Sam wanted to know.

Apparently frou-frou food was lost on my people.

Back at the loft, we found that Chilly had completely eviscerated a throw pillow. He was still pouncing on the poor thing, and did his frozen statue impression when Sam yelled.

"He can still see you." Hannah wrinkled her little nose at her cat. "Chilly and Pa are both naughty."

"Why am I naughty?" I asked her.

"I don't know, Daddy said."

I looked over at Sam.

"You know what you did."

I went to make sandwiches while Sam had a talk with the cat.

After everyone ate except me—I had actually enjoyed my meal—we all sat down to watch a Pixar movie. The bug one was Hannah's favorite, and it was her turn to pick.

Sam suggested they go get the pillows off their beds and we could all lie on the floor. As they flew off, he stretched out and patted the space beside him.

"Oh hell no."

"Why not?"

"My ass is still throbbing from the pounding you gave me earlier. I'll lie on the couch."

"Like I'm gonna attack you in front of my kids."

"Your kids?"

"Our kids, whatever. You knew what the fuck I meant."

I lifted my eyebrow.

"Fuck."

"Sam."

"Sorry, sorry," he mumbled. "Two days hanging out with other cops, it just comes right back."

"Uh-huh."

"Our kids."

"Good," I chuckled. "And no, I don't think you will attack me in front of them."

"Then c'mere."

But I still didn't trust him.

"And throbbing is good," he informed me. "Throbbing isn't pain, throbbing just reminds your ass who it belongs to."

"Is that right?"

The grunt was a yes.

He looked good, all languid and sexy on the thick rug, his eyes heavy-lidded as he stared up at me.

"I want to talk about the gunman in our hotel room."

"It's a long story."

"I took a nap; I can stay up late and hear it."

He patted the rug again.

I stepped over him, standing, gazing down at the man who had been it for me from the moment he'd walked into my life.

His hands slid up the back of my calves. "Sit down."

I sank over him, straddling his abdomen, and he immediately pushed me back so my ass settled over his groin.

The rumble of happiness coupled with his hands sliding under my thighs, first gently and then with more pressure, made me squirm.

"Don't do that," he said sharply.

"Don't do what?" I asked, swiveling my hips, showing off how loose they were, how flexible my body was.

"Stop."

I dragged my crease over his hardening length and squeaked when he grabbed me tight.

"All I can think about right now are those dimples in your ass," he said, his voice a husky whisper. "So stop teasing me before I eat you."

"Oh please eat me," I begged.

His eyes were molten as the kids charged back into the room.

I bent over him, a hand flat on the floor on each side of his head, and kissed him. He opened beneath me, and I felt his erection straining against his zipper as my tongue checked his tonsils.

"Ewww." Kola sounded grossed out.

The heat of the man was searing through my clothes, my skin, and I bucked against him involuntarily.

"Oh you're gonna pay." Sam's breathless growl made me smile as I broke the kiss.

He caught my bottom lip in his teeth, the nibbling gentle but firm, and I sighed because the man's dominance was something I never tired of.

"I want to talk to you," I told him when I was allowed to sit up.

"I'll make you a deal." He smiled wickedly.

I was in so much trouble.

I COULDN'T sleep, and I had no idea how Sam could, so I kept poking him when he nodded off.

"I'm awake," he said defensively, and I worked hard not to smile.

Whenever I caught the man doing something he considered weak—like falling asleep when he was tired because regular humans might need rest but never him—he got snarly. Like how dare I accuse him of needing to close his eyes when he so obviously didn't?

"So the gunman, he works for this guy we now know kidnapped the witness."

"No, basically the dead gunman, Tishman, he worked for Christian Salcedo, who is the one being blackmailed by our witness, Andrew Turner."

"So you were right."

He nodded. "I was right; Turner has something big on Salcedo, so Salcedo took him from WITSEC to keep him from testifying."

"But don't the bad guys usually just shoot the good guys to keep them from talking?"

"Normally yes, but in this case, as I told you last week, Turner's not actually a good guy, and he has Salcedo running scared."

"So then what?"

"Well, now we're kind of at a standstill. We can't reach out to Salcedo because what Turner knows about his operation will put him in jail, but whatever Turner has as his ace is keeping Salcedo on a tight leash."

"So this Salcedo, he's sort of screwed either way. He helps you, he goes to jail, he keeps hiding Turner, he goes to jail."

"Yep."

"But he's running the risk of going to prison forever because he took Turner."

Sam nodded.

"Do you think Turner is with Salcedo now, wherever that is?"

"Yeah, I think Salcedo moved Turner after we almost caught up with him in Phoenix."

"But how did Salcedo know that you were going to Phoenix?"

He made a face but only for a second. Anyone but me would have missed it, but I knew every expression the man made.

"Sam?"

He looked at the ceiling.

"Ohmygod, what?"

His eyes were back on me. "My boss has a theory, and it's a pretty good one actually."

I waited.

"Just to catch you up, Salcedo was the guy who got away back when I was running down that drug cartel in Columbia."

"You never said anyone got away."

"Didn't I?"

"Sam!"

"Fuck," he growled, throwing off the sheet covering him and charging across the room to the window.

I gasped, and he spun around to face me. "Salcedo was a member of the cartel you busted?"

"Yes."

"And?"

"And because he was the last man standing and because we never caught him, he moved up in the organization."

"And? C'mon, this is like pulling teeth. Is your informant in Phoenix the one who ID'd Turner?"

"Yeah, or was."

"Was?"

"He's dead."

"Oh. So someone knew that he got the information to you that Turner was alive and well."

"You're very good at this," he said irritably.

"I've had years of practice." I was snide as I rolled off the bed.

"Jory—"

"And now, all of a sudden, out of the blue, Dr. Kevin Dwyer shows up."

His shoulders slumped.

"Isn't that strange." I stared holes in him.

"Okay," he began, moving toward me. "My boss thinks I—"

"You're gonna use Kevin to catch Salcedo and Turner," I said, putting up my hand.

He stopped. "Yeah."

"So Kevin is connected to Salcedo."

"We think so, yes. The connection is hidden. I don't know how they know each other, but Kevin was the only one who knew when we were moving on the cartel... I drank a lot back then, and I thought I could trust the guy I was fucking."

I was processing.

"So yeah, it follows that my informant made contact with me, they found out, and then suddenly Kevin's back in town."

"But these people must have followed you and seen me and the kids, and this guy Salcedo still thought that sending Kevin here was a good idea? He must have believed that he could tempt you away from your family."

"Salcedo must have seen me with Kevin in Columbia all those years ago. That's the last he's probably seen of me."

"What about his hit man in Phoenix?"

"That guy was sent to my room after me. I doubt Salcedo has checked up on me at all. He just heard that my guy reached out to me and he put Kevin into play. Kevin's the only person Salcedo knows who knows me."

"So you're saying what?"

"That it's doubtful that Salcedo has any idea about you or the kids."

"But Kevin knows now."

"Which is why you're here and not at home."

"So you weren't worried about us because of Phoenix, you're worried because of Kevin."

"Yes."

"How do you think Kevin got the job at County?"

"How did he just show up, you mean?"

"Yeah."

"I think he's probably working there for free. Sanchez and Ryan are checking on it now. Kowalski and Dorsey are tailing Kevin, and White and some guys from Chicago PD are sitting on all the bugs in his apartment."

"Okay." I took that all in.

"So what?"

I wasn't sure what he meant.

"What are you thinking?"

"Just that this Salcedo guy must have really thought that Kevin Dwyer had you wrapped around his finger."

"Please, please, do not get your brain running on this. Whatever anyone else thinks is crap. The important part is what I know and what I believe."

"And so what? What precisely is the play here?"

"I'm not following."

"Do you have to convince Kevin that you want him so he will lead you to Salcedo? Is that what you're supposed to do? Are you supposed to romance him so you can get into his home and check around? How far do you have to take it?"

He was scowling.

"Just tell me."

"You're getting all this from watching TV, right?"

"Don't patronize me!"

"I'm not, just tell me what you think I'll be doing!" he said, his voice rising as he took a step forward.

I took one back. "You'll start by showing up at his work and saying that you have to see him."

He kept coming.

"Then you'll tell him that you've been thinking about him and you can't stop," I said even as my eyes raked all over his body. I looked at him the way I knew Kevin Dwyer had and would. Beautiful man, beautiful body. Even the scars only added to his allure.

"Is that what I'll say?"

I took a shaky breath, having walked myself back into the wall. Sam stopped in front of me, not crowding me, just standing, staring down into my eyes.

"Sam? What will you have to do?"

"I dunno," he said, but his eyes weren't posing a question, they were deviant and hot. "What should I do to catch Salcedo? Turner? How far could I take it?"

My mouth was dry, there was a lump in my throat, and I was having trouble breathing.

"Jory?"

"Kiss him?"

"I should kiss him?"

Oh God, what was I supposed to say? "What does your boss want you to do?"

"My boss?"

"Yeah."

"Well," he said, lifting his hand to take hold of my chin, his thumb sliding over my bottom lip, "my boss, because he's kind of brilliant, doesn't want to see my Valentino impression. Instead, he wants Kevin's place bugged—which we did already—wants him followed everywhere he goes, and wants me and the rest of my guys to basically put the fear of God into him and see how long it takes before he fuckin' cracks."

It took me a second.

He rolled his eyes.

"Sam!"

"Really? You think US Marshals sex people up?"

It sounded really dumb when he put it like that.

"We shoot people! We put them in jail or we protect them. We do not run sophisticated con operations where we have sex to get state secrets. That's the CIA!"

"Sam!"

The noise he made was pure unadulterated disgust.

"I thought that—"

"I only kiss you, idiot."

I scowled at him.

He let out a breath and then I got the grin I loved, the evil one, the one that made his eyes glitter. "And besides, ya know, my seduction skills are kinda rusty, 'cause now I just hafta snap my fingers to get laid."

He saw my eyes go murderous, and started laughing at the same time he grabbed me, wrapping me up in arms bulky with muscle.

"Sam!"

"I only hold you down, I only fuck you, and I only ever sleep with you in my arms. I'm not James Bond, ya know; I don't go undercover and get laid to a Hans Zimmer soundtrack." He was still smiling, but his eyes were locked on mine and pleading. "Baby, Salcedo made a mistake sending Kevin, and we're gonna exploit that."

I nodded because I couldn't speak.

"And now I understand that Kevin Dwyer never had any feelings for me at all. Everything he ever said, everything he told me he felt, was a lie."

"No," I told him. "He might have been in a bad position, Sam, but I saw how he looked at you, and that was real."

But Sam wasn't buying it; I could see it on his face. He had made up his mind and that was it. No matter what Kevin Dwyer ever did, ever said, Sam had passed judgment on him, and it was done.

I needed to get my hands on him, to hug him, hold him, but he was so much stronger than me, so much bigger, and that fact, that he was all about power and control, was the biggest turn-on ever.

"I think you're wrong about Kevin. I think he might be back here under Salcedo's orders, but I have no doubt that his feelings were real all those years ago, and I'll bet, if you're up to it, that he would love to have you back."

"As if I give a damn. That day I went out to talk to him in the hall, do you wanna know what I said?"

I was dying to know. "It's none of my business."

"I think it is."

I nodded so he would go ahead.

"He told me he wanted to see me."

Of course he had.

"And I told him I was married and I had a family and that he was not part of my life anymore. I wished him the best and I walked away."

It was so cold, so final, and if I had been in Kevin's place, it would have killed me. "I said the same thing to you when you charged back into my life after three years away."

"No," he assured me. "You told me you didn't think it would work, but that was only because you were scared I would hurt you again. You didn't have a life yet, you didn't have a husband or kids. There's a big difference."

Yes, there was.

"And I always knew I was the one for you, always. There was never a doubt in my mind."

"No?"

"No." He shook his head. "It was why I couldn't be the guy anyone else needed, because I was already the one that *you* needed."

My heart felt like it was going to swell out of my chest.

"Say something."

I squinted so I wouldn't cry. "So your guys are gonna bug Kevin's house?"

"Like I said, it's done already," he said, his grip loosening so I could get my arms free and wrap them around his neck.

"Sam."

"Yes?"

I swallowed hard. "You know how much you love me?"

"Yeah."

"I love you the same."

He kissed me then, hand on the back of my head, holding me still as his mouth opened mine, wanting in.

I returned the passion, the yearning, the deep, throbbing want, pressing tight against him, moaning as my tongue stroked over his in our familiar dance. We parted at the same time, because there was heat building, but more than that, a sort of breathless anticipation of emotion.

"It's always been... us," he said quickly.

"Yes," I agreed. I licked over his bottom lip, suckled it, bit it softly until he moaned deep. "It has."

"So?

"So."

"Kiss me some more."

"I'm very possessive."

"I know, it's good."

I kissed him so he'd know it wasn't going to change.

ELEVEN

SAM got home on Friday night and was stunned when he heard all the noise.

"What?"

"Lemme get this straight," he said, scowling at me. "I could be in mortal danger here, people could be trying to kill me, but Dane and Aja still let their kids visit?"

"For one," I began, crossing my arms and mirroring him, "if your kids are safe—and they are—then so are theirs, and hello, Aja needs to get laid."

"Oh for the love of God," he groaned, "why the hell did I need to hear that?"

"Because it's true! She needed a date night!"

He was still stunned as he was swarmed by children that came flying in from the other room: Kola and Hannah, followed quickly by Robert, who was the same age as Hannah, and Gentry, who had just turned two. He put up his hands for Sam, who whisked him up in his arms and hugged him.

Gen was adorable, with Dane's eyes and Aja's cheekbones; Robert had gotten his mother's honey brown eyes and long lashes but had Dane's features, his nose and his jaw. I told Aja often that the girls would be waiting in line for her boys.

"We'll see who gets by Mama."

I was betting not many. Just thinking about having Aja Harcourt as a mother-in-law would be terrifying. She was smart and gorgeous. Good luck trying to live up to that!

My plan had been to make dinner, but Regina called and said that she had made lasagna and would we like to come over. I explained about Robert and Gentry, and since she had not seen them since right before school started, she was excited to have them.

Once there, I excused myself when I saw Aaron Sutter's number come up on my display.

"And?" He muttered on his end.

"What? I figured you'd call and tell me." I defended myself.

He sighed deeply.

"That bad? I thought you guys had—"

"He had to go work on a task force thing in New York."

"Yeah, I know. I figured that would be good. If you hated him, it would just be done. If you liked him, you could miss him."

Silence.

"Aaron?" He was never quiet or thoughtful, and it was sort of freaking me out.

"He's in the closet, you know. Like, no one at work knows he's gay."

"Yeah, well, only your friends know you're gay. Even your family doesn't know."

"They know."

"They suspect. Everyone does. But you've never come out to the press or to your parents or your brother. You never go to your big social engagements with a guy on your arm. You and I never arrived together, we never left together. When I showed up on the society pages with you, it was always as your friend. You have amazing friends who would never breathe a word about your personal life. Even Todd, who I hate, or did hate, even him, he—"

"Todd got married and moved to Connecticut, you know. You'd probably actually like him now."

"Don't get crazy," I chuckled, remembering his buddy who had always figured me for trash. "I'm just saying, you have good people in your circle, and they would never out you."

"Yeah, I know."

"So then what?"

"No, I just… it was nice, you know? He gets it."

"Okay. And?"

"And what?"

"And Duncan Stiel? What's the deal?"

He cleared his throat. "When he gets back, he's gonna call me."

"That's it?"

"Yeah."

"So," I drew out the word. "You're not gonna pop up to New York to visit him?"

"No." He sounded irritated. "He's working and I have to fly to Berlin tomorrow to discuss contracts and… things."

"Things?"

"Just—good-bye."

"What about your art auction?"

"I talked to Fallon. You saw the money, right?"

I had. I didn't check the business account every day like I did my personal one but I had seen the transfer. "Yeah, but don't you want to look at what we—"

"No, you know I trust you. Just do it."

He did not sound like himself. "You um, normally try to come on to me, you know."

Nothing.

"Not that this isn't better, and Sam will certainly be thrilled, but… I actually thought I was doing you a favor and not making your life shitty. I'm sorry that you and Duncan didn't—"

"What?"

"Aaron, did you like Duncan? Did he like you? I mean, what the hell?"

He cleared his throat, but there was no great outpouring of information.

"You're really starting to—"

"He's different than I thought."

"And you're different right now than you've ever been," I said, because really, I had never met this man before. For as long as I'd known Aaron he'd been cocky and sure and loud and brash. There had been quiet times, yes; there had been times he tried to get me to move in and see the life he could provide. There had been times he'd tried to change me, make me dependent, make me love him, body and soul. But the man on the phone was unsure, and that was simply not Aaron Sutter.

"Jory."

It was my fault. I broke him. "What can I do?"

"I… I want to go to New York."

"You do?"

"I do."

"And so what's stopping you?" I wanted to know.

"I don't want to push if I shouldn't," he said as he cleared his throat.

"Wouldn't going show interest?"

"Or compulsive tendencies," he sighed deeply.

"So you don't want to look too eager?"

"I don't want to look like I want more than there is." He explained. "That's no good."

"Okay. May I ask what was said when you guys parted that night?"

He grunted. "That was slick, or tried to be. Ask what you want to know."

"Did you sleep with him?" This was the heart of the matter.

"Yes, I did."

"And?"

"And there is no way in hell I'm telling you what went on in my bedroom."

"You always tell." I was indignant.

"Not this time."

Not this time. "You didn't use to tell your pals about us."

"What in the world does that—"

"You didn't," I cut him off.

"And so?"

"Why didn't you?"

"That's ancient his—"

"Why?"

"Because you were special." He was matter of fact and annoyed at the same time.

"Did you tell anyone about Duncan?"

"You're the only one who knows about me and the detective."

Uh-huh. "So he knows who you are, since you took him home with you."

"Yes."

"And how did that go?" This was getting good and the digging was killing me.

"He's in the closet, so am I. He liked that I got it, I appreciated that he did."

"So that part was perfect."

"It was." He agreed with me.

"Oh for crissakes, Aaron, you're driving me nuts!" I yelled at him. "Do you want to see Duncan again or not?"

"I—"

"Aaron!"

"Fine! Yes, I want to see him! Why the hell do you think I want to go to New York?"

"What did he say? What did you say? Jesus, what is this, junior high?"

"He said when he got back, he wanted to see me and he wanted to know if that would be okay?"

"And you said, hell yeah, Detective, I would love to see you."

"Pretty much."

Pretty much? "Aaron Sutter, you sound a little flustered."

"Yeah."

Yeah? "Aaron?"

"I'm hanging up now."

"Don't you dare," I threatened him. "Talk to me."

"I can't."

Holy. Shit. "Try."

"I liked him."

"Yeah I got that and so?"

"And so... I mean he told me everything."

"What's everything?"

"Just about him, about how he's been screwing nameless, faceless guys and how there was one guy, a special guy, but it didn't work because of him."

"Because of who?"

"Duncan. I mean, like I told you, he's not out and the guy was and so he needed me to understand that and of course I do and you should have seen how relieved he was and... he was just and I want to... shit."

"You want to what? Move him in? Lock him in?"

"He's the kind of man who needs to belong to one person. You can tell."

"Desperation is not sexy."

"No, not normally, no."

Oh dear God. "But he wants to belong, and you what?"

The growl was deep.

"Aaron?"

"The thought of him just living like he's been when he so wanted to stay... I... and I don't even know if... I don't know."

The weight of it, of what I'd done, hit me. I thought I knew people, thought I knew things, but maybe I didn't, and when all was said and done, Aaron Sutter had turned out to be a friend, someone I could count on.

"I'm sorry I—"

"Why would you be sorry? Don't be sorry yet."

I took a breath.

"I'll let you know what happens."

"When?"

"When I get back from New York."

"So you're going?"

"I guess so."

And since I had no more advice to give, I shut the hell up and let him hang up on me.

"J?" Sam was concerned when I reappeared in the living room.

"Sorry, I had to talk to Aaron."

"Oh? And how are he and Duncan getting along?"

"I have no idea."

Sam nodded and then pointed at me. "If that ends in gunfire, it's all on you."

"Really? You think that's a nice thing to say?"

"I'm just saying, cop, playboy... how did that make sense in your head?"

Nothing ever made sense in my head—that was the problem.

SAM had cancelled fishing with Chaz and Pat, but since making him go to the movies was cruel and unusual punishment, I met the others—Dylan and her two kids; Stuart and his mother, Jessica; Tess and her father, Gordon; my buddy Evan and his two boys, Bryce and Seth—at the movies right after eleven the next morning. It was a production with that many kids—ten in all—to get everyone seated with popcorn and a drink and napkins. Halfway through the movie, Gentry had to pee, but it was more than fine, and since, as Aja had told me, he was on the cusp of being potty trained, when he said he had to go, we went.

Afterward we took the kids out for lunch and then to a playground close to Dylan's house. It was nice, all of us sitting and talking. I had not seen Evan in a couple of months, and it was good to catch up. Gordon and Jessica seemed to be hitting it off, and since they were both single parents, I was sort of pleased with myself.

"You are the love god," Dylan teased me.

"I still got it."

Evan rolled his eyes, and I took that opportunity to ask about Loudon, his partner, his husband, the man he'd always said he would never find and whom he had been married to for the past eleven years. They were made for each other. Evan was sort of a high-strung worrier, and Loudon was calm and grounded. I had seen them in action many a time, and sometimes Evan's obsessive personality was a good thing—it kept the ball from getting dropped. Other times Loudon reminded him that stopping to breathe and refocus was the thing to do. It was nice to see that their boys, Bryce and Seth, had facets of both. Like Sam and I, Evan and Loudon had adopted, Bryce from Spain and Seth from South Africa.

As Dylan went to see why Mabel and Mica were hanging upside-down from the monkey bars while Seth counted underneath them, Evan leaned forward and put a hand on my knee. I quickly covered it with my own.

"What's up?" I asked him.

"Hey, uhm, Loudon and I have been talking, and we both agreed that if, heaven forbid, anything ever happened to us, we want you and Sam to take the boys."

I panned slowly to see his face.

"Okay?"

It was a shock. "Are you sure? I mean, Loudon's always said how much he worries about Sam's job, and—"

"Yeah, but Loudon knows, just like I do, that no one will take better care of them than Sam. He won't let anything happen to them, and you worry as much as I do."

"Why do people keep saying that? I don't worry."

He gave me a look.

"What?"

"Come on, Jory. You're very protective, and I love that. And Sam's gonna be like a prison guard, and I like that too. I mean, when all the kids get older and they start to run around wild, because if the curse is true and you get a kid just like you—oh honey, how out of control will our kids be?"

I shuddered to think. "Just, what's your point?"

"Sam's going to be the one we all turn to. He'll be checking up and ruining parties and putting the fear of God into whomever our kids see and letting those people know that if they mess with them, sell them any drugs, smoke with them, drink with them, that he'll be there to put a bullet in them."

I nodded because it was very possible. Not the actual killing, but the threatening and the fear that Sam Kage could, and would, inspire.

"And he has all those cop friends, and I've met his buddies— Chaz and Pat, right?"

"Right."

"Yeah, see, and I've met their kids, and they've got nice ones, so—"

"They have mothers, you know, those kids. It's not just fathering that's happening."

"No, I know, I just mean that they're law-enforcement types and their kids turned out okay, and since we're all counting on Sam to watch out even peripherally for our kids, then for sure if Loudon and I both go down in a fiery ball or get hit by a crosstown bus, then you and Sam would be the ones we'd want to step in for us."

"But your mom would—"

"She's older, Jory, and the kids will need hands-on parenting, two people who can keep up physically as well as anything else."

I studied his face and saw only absolute seriousness.

"I see Hannah and Kola, and they're weird"—he shrugged—"because you're weird, but so are mine, and for the same exact reason. My boys are going to be messed up a little because Loudon and I are. No way around it. You're a good father. I always figured you would be."

"Really?"

"Yes, baby." He squeezed my knee. "You have the best heart."

I sighed deeply. "Okay. Sign me up. It would be an honor to be the guardian of your kids."

He nodded. "You don't have to ask Sam?"

"Oh no." I shook my head, turning to look out at the playground, watching Hannah growl at Gentry as she chased him and he laughed and ran. "Sam accepts that kind of responsibility as an honor. It's the same way he took the news when I told him that Dane and Aja wrote us into their will to be Robbie and Gen's guardians. He was deeply moved. I mean, they're trusting him with the most precious part of their lives, their kids. He takes that very seriously."

"I know." Evan patted my leg, smiling at me. "And you guys will do the very best you know how. Can't ask for better than that."

I nodded as he got up to go see what was happening, since Dylan was talking to her daughter, who was upside-down now, and Mica was holding his breath.

Looking around, I saw Gentry on the ground, twitching every time Hannah pretended to dig into his head with what looked like, the way she was holding her hands, an imaginary knife and fork. I stopped Kola as he ran by me with Stuart and Tess.

"What is your sister doing?" I asked, pointing her out for him.

"Oh, eating Gentry's brains. She's a zombie."

"With utensils?"

"You always tell her not to use her hands," he said with a straight face.

"Oh, yeah, of course."

He shrugged and ran away. Moments later, Robbie passed me, howling.

"And you're what? A werewolf?"

He stopped to look at me. "My daddy says there's no such thing. I'm a rabid wolf."

Rabid. He was so Dane's kid, even though he was only four. I nodded. "Carry on."

His smile was huge as he raced off. Minutes later Kola was a rabid wolf with him, which made Robbie light up. I was so happy my kids and my brother's kids got along so well.

"Mica wants to be an evil scientist when he grows up," Dylan told me as I sat on top of the monkey bars with her. It was easier to see the whole playground from higher ground, and the kids all thought it was awesome that we could get up there. Of course I had to then inform them that it was bad.

"You're an example of what not to do?" Evan asked from below, arms crossed.

"My life serves as a cautionary tale for many things," I reminded him.

"I can't argue with that." He shrugged before he walked away.

"So, spill? Kola's career goal?" she prodded me.

"Veterinarian." I smiled. "At least this week. How about Mab? What's her life goal?"

"She wants to be a US Marshal."

"Are you kidding?"

"Nope. Sam said girls can do the same things that boys can. And I love him for that, but I hope to God she grows out of it."

"Me too," I agreed.

"If I die, though, it's all over."

I turned and squinted at her. "Sorry?"

She shrugged. "If Chris and I die and you get Mica and Mabel, she'll be living with her idol at that point. It'll be game over."

"Do you realize how many kids I'll be raising if all my friends and my brother and his wife all die in a tragic cruise ship disaster?"

She started chuckling. "Yeah, you better make sure we don't all vacation together without you."

I grunted. "I'll keep it in mind."

"You do that," she laughed, and I grabbed hold of her to make sure she didn't fall off the monkey bars and crack her head open. I didn't want to have to explain that to her husband.

SAM had thought that the idea of Duncan and Aaron together was absurd, and then when I told him that two of Kola's classmates' parents had traded numbers at the park, Sam had rolled his eyes.

"What? I remain...." I paused dramatically. "The love god."

He waved me over to him. "Come here, love god."

I ran but he caught me easily, and when I was under him on the floor in the hall, his eyes sparkling with mischief and heat, I melted.

"God, I love you."

He waggled his eyebrows at me.

"Do you realize how many kids we'll have to provide for if everyone dies at once?"

His scowl was fast. "I'm sorry?"

"Evan and Loudon are making us the legal guardians of their kids."

"They don't even like me!" He was indignant.

"They love you. Everybody loves you."

"Since when?"

"Since they've seen you take care of me, take care of our kids, and love us all with your great big heart. It's hard not to adore a man that you know is all thunder and lightning on the outside and warm, gooey goodness underneath."

It took him a second to process everything I'd said. "I don't think any of that was a compliment."

I laughed myself silly.

That evening Sam and I made pancakes and eggs and bacon for dinner since we were having brunch the following morning and not a traditional breakfast. I hated having two meals exactly alike back to back. It was fun to watch Sam take requests for shapes of pancakes and then try his damndest to make them.

"Stop sighing," he grumbled at me even as he bent and kissed my nose.

TWELVE

THE place Dane and Aja wanted to meet for brunch at eleven the following morning was downtown, and they were waiting outside for us when we came up the sidewalk. Gentry saw his mother when we got close and bolted toward her. I waved so she'd notice us, since she was talking to her husband, and then pointed at her kid. She knelt and held out her arms, and he slammed into her like little kids did, face in the side of her neck, and inhaled her scent as he hugged with everything he had. The look of absolute bliss on her face made it a picture-perfect moment.

Robert rushed to his father, and Dane hugged him tight before he and Aja switched kids. They both looked better, Aja rested, Dane smiling like he never did. Dane was more of a habitual scowl guy than cheerful. They had needed the weekend alone, and I made the offer again: anytime. Sam gave his slight nod so they knew that really, it was fine.

Quickly, so no one else saw, Aja whipped back the collar of her blouse, showed me a hickey, and then covered it back up. Dane turned to look at us when he heard my snicker.

"What?" I asked him.

"What?" she echoed.

He turned, brows furrowed, and gave both Aja and me a look before leading Hannah and Robert into the restaurant with Sam right behind him.

"So." I smiled slowly at my sister-in-law.

She looked like the cat that swallowed the canary.

"Nice couple days? You sleep well?"

"Sleep?" She coughed.

I started laughing, and Sam glared back at us.

"Thank you for giving us a couple nights off." She smiled at me. "We don't need it every week or even every month, but it's nice to know we have the option."

"You're welcome."

"And the same goes for you and the marshal."

"Nah." I shrugged. "We can just have a quickie in the car."

And of course that came out right as we reached the table and the waitress had just asked if the table was good.

Sam groaned and let his head roll back and hit the booth. Dane went face-first into the palm of his hand.

"What's a quickie?" Hannah wanted to know because she had scary cat ears, and she turned to look at her uncle in anticipation of an answer.

The waitress started giggling, Aja choked, and I told Hannah that a quickie was going through the drive-through.

She looked confused and her brother told her she'd understand when she was older. He looked very pleased with himself.

AFTER brunch, after clothes and backpacks got switched out, Dane told Sam how good it was to have him back and that he would expect to see him the following day in his office. Sam nodded and then they were gone.

"What are you meeting Dane about?"

"Oh, you know perfectly well what."

I had no idea, and then it blinked into my head. "Oh, the house."

"Yeah, the house," he grumbled. "I should know better than to ask him to keep a secret from you."

"Yes, you should," I said pointedly. "And so?"

He wrapped his arms around Kola's legs, as my son was sitting on his shoulders and I was carrying Hannah because her stomach hurt. "So what do you think?"

"I think I love that house, but I don't know if we can afford it."

"You've always loved it."

Yes, I had.

The large two-story Queen Anne located in Oak Park's historic district was bigger than the house we were in now. It had close to thirty-five hundred square feet of living space, a big attic, high ceilings, hardwood floors, and a completely renovated basement with a washer and dryer. When I had first seen it, years ago when Dane and Aja moved in after they were married, I had been sick with jealousy. Of course, because it was my brother, I got over it, but when they had moved... the desire had kicked in all over again. The fact that Sam and I were so in sync that he had wanted it too, for me, for him, for the kids, made me deliriously happy. And I knew that Dane was basically selling it for a quarter of what it was worth, for a quarter of what he had paid, but I also knew that to him, that wasn't the point.

"I've never seen you like this about something," I said to Sam.

"I've never wanted anything for you guys like this."

"You've been thinking about this for a while, huh?"

"Yeah, and I think we can swing it. The mortgage will be more than we're paying now, but not by that much, not like by another grand. And the house is bigger, and it's in a better neighborhood, and the schools are good, and most importantly, your brother is giving us a deal."

I turned so I could see his eyes.

"I finally get that Dane really does say exactly what he means."

"It took you this long?"

He shrugged. "Yeah, but now I know if he says he wants me to have the house for you and the kids because he appreciates me taking care of you all, even though it's not his place to reward me for doing something I love, for doing something that's part of my nature, I get it."

"An epiphany. I think I'm getting all verklempt."

"I am trying to have a serious conversation with you."

"Yes, dear."

He draped an arm around my shoulder and hauled me close, and it was nice, the four of us together, my family.

"So you were saying?"

"I want us to move. I want the house."

"Okay." I breathed in, leaning on him. "I do too. I've always loved that house. I was sick when they moved out of it."

"I didn't care that they moved, I just wanted to get there before he sold it. I knew he had offers even before they put the For Sale sign up."

"And you asked him to do what?"

"Just hold onto it until I could get some capital together."

I waited.

He sighed deeply. "Which your ass—"

"Carrying a kid," I reminded him.

"Which your brother took to mean…." Sam coughed. "Doctor the reports so the marshal can afford it."

I leaned my head back so I could kiss under the man's jaw.

The contented rumble made me smile. "He's really something."

"Yes, he is."

"I mean, he went off about a house needing people the same as people need a house… what is that?"

"He's an architect. He believes that houses need to be loved to become homes."

He groaned. "This is not about stature for me; it's about the place I plan to raise my kids, where we're going to spend our holidays and put lights up and take them down. It's where I'm gonna be until I die. We're not moving to Florida or Arizona or someplace like that when we're old. This is gonna be the place our kids will come back to when they go off to college, the place they'll bring their families for holidays. You get that?"

"I do."

"I just, it feels like home."

"Then let's do it. Tomorrow, go sign whatever you need to with Dane to get things started, and I'll call Mrs. Souza, our Realtor, and get our place listed."

He was really happy, and when I saw the joy, my stomach flipped over.

"You should have told me you wanted this so badly."

"Yeah, I know. I promise to tell you next time."

It didn't matter, only the way I was being hugged, his warm breath caressing my ear, and the lips sliding over my cheek. That was all my brain was processing.

AS WE made our way back down the Magnificent Mile toward the loft, we stopped into Water Tower Place because I needed a new lunch box for Hannah, a dress for her for Thanksgiving, and a new backpack for Kola.

"What happened to the old one?" Sam asked me.

"Chilly," Kola and Hannah said together.

"Really?"

"You saw how he killed that pillow the other night," Hannah told her father.

The pained expression I got made me throw up my hands. "What? He's a destructive force of nature. What do you want me to do?"

Sam shot himself in the head with his finger.

I rolled my eyes at him.

Shopping was fun for me, and Kola was a fan as well. Hannah and her father wanted to sit and eat ice cream. I finally gave up and told them we had to call it quits on the fun shopping because we had to go to the grocery store. Not surprisingly, they were no more excited to do that.

When we got home, I made the mistake of lying down on the couch and getting snuggly with Hannah instead of simply grabbing the car keys and heading right back out to go to the grocery store, which was not within walking distance.

"Are we going?" Sam asked me, but I could hear the humor in his voice.

"In just a second," I promised, even though it was cold and overcast outside and all I wanted to do was curl up and not move.

"Your cat is in a ball in the middle of our bed."

He had the right idea.

Sam made a fire and turned on the TV, and when he was done, he shoved both Hannah and me off the couch and took our spot.

"Daddy!" She was indignant.

He grunted at her.

I got back up and lay down on top of him, draping myself across his chest, my head under his chin. Hannah snuggled down in his left arm. Kola joined us, PSP in hand, head on the other end of the couch, his legs between mine, on top of Sam's. We were a warm pile all crushed together, and I could not keep my eyes open.

"I like it when there are other people here," Kola said after a few minutes of only the sound of football. "But I like it when it's just us too."

"Me too," Sam said, and I felt the rumble of laughter deep in his chest.

"What?"

"Your daughter," he said, and his grin was wide when I opened my eyes.

Head back, eyes closed, my sweet little angel was snoring like a drunken sailor.

"I told you," Kola grumbled from the other end. "She's really a boy in there. She farts too, you know."

Yes, I knew.

WAKING up from a nap in the middle of the day is never good. You rise grouchy and ready to go back to bed. So I was in a foul mood as we headed over to the grocery store.

Once there, Sam and Kola went to get milk and bread and the rest of the essentials, and Hannah and I went to grab fruit. I had apples and grapes and I was picking out some bananas when someone said my name. Before I could turn, I felt a hand on my shoulder and then a gun—and I knew what one felt like firsthand—pressed to the middle of my back.

"Come with me."

"Okay," I said because I just wanted to get the man away from my girl.

"Pa." Hannah looked up at me, tugging on my hand, trying to move me forward, only then seeing the man and trying to move around me to see my back. "Come on."

"No, love," I told her. "Go find Daddy."

Her face wrinkled up and she started the blinking she always did before the tears.

"B," I directed her as I felt the gun shoved hard against me, "run."

She didn't argue. She was feisty, my girl, but she understood what my tone meant, and the sound of my voice had left no room for argument. She bolted away from me to go find Sam. The idea of my munchkin alone in a store would normally have made my stomach hit the floor, but she had started to scream. I heard her—I was certain dogs all across the tristate area did too—as she began to wail for her father.

"Shit," the guy muttered behind me, and I sent up a silent prayer that kidnapping kids had not been on his agenda. I had no idea what I would have done to keep my baby safe.

The man grabbed my bicep tight and walked me away from the produce department and then out the front door where a black sedan was idling halfway across the parking lot. We were close to it, almost on top of it, when the door opened. I saw dress pants, but no one leaned forward so I could see a face.

"Freeze!" I heard Sam yell from behind me.

It all happened so fast.

"Drop your weapon and get on the ground!" His furious roar blew through me.

My kidnapper shoved me forward at the same time, and only then did a man with a gun lean out.

All I had was my own body to shield Sam with to make sure that no bullets reached the man I loved.

"Drop!"

But the command hit me, and for once I didn't second-guess him or worry or even think. Normally I acted, but I was so used to him now, to our life, to a clear division in our home. I did the everyday stuff, Sam did emergencies. I handled homework, he handled people with guns. It was our way. So he gave me an order and I obeyed it. I simply collapsed onto the asphalt.

There were shots and yelling. The car's engine gunned, tires squealed, there was a volley of gunfire, and then, when I lifted my head up just a little, the car fishtailed and its back window exploded before it crashed into a parked car.

"Stay down!" Sam yelled as he pounded by me.

I watched him run to the car, stop, crouch down on the side, and yell from where he was, pressed behind the back door on the driver's side. Anyone who could get out of the car needed to do it right fucking now before he started blowing holes in it.

There were sirens, then a whole wall of sound, and when I looked, I saw the driver's side door open.

A gun was tossed out before a man emerged, fingers laced together on top of his head. He went instantly to his knees before Sam ordered him to spread-eagle on the ground.

As soon as the man complied, Sam yelled at whoever was left in the car to come out. He didn't rush forward; he didn't throw open doors, just waited. After another moment, the back door opened and a man fell out onto the ground. He was clutching his right shoulder, and there was a lot of blood.

Sam still didn't move until there were police cars surrounding him. Officers swarmed the car, Sam pointed, and they ducked down and came around the other side. Doors were grabbed and flung open, and then I watched as a collective breath was taken and guns started being holstered. An ambulance parked, and only then, as I lifted up, did I realize that maybe five feet from me was a dead man.

It was a blur as Sam came loping back to me and dropped down on one knee.

"You're amazing." I caught my breath, beginning to shake.

"Baby, you listened." He smiled big even as his voice cracked.

"For once, huh?"

"It was the perfect time to start," he assured me as he crushed me in his arms, hugging me so hard I thought my ribs would snap. "Okay, come on, you gotta move."

He dragged me to my feet, threw me over his shoulder in a fireman carry, and then yelled for help. Two officers were there fast, parting the crowd, and I was back in the store and being put down right inside the front door, off to the left, where the shopping carts were. It was also where Kola and Hannah were.

When the kids saw me, they ran. As soon as Sam put me down, I was mobbed by little people. Sam ordered the officers to guard me and the kids and not let anyone near, he didn't care who it was.

"I'm authorizing deadly force, do you understand?"

They did.

Sam was gone then, charging back out through the doors.

"Pa, what happened?" Kola asked me, sitting down beside me on the floor, holding my hand between both of his. "Hannah said there was another man, but we didn't see him."

"It's okay, I'm okay, he didn't hurt me," I told my son before turning to my girl. "You did a good job going to get Daddy, B. I'm so proud of you."

She nodded, and I saw how puffy her eyes were then and guessed what had happened. As I pulled her into my lap, I looked back at my boy.

"Good job translating what she needed, Kola," I told him. "I bet she was crying really hard and Daddy didn't understand."

His smile was huge. "He didn't, but I did."

I put a hand on his cheek. "Good job, love."

He was beaming with pride, Hannah started hiccupping, and I clutched them both tight to me as chaos swirled around us.

As I listened to Kola talk to Hannah, tell her that when they got home, if she wanted, he would play Candy Land with her before bed, and felt her nod and start telling him who she wanted to be, the cold knot of fear in the pit of my stomach slowly started to unravel. There would be time to sort out my head later. Right that second, for the kids, I was their rock. I was fine, so they were fine. It was how it worked. Who knew that someday I was going to be the grown-up?

THIRTEEN

I HAD to go home without Sam. There was no way around it. I was okay to drive; it was normal, and so I did it. Of course we had a police car in front of us and one behind us and four officers escorted us to the loft, which was thoroughly checked before we were allowed inside for the night.

Once we were home, I did normal things. We had dinner; I made grilled cheese sandwiches and tomato soup with Goldfish. I had the kids take showers and get into their jammies. We got clothes out for the following morning, filled Kola's new backpack with the things from the old one, and then, because Hannah didn't want to play a game, we sat together on the couch and watched *Schoolhouse Rock* on DVD because Hannah liked the songs and Kola was getting the math.

Hannah fell asleep right after seven, which was her bedtime anyway, and I put Kola to bed at eight, which was his on school nights.

When there was a knock on the door, I checked the peephole and was surprised that standing next to one of the officers was Chaz.

I opened the door, and he looked pained. "What's wrong?"

"You gotta go downstairs. Sam's there. Me and Pat...." He stopped, looking down the hall as the elevator dinged and Pat got off. He was jogging toward me when Chaz put a hand on my shoulder, returning my attention to him. "Okay, me and Pat are gonna stay with the kids. You need to go."

"Where am I going?"

"To Sam, downstairs," Chaz reiterated. "Where's your coat?"

I went and grabbed the first thing in the closet, my trench coat, pulled it on over the jeans and sweater I was wearing, along with my sneakers. I normally walked around the house in only socks if I was planning on staying in.

After Chaz locked the door behind me, I headed down to the elevator to find Sam.

He was outside with, as far as I could tell, his entire team of marshals, more men in suits, and then some uniformed patrolmen. As I reached him, he looked up and gave me a faint smile.

I knew it pained him not to be able to grab me, put an arm around me. I knew the guys who worked in his office were cool with Sam living with me, or at least they said nothing to his face, but this was a professional situation, and in front of our building, there were a lot of people who didn't know me or Sam.

"Okay, here's the deal," he told me, his eyes locked on mine. "It turns out that the guy I shot, and the other two, both work for Salcedo. They were looking to pick you up tonight because they got a tip that I was out of town. Who would know that I was out of town, Jory?"

I cleared my throat. "Kevin Dwyer."

"Yes," he agreed. "He saw you the other night at Dane's party without me. When he asked, he was told that I was out of town, and when he asked Dane when you were expecting me back, he told Kevin that he didn't know."

"And you know this how?"

"From the planted bugs in Dr. Dwyer's residence, and it was confirmed from text messages he sent from his cell to others. We cloned his phone at the same time we bugged his apartment."

"Okay." I took a breath. "But why am I out here in the cold instead of upstairs with my children?"

"Salcedo doesn't know that he didn't acquire you yet."

"You mean he thinks his guys are still on the way with me."

"Yes."

"And so what?"

"And so in exchange for being allowed to turn state's evidence, Mr. Morelos, who's in the car—the man who was driving—has agreed to escort you back to the rendezvous point with Salcedo. We need you to go in with Mr. Morelos, wearing a wire, to draw Salcedo out so we can arrest him. None of us have ever seen the man. Even me. I heard of him. We were even supposed to meet once, but it fell through. So nobody knows what he looks like. If you go in, he should be easy to identify."

"And if I don't go?"

"If you don't go, they'll know we popped their guys and they're back in the wind. We need you to be the bait."

I saw it then, the quick cording of muscles in Sam's neck, a slight narrowing of his eyes, and understood this was not his call and not his idea in any way.

"Mr. Harcourt?"

Turning, I found Clint Farmer in front of me.

"We find ourselves in a unique situation. Obviously Mr. Salcedo sent Dr. Dwyer here to keep tabs on Sam because they felt he was getting too close to finding Andrew Turner. They tried to kill him twice in Phoenix and now, tonight, tried to acquire you. So we need to stop this before they come at him again. The problem being, of course, that we have no idea what Mr. Salcedo looks like."

I nodded.

"I need to slap a wire on you and I need you to walk into that warehouse in the shipyard and meet with these people."

"Okay."

He took a breath. "We would never ask this if we thought they truly wanted to do you any harm. You were being kidnapped for leverage and that was all. It is our understanding that no one actually wants to hurt you."

"Sure."

"That being said, there is always a danger that something could go wrong."

"I understand."

"Unfortunately you're the only one who can do this."

"Yeah I got that."

"Okay so, are we good to go then, Mr. Harcourt?"

I couldn't for the life of me answer. Yes, I wanted this whole thing to go away, but on the other hand, it wasn't just me anymore. Me being dead affected the man I loved and the two short people who lived with me.

He waited a moment and then took hold of my arm and walked me out of the circle of the other men before he turned and looked at me. "Three years ago my wife, Maggie, got in the middle of a mob hit."

He had all my attention.

"I'm still a bit fuzzy on the details, but she works in PR, and her firm was putting on an event, and this dear sweet old man gave her a letter to pass on to his son. I mean how *Breakfast at Tiffany's* can this get, right?"

His tone, the reference—I was liking him.

"Okay, so all of a sudden, we have hit men following her, trying to kill her, and she had no idea what the hell's going on, and then one night when I'm trying to decide whether to lock her up or kiss her, she says, 'Oh yeah.'" He paused. "I think that old man gave me a letter that I forgot to deliver. It's filed under *F* for 'favor' in my file."

I smiled at him.

He made the international sign of strangulation, and I understood that his wife was driving him insane. "I love her, but I was going to throttle her."

"What happened?"

"I had to send her alone and wired for sound into a room with men I didn't know or she was going to be running for the rest of her life. So I get it. I get what we're asking of you, of the marshal, of your family. I understand, so the choice is yours."

"Was she okay? Your wife?"

He lifted his phone and showed me a picture of a woman smiling at him in the midst of what looked like a demolished kitchen. There wasn't a part of her not covered in baking flour.

"Cookies for my daughter's third-grade class this afternoon. There's no telling what it looks like currently."

I took a breath. "If its crap, it's really good crap you just laid on me."

He lifted his hand so I could see the thick band of gold. "It's not crap."

"Okay."

"Okay," he sighed and motioned with his fingers. "We'll come running in a heartbeat, Mr. Harcourt."

"Call me Jory."

AN HOUR later, we drove in silence toward the warehouse district.

"Would you please talk to me?"

"I'm sorry," I told him. "I'm wearing a wire, Marshal; I don't think that right now is the appropriate time to be asking me questions."

He growled at me.

I crossed my arms.

"Why are you mad at me?"

"Oh I don't know," I said snidely, "what could it be?"

I read it on his face when he got it, the heavy sigh before he turned to me. "It was nothing."

"Your boss seemed to think that a man trying to kill you was, in fact, not nothing."

"Yeah, but—"

"This is just like you and Rico having to shoot your way out of something, this is like you having to go to work every day and take your life in your hands and then coming home like nothing happened and asking me what we're having for dinner!"

"Jor—"

"You killed a man tonight, Sam, because of me, and—"

"Listen," he said, grabbing hold of my chin and yanking it sideways so he could see my face. "I shot that man because he turned and fired on me. I was terrified of hitting you, but I was not letting him put you in that car. But anyone in that same situation, I would have fired, do you understand? You being there did not change the use of deadly force. Do you get it?"

I tugged free and leaned back. "Yes, Marshal, I got it. Anyone there and you would have acted the exact same way. I hear you loud and clear."

We rode in silence.

"You're not listening at all," he muttered under his breath.

"I would be listening, but you never say anything. You need to tell me what's—" I reminded myself I was wearing a wire. "—never mind."

The car finally stopped close to the docks, and I saw a light halfway down a small pier on the left. The driver, Mr. Morelos, got out first, and I was about to follow when Sam grabbed my wrist tight and dragged me off my seat and into his lap.

"What are you doing?" I whispered.

He knotted one hand in my hair, wrapped the other around my throat and tipped my head back. That quickly, that easily, I was at his mercy.

"I will kill anyone who ever tries to hurt you, do you understand?"

My eyes met his and I saw the heat there, the possessiveness, and understood. I listened. "You're thinking I feel guilty about that man you killed, but I don't."

He let me go and I turned, sitting up, straddling his thighs.

"If the man had thrown down his gun and put up his hands, you wouldn't have killed him. You think you might have because the guy's intention was to take me with him, but Sam, you would never hurt an unarmed man."

His hands went to my hair, pushing it back from my face.

"I know if the guy had surrendered that you wouldn't have killed him. But he fired back at you, there was no choice. You had to save me and you had to save yourself. You have kids, Sam. You have me, so there's no question if you come home, there's no question if it's you or someone else. It's you."

"I know you're pissed that I don't share enough of this crap with you, but when I get home I'm just so happy to be there... I have you and the kids and the stupid cat, and honestly I feel so different that my head just isn't in that place anymore."

I stared deeply into his gorgeous eyes.

"I swear, I will tell you more. I will work on it, I will. But just walking through the door and seeing all your sweet faces—fixes me. Do you get it?"

"I do now, you big dumb jerk," I sighed, smiling at him.

He pulled me forward fast, violently, and the kiss I got was ravaging but fast, and then I was outside the car, standing there, dazed, and wobbling just a little.

Fortunately the driver had seen nothing and so grabbed my bicep tight as he walked me down toward the door marked fifteen.

"How did you first embark on a life of crime?" I asked him, trying to draw him into conversation. "I have kids, so I'd like to keep a lookout for the warning signs."

After a moment he turned to look at me. "This is your banter? You're trying to insult me?"

"Well, I was just saying to my best friend the other day that I think everyone's life can either be an example or a lesson, don't you think?"

"Best friend? Who talks like that?" he asked as he opened the door and shoved me through it.

"You don't have a best friend?" I asked, making a mental note of that, turning to look over my shoulder at him.

"I—"

"No, it's fine," I said absently. "God, I wish I had my phone so I could make a list. My memory's not quite what it used to be."

"Who the fuck are you?" he asked as he got out his gun from the holster under his jacket and pointed it at me before we walked toward the light.

"I'm just trying to stay calm. Aren't you nervous?"

He didn't answer.

"Man this light I'm walking toward is bright," I said to Sam and everyone else listening to me. "And that's not supposed to be a good thing, ya know?"

It was a huge warehouse, but we didn't go in that far. When we stopped, there were five men there, and I knew one.

"Dr. Dwyer," I said.

He tipped his head sideways and squinted.

It took me longer than I would have liked, I prided myself on being quicker. "Oh," I breathed out. "You're Salcedo! That's brilliant."

He said nothing.

"And even talking about yourself to yourself? You're a genius."

"Where are the others?" a man asked Mr. Morelos.

"I have no idea. I did my part and we got outside, and there was nobody there. No car, nobody. They both bailed."

"You were supposed to be driving."

"Javi changed the order. He decided to drive, and Cranston was backup in the car."

Silence.

"Cranston was a marshal. He wouldn't have bailed."

"The marshal from Vegas," I clarified. "The dirty one."

"Shut up."

"We took him at the—"

"What the fuck is this?" a guy asked, moving forward into the light.

"Mr. Turner," I said because I recognized him from the photographs Sam had shown me that day at our house.

His eyes met mine. "Who are you and why are you here?"

"I'm here, supposedly, as leverage to make Marshal Sam Kage back off, but I suspect what's really going to happen is that I'm about to die and you're about to die, because I'll bet you Salcedo's dead." I said, pretending I didn't know who Salcedo was so the wire I was wearing would get it all, every confession, every truth. What was the point of everything that went on around me being recorded if it wasn't incriminating.

"He's not dead, you dumb prick!" He pointed at Dwyer. "He's right there, and—"

"Ah-ha!" I yelled. "You, Kevin Dwyer, are Salcedo! How the hell did you do that?"

"Of course he's Salcedo. What the hell is—"

"You're so dead," I told Turner. "Salcedo is gonna die, and there will only be Dr. Dwyer, and so whatever you have, or think you have, on Salcedo—is it video? Porn? Anyway, whatever it is, it won't matter because he'll be dead and he gets to start a whole new life here, with my marshal, after you die and I die right here."

Turner pivoted around to look at Dwyer/Salcedo. "Is that true? You're going to disappear into the life of the doctor you created?"

"Are you actually a doctor?" I asked.

"Yes!" he yelled at me, and I saw the gun.

"Did you have sex with Randall Erickson the other night?"

Why that was the most revolting part of it all, I had no idea, but God, it so was.

"DEA!" came the first yell as there were flashlights and lots of feet pounding across concrete. "Everybody down!"

I dropped to the floor.

"Hands behind your head!"

Doing as I was told, I laced my fingers behind the back of my head and waited. It occurred to me that Salcedo had been in Dane and

Aja's loft and that he had used Randall to make that trip just so he could ask my brother if he knew where Sam was. I hated that he had used Dane to get to me and to Sam. Even worse, he had used Randall. That would be quite the ego blow.

"What the hell is going on?" I heard someone yell. "Why do I have US Marshals outside and Chicago PD?"

It was confusing because there were too many people with too many agendas. I ended up in a small room, handcuffed, sitting on the floor across from Dwyer/Salcedo, who was sitting between the driver and Mr. Turner.

"So what do you have on him?" I asked Turner. "All the documentation that he and Dwyer are the same person?"

He nodded. "Yeah. I have everything that proves he's the same guy."

I looked over at Dwyer. "And so because you didn't want to go to prison, you busted him out of WITSEC."

He was just staring at me.

"But what I don't get is, why didn't you just go into witness protection too?"

"Because that was never on the table for me." He made a face. "What does... I don't understand."

Men came in then, and I saw the DEA badges, and everyone was taken out except me and Dwyer/Salcedo.

"Before," I began, "when you started to say you didn't understand, you meant me and Sam, right? You don't get us, how we're together or why."

His eyes narrowed with hatred. "Yes."

I understood. He was a gorgeous man himself. "He doesn't think there was ever anything between you two. He thinks you used him that entire time."

He started nodding. "He's right."

But it was crap, and my proof was right there on his face, in his eyes. "He's wrong. Tell me. It was new back then, this identity. You went to medical school. Come on, tell me the story."

"It wasn't supposed to be my path. But the others weren't smart, and it came time to step up or step aside... and then we had to get information from an idiot Chicago Police detective working undercover with a federal task force. He had information because he ended up busting a friend."

Dominic. "So you and Sam... you talked."

He shrugged. "He was broken then. His closest friend, everything was a mess, he drank so much, and then when he got hurt and came to the hospital...."

"What?"

"Once I had my hands on him... there was more I wanted." He exhaled.

I needed to hear it all from Sam, not this man. "So now everything you were afraid of ended up happening anyway."

"Yes, it did."

"You had a lot of people on your payroll, your own marshal, even—that Cranston guy from Vegas."

"You have no idea."

"And for what?"

He shook his head.

"Were you done with Sam, or were you always planning to reappear in his life?"

"When he left he was very specific about what he wanted for his life and who... and like he told you, it was never anything at all."

I shook my head as the door opened. "You're both liars."

"I suspect some truth in that," he said as he looked up at Sam's boss.

"You know you're still wearing a wire right?" Farmer gave me the same pained expression I got from Sam quite a bit.

"But you're gonna erase everything from once the bust happened, right?" I smiled up at him.

"Consider it done."

"Thanks."

FOR the second time that night, I was home alone without my man. After I relieved Chaz and Pat, I took a long hot shower and washed away the day. I tried to wait up for Sam but finally passed out sometime after two. I had to get the kids up for school in four and half hours.

FOURTEEN

SAM still wasn't home in the morning, and I was disappointed because I wanted him to go with me to take the kids back to school. The text message I got told me he was still being debriefed, though, and as it turned out, Dane was there waiting for me when I rolled into the parking lot.

"Is your manic husband better today?" he asked peevishly.

"I have no idea what that means."

Apparently Sam had called Dane at some point in the night or early morning, and they had spoken at length about the house, and then Sam had asked Dane to be my backup because he knew he would still be sitting with the guys from DEA.

"I don't want to know. All I do know is that it sounds as though you will not be returning to your home but will instead be moving from my loft into the house in Oak Park. There are movers and cleaners going to your current residence today. I'm having Pedro take care of all the change of address forms."

"My neighbors are going to be so confused."

"I suspect Sam doesn't care about that."

"I wonder what the new ones will be like." I squinted up at him.

"Different," he informed me as we started up the stairs, me holding Hannah's hand and him holding Kola's. "You own a home in historic Oak Park now. I took the liberty of contacting the man I have taking care of the grounds now, Mr. Kincaide, and telling him that you will be taking over the billing. If you or Sam want to do it yourselves, you can, but there are very specific rules about how the yard must be maintained and—"

"Can we put up Christmas lights?"

"What?"

"It's a deal breaker, Dane."

"Of course you can put up Christmas lights. What kind of—"

"I just wanted to be sure."

"If I live to be a thousand, I will never understand all the different places your mind goes."

I was certain that was true.

We walked Kola to his room first, where Miss Taylor was now and not Mr. Michaels. Poor girl—I thought she was going to liquefy as she stood there, gazing at Dane. When he finally turned and smiled at her, she puddled and I groaned.

As we walked Hannah to her room, she explained to her uncle about getting in trouble for the water gun.

"Never carry a big gun," he cautioned her. "You just get a tiny spray bottle like you use when you iron clothes and you use that. That way you can test to see if you've got a witch without alerting them that you're onto them."

Her eyes got big and she nodded.

"I'm sorry, *my* brain works oddly?" I said irritably.

"I have no idea what you're talking about."

Dane charmed Ms. Brady as well, the older woman simpering under his charcoal-gray eyes. And yes, he was handsome, but it was more. I had always had the feeling that Dane was simply larger than life. I was so thankful that I had him in mine.

"I don't tell you like I should," I said as we were walking back down the hall toward the front door, "but I appreciate everything you do for me, and I love—"

"Yes, same. Good." He was brusque as he patted my cheek before he turned and took the stairs down the front stoop, waved without looking back, and started across the parking lot.

I should have known better.

"Mr. Harcourt?"

Turning, I found Mrs. Petrovich.

"I'm sorry about my husband," I told her. "He's a yeller."

She nodded. "I'm sorry for Mr. Michaels, who has been dismissed, and Mr. Parker, who has been barred from school grounds."

"Okay."

She reached out and took hold of my arm. "You and your family have been part of ours for the past three years, Mr. Harcourt, since Kola started when he was in preschool, like Hannah is now. You didn't think twice about enrolling her with us because he was doing so well here. I don't want that to change because of this incident, but mostly because I don't want you to think that we don't care about your children. All the kids mean the world to me, I wouldn't be here if that wasn't the case, but Kola is just a jewel, and Hannah...." She started to smile. "I just don't know what goes through that girl's head sometimes, but I just can't wait to see her every day."

"Okay."

"So I sincerely hope that we can all get past this incident and back to how things were before. That is the first such occurrence we've ever had at this school, and I can assure you that it will most certainly be the last."

I smiled at her. "You're adding aides to all classes, aren't you?"

She cleared her throat. "Whatever do you mean?"

"You've been pushing that for a while, but the board wouldn't budge." I nodded, grinning at her. "I read the newsletter and that's a very good way to prove your point."

She took hold of my hand. "You know that I would have never chosen to have—"

"I know, you didn't want a child hurt to illustrate your concerns, but the point was certainly made, wasn't it?"

"Oh yes it was." She exhaled, releasing my hand. Such an attractive woman in her Donna Karan suit, short, stylish haircut, reading glasses hanging on a chain, pearls, makeup immaculately applied, and her dark-blue eyes locked on my face. I had found her so polished the first time we met, and the perception had never changed.

I crossed my arms. "Did Rick Jenner scare the board?"

"Mr. Jenner terrified the board. Jenner Knox is a very well-known law firm here in Chicago."

"But it's not even a year old," I said, making my eyes big for her, all innocence.

She cleared her throat. "Richard Jenner may have just started his new firm, Mr. Harcourt, but we all know that he was the managing partner at his old firm for many years."

I arched an eyebrow for her.

"He's quite intimidating."

"Yes, ma'am, I know."

She squinted at me. "I must say that when you applied here, you and the marshal, I did not suspect that if there was ever a problem that a man like Richard Jenner would be who I would find in my office."

"My brother, who you just saw… did you see him?"

"He would be hard to miss."

"Yeah, well, he watches out for me, he's the scary one, and—"

"Make no mistake, Mr. Harcourt, the scary one in this scenario has always been and I suspect will always be Marshal Kage."

I cleared my throat. "Again, sorry he yelled."

"He had every right to."

I reached out and squeezed her arm. "We'll get past this."

"Good," she whispered. "We'll see you after school."

"Yes, ma'am."

I was smiling when I reached the minivan.

After pulling out of the parking lot, I took a left, and a car passed me and then cut in front of me sharply and came to a stop. I had to either slam on my brakes or ram into it. I hit the brakes.

The car door flew open and the second I saw Mr. Parker get out with a baseball bat, I grabbed my phone and dialed 911. As he yelled at me to get out of my faggot car and get my faggot ass out there, I talked to the operator. When he started beating on the hood, the operator asked what that noise was. I explained that he was hitting my van.

"And it's new," I groaned, because really, I was safe as long as I didn't get out.

She sounded more frantic than I was.

He hit the window and by that time I had the operator on speaker and my phone shooting video because there was nothing else to do—I was stuck until the police got there.

"Mr. Harcourt, did you call in a 211 the other night?"

"Yeah."

"That was wonderful, what you did. I just… we weren't allowed to contact you or… any…."

"Which one?" I asked as Mr. Parker took out the passenger side mirror. What was I going to tell Aaron?

"Detective Everman is my brother-in-law… we're all very thankful."

"Are both of them all right?"

"Yes." She sighed deeply. "Both of them will make a full recovery."

"Good, I'm—shit."

"What's wrong?"

He had retreated to his car, and now he had an ax. "Tell the officers coming that this guy has an ax now."

"Will advise. Move away from the windows, Mr. Harcourt. ETA is one minute out."

"Okay." I took a breath, scrambling into the backseat as Mr. Parker charged the van and swung at the windshield.

I was really sick of hearing sirens, hearing the yelling, but the sea of blue uniforms was cool, and the way they held their guns on him until he dropped the ax was like a scene out of a movie.

He was on the ground, and it was overkill, in my opinion, but they had no way of knowing what the man was on, and he was big and strong. But there was a knee driven down between his shoulder blades, one in the small of his back, and the last guy sat on his legs. It could not have been comfortable.

They sort of hog-tied him with PlastiCuffs and carried him to the back of one of the police cars. Once there, they came for me. The street in the little suburban neighborhood was full of working families, so there was no one out on the sidewalk to witness any of the excitement.

I gave my statement to Officer Fields as more men in blue joined us, clustering around. They asked if I was okay, and I explained again that I had not gotten out of the van. It was picture-taking time after that. When my phone rang, I saw that it was Sam and excused myself.

"Where are you?" he asked me.

"Where are you?"

"I'm finally home. I took a shower and—did you go to work? I want to talk to you about everything and just… I need to see you, so can you come home?"

I coughed. "I'm actually with the police."

There was a brief silence.

"What?"

"Mr. Parker just attacked me after I dropped off Kola and B, but I'll be home after I finish with the police and then call Aaron to figure out where to take the—"

"Attacked you?"

"Well"—I gestured at the poor Mercedes he couldn't see—"yeah, I mean the van, not me. Well, yeah, me, but mostly the van. It would have been me if he could've reached me, but—"

"Jesus Christ, Jory! Are you hurt?"

"No, I'm not hurt, were you listening? I was in the minivan and it just got beat to shit."

"Where—" His voice cracked, bottomed out. "—are you exactly?"

I read him the street sign I could see from where I was and told him to hold on because the policeman had to talk to me.

"Put him on the phone."

"But Sam, I—"

"Put him on the phone," he growled.

"Fine, God, don't make that noise," I snapped, passing my iPhone to the officer. He looked confused.

"Just—" I nodded, gesturing for him to put it to his ear. "Talk to the Federal Marshal."

Fun to watch the man's eyes go all big and round, and he started answering questions that were being fired fast, judging from the brevity and quickness of the answers. Apparently Mr. Parker's ex-wife was now suing for sole custody of their son based on the incident with Kola at the school. Until the custody got sorted out, Oliver was with his mother, and she had filed a restraining order against her ex-husband as well.

If Sam had not been a marshal and an ex-Chicago Police detective, he would not have been given all that information, but as it was, the officer spilled it all and did a lot of yes sir, no sir, very good sir until the phone came back to me.

"Don't move. Sit your ass down on the curb and wait for me."

"But what about the—"

"I'm sending a tow truck for the van. Just… sit."

"How in any realm of possibility can this be my fault?"

"You're a trouble magnet."

"I am not!"

"I bet you said that with a straight face!"

"Sam!"

"Get off the phone. I have to call Aaron Sutter, which is gonna make my whole fuckin' day!"

"He really likes Duncan, you know."

"Oh that's fantastic news."

"The sarcasm is not lost on me."

"I could give a fuck! The only—"

"Oh come on, you care a little, I can tell. You and Duncan Stiel are—"

"Like I started to say, the only thing those two are gonna fuckin' do is make each other fuckin' miserable, but they're both bastards, so they deserve each other!"

"Back to swearing, are we?"

"Jory!"

Oh he was mad, and for whatever reason, I couldn't stop smiling. God, I loved Sam Kage all pissed off. It made for the violent rush toward bed that made my heart stop. Because when Sam was furious, he went silent and cold, but right now, pushed and prodded, he was like one of those rodeo bulls that just charged out and decimated whatever was in its path. I couldn't wait to get home and have him throw me down on the bed and hold me down. Oh, I was so in for it—I would be completely and utterly ravished. I shivered just thinking about it.

"Dane said we're moving," I baited him some more.

"I already told you we were moving! Do you ever listen to anything I say? Ever?"

This was fun. "And so Dwyer and Salcedo were the same guy, huh, Sam? I guess love is blind and you missed it."

"What? What did you say to me?"

I cackled. There was no way not to. "It's okay, you loved him and he loved you, but you had to come home to—"

"I came home because the op was done and I had to get back to you! I needed you! I wanted you! I loved you! That's why I fuckin' came home!"

"Loved?" I pressed him.

"Jory, I swear to God, I will fuckin' beat you if you don't—"

"So you love me? Sam? Do you? Am I it? The only one? Am I?"

"I'm gonna kill you!"

"Oh come on, say you love me. C'mon, Sammy, you can say it… come on…."

"*Sammy?*"

I lost it in heaving laughter, his complete indignation slaying me completely.

He roared and the phone went dead, and I had the sudden urge to hide or run, but instead I called Aaron Sutter.

"Can't talk now," he told me when he picked up. "Your man is on the other line."

"Yeah, but you like me better."

"Yeah, but Duncan… he mentioned that he respects Sam quite a bit, and he was thinking that he might want to follow the same path as Sam did in becoming a marshal and was hoping he could get Sam's help with that."

"You don't just decide one day to become a marshal; it's like, a real job, you know."

"No, I know, he knows."

And it hit me. "Jesus, Aaron, you way more than just like Duncan Stiel."

"I'll talk to you later," he said and hung up on me.

It took me a minute to wrap my brain around Aaron Sutter hanging up on me. Usually I hung up on him, not the other way around. But I had taken a backseat; I was finally clearly in the friend column, because the real guy had finally shown up.

I always thought that not being the guy Aaron Sutter wanted would be a letdown. It was an ego boost to be the ideal, someone else's heart's desire. I thought I would miss it when the day came that I tumbled from my pedestal. I figured, in my secret heart, that I would be sad, but faced with it now, faced with forever being just his friend, I was thrilled… and terrified.

What if Duncan was not ready for the force of nature that Aaron was? What if he ran? What if….

I would help if I could, but that was all I could do. All my life I had fixed everything—or tried to—but really I had no control over any of it. I had power over just me, influence over a few others, and the ability to make Sam and my children happy. What more could I ask for?

I turned my head at the roar of a motor, saw Sam's monster car, and ran down the sidewalk. He pulled up alongside me, the door flew open, and he got out and rushed around the front of the car to reach me.

I held out my arms.

He froze.

"Come here." I wiggled my fingers.

"What is this?"

"This is me delirious to see you."

"Why?"

"Because I love you." I glared at him. "Now come here."

"I love you too," he growled and pounced, and I was in his arms, crushed in the iron embrace, his face pressed to the side of my neck as he shivered hard.

"Not leaving you, never leaving you. We're good, we're solid. But for you, where would I be?"

He just breathed me in.

"I don't care who you loved or who loved you. I'm not jealous because look where you are. You chose me and our life, and you're not going anywhere without me or the kids."

"No," he promised as he lifted his head and took my face in his hands. I saw it in his eyes, the emotion surging through him, and then he was kissing me violently, completely, missing nothing as he devoured my mouth. "Never—" He kissed harder, deeper, his mouth so hot and wet. "—leaving you, you're mine, you make it all work."

I couldn't think of anything better.

MY TORRID sex fantasy got waylaid by Sam and I having to go down to the police station to press charges against Mr. Parker, which took a lot longer than I thought it would. They asked me if he had yelled anything when he was attacking the car, but I lied and said no. I knew why he was enraged, and it honestly had less to do with my sexuality and everything to do with his ex-wife and his kid and pinning his anger someplace. Me being gay was not the issue; the issue was displacement. I was not the victim of a hate crime; I was the scapegoat because he had anger issues. And just because I didn't want to think about it anymore, I deleted the video of him coming at me first with the bat and then the ax. I didn't want to be caught in a lie and saying that it was too painful to keep sounded plausible.

I wasn't sure how things were going to work out for him. This was his second time in jail in days—Chaz and Pat had picked him up for breaking Kola's finger—and he would not be arraigned until the following morning.

As we were leaving the station, I asked Sam what would happen.

"You heard what Officer Marion said. He told us that Mr. Parker confessed to finding out from his ex what day you would be bringing Kola back to school under the guise of apologizing, but instead he ambushed you."

"He won't go to jail, will he?"

"That depends on his priors. We don't know what the deal is with him and his ex."

"I thought there would just be a lot of court-ordered therapy."

"Maybe, I don't know."

"Yes, you do," I pressed him. "You were a cop for how long? You know."

He turned his smoky gray-blue eyes on me. "He's lucky he was there when the cops showed up."

"What are you talking about?"

"If he had run and tried to hide after what he did to you...." He took a breath. "Do I strike you as a reasonable man?"

"Yes," I assured him.

"No," he corrected me, shaking his head. "Get in the car."

I had followed directions, and the hand on the back of my neck hauling me close made me smile. Sam was just reminding himself, as he mauled me, that I was okay. I was not surprised that when he got me back to the loft, behind closed doors, he needed to be skin-to-skin close to assure himself that I was all in one piece. We didn't even get out of bed to eat.

He left me to shower and cook while he picked up the kids from school. I didn't even realize it was raining outside until they got home and came through the door looking like a band of drowned rats.

Sam just glowered at me as he ordered everyone to strip down to their skivvies and run to opposite bathrooms. Once the kids were showered and changed, he did the same, since he had rolled out of bed, sticky and sweaty and smelling like sex, to go get them. He came shuffling back out to the living room and collapsed on the couch in old jeans, a T-shirt, and sweat socks. His eyes were heavy-lidded, his hair was sticking up, and he was flushed from the heat of the hot water. He was completely irresistible, and standing there, leaning over the back of the couch, I could barely keep my hands off him.

I loved looking at him, the golden lashes resting on his cheeks, the rise and fall of the massive chest that held his great heart and the power and strength in the man even at rest. When I traced down his nose with my finger, he scrunched up his face, and I couldn't help leaning over and kissing his forehead. The rumbling purr made me smile.

He was exhausted, and since he had been awake for a full twenty-four hours, I was not surprised. But still, when Hannah shook him a couple of hours later, he woke up. The trumpeting sound she made caused a little bit of wincing, from the volume, but since I knew it was just to announce her entrance, I didn't ask her to tone it down. I was not a fan of being told to *quiet down* or *calm down*, so I tried to not do it to my kids. I was loud and I was raising loud people. They had to count on learning restraint from Sam.

"What are we doing?" Sam asked, his voice full of gravel, as he sat up on the couch, rubbing his right eye with the heel of his hand.

He had not been in a deep sleep, because honestly he had to be in his bed with me either wrapped around him or him spooned to my back. Only with me was he completely relaxed, so napping on the couch had not put him all the way out. But it was enough to make him rumpled and bleary as he fought his way back to full consciousness. Hannah's flourish of horns, or what she approximated that sound to be, had jarred both him and Chilly, who had been curled up on his chest. They had made an adorable picture together: the big strong man and his fluffy cat. It was one I would have been murdered over taking, so I refrained.

"J?" He grunted again, yawning, eyes watering for a minute as he clasped his forearms behind his head and did the all-over body stretch.

"Halloween costumes," I explained from behind him as Hannah skipped around in front of her father and struck a pose.

It was cute how Chilly meowed indignantly and did his own stretch before jumping off the couch. Clearly he was irritated that he had been woken up for a fashion show.

Sam cleared his throat. "Uhm, not sure."

Hannah was still holding her head-tilted-in-place, arms-thrust-forward, curved-back, worship-me position for him. It was, I guessed, her version of a runway model stance. The fact that she more resembled Frankenstein ready to rip someone's head off was hardly her fault.

I leaned over close to his ear and whispered, "Ninja fairy."

He grunted and nodded. "Well, that explains the fuchsia wings, the glitter ninja outfit, the wand, and the sai."

"The what?"

"The knives there." He tipped his head. "Like the ones Elektra carries."

"Elektra fan, are you?" I learned something new about the man every day.

"Are you kidding?" he said like I was stupid.

"Should I be worried that you have a fetish for hot women in red leather?"

"I think, actually, Daredevil was the one who wore red leather." He grinned lazily, tipping his head back so he could see me. "But if you want to wear any kind of leather for me, I'd be more than happy."

"Stop flirting with me. Your daughter's gonna cramp up."

He was chuckling as he turned his attention back to Hannah, studying her. "Okay, so you're gonna throw razor-sharp knives at people and, if they get hurt, wave your magic wand and make them all better?"

She unfroze and turned big eyes and a bigger smile on her father. "Yes!"

Obviously he was brilliant, and the way she launched herself at him, crossing blades and a sparkly wand behind his neck as she squeezed him, told him so. I could not stifle the sigh as he hugged and kissed her.

He put her on his lap as Kola ran out and froze in the same place Hannah had, on the rug in front of the fireplace.

"I like your cutlass," Sam told his son.

"I'm a pirate."

"I can see that," he told him, turning to look at me with one arched eyebrow.

"What?"

"He's the prettiest pirate I've ever seen in my life."

"What?" I was defensive before the whine popped out. "No, he's scary."

"I think he can walk right out on a Broadway stage in that and be okay."

"No, he's evil."

"He could be a singing pirate."

"Sam!"

"He's a *Pirates of Penzance* pirate."

"No, he—"

"We need to get you an eye patch, buddy," Sam told him. "And we can draw on some scars and maybe rip the sleeve on your coat and—"

"Rip it?" I interrupted.

"Oooh, yeah!" Kola was excited. "Can we put fake blood on me too?"

"Oh now you're talking." Sam was nodding, gesturing his son over to him. "And we need to get you some ugly teeth because pirates had scurvy."

"What's that?"

"It's a disease you get if you don't get enough vitamin C where some of your teeth fall out and the rest are all brown and disgusting."

"Awesome," Kola breathed out.

"Not awesome," I grumbled, walking back to the kitchen to check on the meatloaf we were having for dinner. The mashed potatoes were done and on the stove; I just had to toss the salad and finish steaming the broccoli. Not that I was going to get the vegetables down anyone in my house, but I was working on it. Sam was just as bad as the kids as far as roughage went.

As I put the salad on the table, there were suddenly arms around me and I was drawn back against the wall of hard muscle that was Sam.

"Yes, costume killer?"

He kissed behind my ear and down the back of my neck, and it felt amazing, so I tipped my head sideways so he could reach more. "I'm improving, not killing, and I had too nice a day once I got home to fight with you about anything, so if you don't want me to—"

"No," I said, my smile quickly turning to laughter as he turned me in his arms and dipped me. "You and Kola fix it up and—are you okay?"

"I can't dance with the man I love?"

We never danced, but as the kids returned in their jammies, we were swaying around the dinner table. The afternoon thunderstorm had blanketed everything, and it was still pouring outside at six at night.

"What are you doing?" Kola asked as he started setting out the plates and napkins like he did every night. Hannah's job was the silverware.

"Dancing with Pa," Sam said, pressing me closer, his hand on the small of my back. "What does it look like I'm doing?"

Kola shrugged. Apparently we were too strange to deal with, but Hannah smiled and nodded.

"Me next!"

"Yes, ma'am," Sam agreed before he spun me into the living room and then lifted me off my feet. "Wrap your legs around me."

"You realize you have children right there," I reminded him even as I complied, sliding my legs up his thighs and over his hips as his hands went to my ass, holding me against him.

"I liked spending the day in bed with you," he said, and his voice was low and husky. "Tighter."

I pushed closer, my groin pressed to his hard abdomen. "We talked too," I reminded him, unable to contain the deep, contented sigh when the man was looking at me with soft eyes and the sexy curl of his lip. "We talked about everything."

"Yeah, we did."

And we had. Sam had explained to me that Andrew Turner and Dr. Kevin Dwyer, or Christian Salcedo—whichever name you preferred—were both going to federal prison for a very long time. My heart went out to Kevin/Christian, because if I had lost Sam, I too would have been heartbroken.

"It was never love," he'd told me as we had lain together on sweaty sheets, me draped over him, him making sure I couldn't move. "You're the only one, J, you know that. Just you."

Just me.

"Hey."

I realized my mind had been wandering. "Sorry, what?"

He chuckled as he leaned in and kissed me.

"We talked about that," Kola told us.

"I like it," Hannah giggled. "They love each other."

"Yeah, but Auntie Dyl and Uncle Chris don't kiss all the time."

"But Uncle Dane and Auntie Aja do."

"So maybe because Uncle Dane is Pa's brother," Kola offered sagely. "That's why they kiss who they're married to."

Hannah nodded.

"'Cause they're brothers makes them the same."

"Like me and you."

"We're not brothers."

"Yeah, but we're family."

"Yeah," he agreed. "We're family."

I couldn't stop the tears, and Sam wiped them away before he kissed me.

"You have such a soft heart."

For him and my kids, yes, I did.

MARY CALMES lives in Lexington, Kentucky, with her husband and two children and loves all the seasons except summer. She graduated from the University of the Pacific in Stockton, California, with a bachelor's degree in English literature. Due to the fact that it is English lit and not English grammar, do not ask her to point out a clause for you, as it will *so* not happen. She loves writing, becoming immersed in the process, and falling into the work. She can even tell you what her characters smell like. She loves buying books and going to conventions to meet her fans.

Read more about Jory and Sam

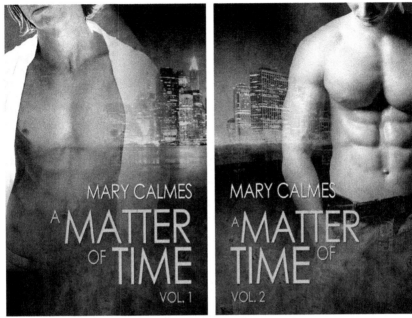

Romance from MARY CALMES

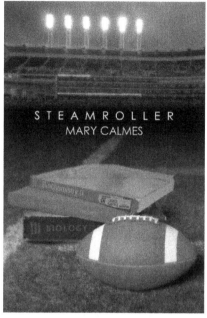

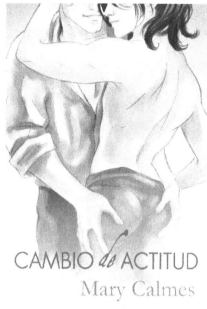

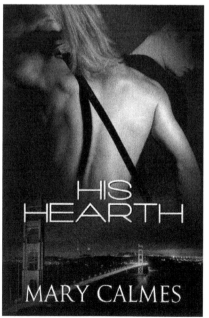

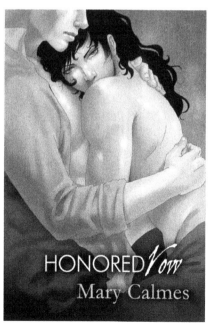

http://www.dreamspinnerpress.com

9 781623 800260

BUT FOR *You*

MARY CALMES

Sequel to Bulletproof

Jory Harcourt is finally living the dream. Being married to US Marshal Sam Kage has changed him—it's settled the tumult of their past and changed Jory from a guy who bails at the first sign of trouble to a man who stays and weathers the storm. He and Sam have two kids, a house in the burbs, and a badass minivan. Jory's days of being an epicenter for disaster are over. Domestic life is good.

Which means it's exactly the right time for a shakeup on the home front. Sam's ex turns up in an unexpected place. A hit man climbs up their balcony at a family reunion. And maybe both of those things have something to do with a witness who disappeared a year ago. Marital bliss just got a kick in the pants, but Jory won't let anyone take his family away from him. Before he knew what it felt like to have a home, he would have run. Not anymore. He knows he and Sam need to handle things together, because that's the only way they're going to make it.

www.dreamspinnerpress.com

ISBN 978-1-62380-026-0

51499